ANNETTE G. ANDERS

D1714701

Bellini's Mimosa

COLORS OF HAPPINESS BOOK I

Bellini's Mimosa

Colors of Happiness Book I

Annette G. Anders

AMICA PRESS

Copyright *BELLINI'S MIMOSA* © 2022 by Annette G. Anders.

Email: Author@AnnetteGAnders.com

Editor: Faith Freewoman, www.demonfordetails.com

Cover designer: Brandi Doane McCann, www.ebook-coverdesigns.com

First edition

ISBN: 979-8-9857443-0-9 (e-book)

ISBN: 979-8-9857443-1-6 (paperback)

To receive my newsletter, please sign up at:
www.AnnetteGAnders.com

To Axel and Mika,
and our unforgettable vacations in Italy

*"There is only one happiness in this life,
To love and to be loved."*

~ George Sand

Chapter 1

Mimi

"I speak three languages," a guy boasted in English with a strong German accent.

"Ohhh!" a chorus of female voices gushed.

"I'm fluent in Dumb, Moron, and Stupid," the guy's unnecessary explanation sliced through the chaotic mixture of voices in the crowded café overlooking the Grand Canal.

Seriously?

Unable to stop herself, Mimi glanced over her shoulder and spotted three giggling young women standing around a blond twentysomething guy.

"Do you know you look like triplets?" he asked his easy-to-impress fan club while casually propping himself against the wrought iron fence surrounding the outdoor tables and folding his arms oh-so-casually.

Another peek confirmed what Mimi already gleaned from the first one—*their three different ethnic backgrounds say otherwise*—but the apparently smitten teenagers continued to giggle.

If that guy's the catch of the day, I'll gladly wait a little longer before I date again.

1

Since she wasn't the guy's target audience, Mimi tuned him out and took a selfie with the Rialto Bridge in the background, then began to type a message to her sister—and almost fell off her stool when an elbow rammed into her ribs.

Her head whipped around.

"Hey, watch it..." she said when two hands gripped her shoulders —and she looked directly into the trilingual moron's face.

"You look familiar. Have we met before?" he asked, apologies apparently not in his vast vocabulary.

How original!

Mimi shook off his hands and returned her attention to her phone —international language for "leave me alone."

He squeezed his khaki-clad butt between the next chair and hers, also without bothering to apologize to the person sitting there.

"I remember! I saw you on the Bridge of Sights," he said, proud and loud.

Bridge of Sights? Mimi cringed at his misnomer.

"Are you waiting for someone?" He put his foot on the bottom rung of her stool, smack between her feet.

Which. Pissed. Her. Off.

She knew it was impossible to avoid bumping shoulders with strangers in a jam-packed restaurant, but she was still extremely sensitive after her experience with Derek.

She shuddered. *Don't think about it. Shake it off.*

"Yeah, I'm waiting all right...for you to leave me alone." Mimi glared at him, then emptied her glass in one long gulp.

Anger—and frustration—stirred deep in her gut and she dropped her phone into her purse.

This was supposed to be *her* weekend to say goodbye to the city she'd fallen in love with over the past five months. How dare he ruin it for her?

But instead of wasting time with this fool, she'd be better off if she went ahead and paid the waiter and then found somewhere else to bask—uninterrupted—in Venice's venerable beauty.

2

Mimi signaled for the check when she saw a man about her own age winding swiftly through the crowded bar. Hip-hugging jeans covered long legs. A linen blazer hung by a hooked finger over his shoulder, sinewy forearms strained the rolled-up sleeves of his white button-down shirt and hinted at an overall toned body. Short, dark hair and three-day stubble perfected the look.

She fought the urge to fan herself with the menu and hoped her eyes weren't bulging as much as his biceps.

And almost toppled off the chair for a second time when Mr. Hot stopped next to her, removed his sunglasses, and grinned at her with the most stunning blue eyes she'd ever seen.

With a hand on the low back of her chair, he said in English tinged with a melodious Italian accent, "*Ciao, cara.* Sorry I'm late."

His baritone voice and rolled *r's* oozed over her like hot fudge over vanilla ice cream.

Suddenly, Mimi craved a scoop of gelato—and wouldn't mind sharing it with him. Only one spoon needed, of course.

With a flick of his wrist, Mr. Hot suggested to Casanova that he should try his luck elsewhere, and Mimi barely suppressed a chuckle when she watched the kid open his mouth, then close it again and slink away.

"Phew, thank you," she signaled again for her check.

"Can I persuade you to stay for a drink?" Mr. Hot asked.

"I..." she started, then imagined her BFF poking her, *Have some fun, Mim. You're surrounded by hundreds of tourists.*

Mr. Hot's hypnotic gaze was still on her, and it was hours before she had to catch her train, so she threw caution to the wind and nodded.

"Okay, why not? I couldn't enjoy my first one."

Mr. Hot turned to the waiting bartender and said in flawless Italian, "I'll have an *Apérol Spritz* and for the lady, whatever she wants."

Mimi ordered another mimosa and mused about his language pattern. He'd dropped the erotic Italian accent after he greeted her, and now he sounded suspiciously New Englandish. Since she grew up in Boston, it was a very familiar accent.

"Out of curiosity, what made you come to rescue me from the wannabe Casanova?"

He laughed and scratched his chin. "Well, it wasn't quite as knightly and altruistic as it might have appeared. I was trying to win the race for a table over there." He pointed to a table for two where new guests just settled.

She followed the direction of his finger and scrunched up her face in a *Sorry* expression. "Oops...too late now."

"I got a weird feeling when I saw him cramming you in and assumed you didn't know him. Something just rubbed me the wrong way." He studied her intensely. "Please tell me I didn't interrupt an amorous little chat!"

She laughed. "A little late to ask now, but no, you didn't. So, seriously, thanks again for getting rid of him."

"You're welcome! By the way, I'm Jake." He stood close enough that she got a whiff of cedarwood, sage, and something earthy. It suited him, and she liked it.

"Short for Jacob, Jacopo, or Giacomo, depending on who you ask," he whispered right next to her ear, sending delightful shivers down her spine.

Which she also liked.

"Mimi. Or Emily, only Emily." She matched his tone and held up both hands in a "what can I say" gesture.

"Nice to meet you, Mimi." The woman behind him vacated her chair and Jake promptly snagged it. "Is this your first time in Venice?"

"No," she shook her head, "I've been living in Verona and visited here several times. But I'm leaving soon and decided to take my time saying goodbye." She wasn't quite sure why she told him that but didn't want to analyze it. "And you?"

"I'm here frequently for business, but don't always take time to visit. Now I'm glad I decided to spend a few extra hours." He winked at her, not much more than a flutter of his eyelid, but it was sexy as hell.

After their drinks arrived, they chatted about favorite things to do in Venice and discovered their mutual fondness for exploring the narrow, off-the-beaten-path streets rather than the busy main drags, as well as visiting Murano, the group of tiny islands with world-famous glassmaking studios.

When Jake checked the time a little over an hour later and said he had reservations for the five o'clock train to Florence, Mimi was oddly disappointed. She couldn't remember having a more enjoyable afternoon in a long time—or being so at ease with a man in an even longer time.

Too bad they didn't meet months ago, when she first arrived in Italy.

You probably wouldn't have accepted his invitation for a drink then.

"Would you give me your phone number?" he asked. "If you don't mind. I'd like to get in touch next time I'm in the area."

Mimi wrote the number of her Italian burner phone on a scrap of paper without reminding him that she was leaving soon. There was no reason for it—nor for giving him her American number. Once she was back in Boston, today would only be a nice memory.

His thumbs flew over his phone and a moment later, her mobile buzzed. "That's me. Now you have my number too. If you happen to come to Florence, call me and I'll show you around."

After he paid, they walked toward the nearest *vaporetto* stop so Jake could hop on a water taxi to the train station. When the boat docked, he air-kissed her cheeks, his lips never touching her skin—a perfectly executed informal Italian hello/goodbye greeting.

"It was a pleasure meeting you, Mimi." When his gaze landed on her mouth, a balmy warmth surged through her that had nothing to do with the mimosas she consumed earlier.

He closed the distance and breathed the hint of a kiss on her lips.

"*Arrivederci, Mimi.*"

Chapter 2

Jake

Jake stowed his carry-on bag in the overhead compartment, leaned back in one of the comfortable first-class seats on the high-speed train, and ordered a double espresso when a waitress offered him a complimentary drink before the train even left Venice's Santa Lucia station.

Normally he'd take advantage of the next two hours and pull up an e-book on his tablet or jot down notes regarding the business meeting he'd attended in the city. But not today.

The train rolled out of the station and crossed the bay to the mainland—the port of Venice, with its cruise ship hub to his left, snow-capped peaks of the Dolomites in the far distance to his right—and Jake's mind circled back to Mimi.

He was hard-pressed to say what made him approach and pretend to know her. Maybe because of having been in the other guy's shoes about a decade ago himself—more than once crossing the blurry line between being dorky and being inappropriate—and knowing that nothing stopped unacceptable behavior faster than a territorial male friend showing up.

But more likely it had to do with the sharp pinch he felt in his chest when he spotted her. He'd have to be blind—or stupid—to not notice a beautiful woman sitting smack in the middle between him and the empty table he wanted to snag. And he was fairly certain he was neither blind nor stupid, even though his cousin Mikaela occasionally told him otherwise.

Yet there was something more about Mimi.

Jake could already hear his Aunt Francesca say, "Ah, it was Cupid's arrow that struck you." Followed by a retelling of her personal interpretation of Cupid and Psyche's love story, until she'd finish with two smacking kisses on his cheeks and say with disturbingly moist eyes, "I pray every day for you to find a good woman, Jacopo."

Yeah, better not mention Happy Hour in Venice.

His first image of Mimi flashed in his mind's eye again. Her brown hair falling in soft waves over her shoulders, her white sleeveless blouse so bright in the sunlight that it almost blinded him, and the fire in her eyes when she told the kid to leave her alone.

If fury caused such a blaze, what would she look like in the throes of passion?

Which will forever remain a mystery to you, Romeo.

Jake cleared his throat and crossed, then uncrossed, his legs, but couldn't get comfortable.

After the waitress served his espresso and a biscotti, Jake looked out the panoramic window but didn't pay attention to the scenery while the train gathered speed on its way to Florence.

He replayed Mimi's laughter, clear as glass, when she held her slim champagne flute closer to his bulbous wine glass and said, "Look at the colors. Don't they make you happy?"

THREE HOURS LATER HE ZIPPED DOWN THE FAMILIAR STATE highway between Florence and Siena in his Alfa Romeo Stelvio at ninety miles per hour—ten over the speed limit. Driving on the highways in Europe was so much more fun than in the States, since the roads were built for speed, and not dotted with potholes the size of bushel baskets.

Tree-covered knolls lined both sides of the four-lane *autostrada*, industrial parks alternated with residential neighborhoods, and here and there he spotted an ancient castle towering on a hill. The evening sun kissed the vineyards, orchards and olive groves and bathed the Tuscan landscape in a spectacular display of light.

After taking his exit and following a country road, he braced himself for his favorite view behind the next sharp curve. And, as always, it didn't disappoint.

The medieval towers of San Gimignano welcomed him back, even though he'd only been gone for two days.

He briefly wondered if Mimi had ever visited San Gimignano and strolled through the stunning walled hilltop town. Not only had it existed since Etruscan times, but it had also been used as the backdrop for numerous movies, books, and video games—and it was the place Jake called home for the past five years.

Reaching the sign advertising Bellini's Winery and *agriturismo*, he turned off the country road and steered his car down the long, winding gravel driveway that eventually ended at his aunt and uncle's private farmhouse—an understated term if he ever heard one, given its size.

To avoid leaving an enormous dust cloud in his wake, he slowed down and crept past his aunt's B&B, waving to guests sitting under a wooden pergola. With some pride, he recognized the wine bottle on their table.

The Chianti Classico *Gran Selezione* was produced from estate-grown grapes, had oak-aged for over three years, and he loved its underlying notes of vanilla and tart cherries and how full-bodied and smooth it was.

Bringing his SUV to a stop in front of a multi-door garage, Jake glanced at the digital clock on his dashboard. Almost nine.

Mimi had mentioned taking a train back to Verona. Did she have to go far from the train station to where she lived? He itched to text her and ask if she made it back all right.

But why? He absentmindedly rubbed a hand over his chest and licked his lips.

His mouth was dryer than the sun-scorched clay soil where his uncle's Vernaccia grapes thrived, and even though he knew it was impossible, he still tasted the mimosa on her lips.

Another spontaneous act he didn't want to analyze too closely right now.

It wasn't as if he didn't enjoy kissing beautiful women, and what it often led to—a casual fling, great sex, no strings attached.

But kissing Mimi felt different, and he couldn't say why. He only knew he'd needed to force himself to step away from her or he might've missed his train.

Jake grabbed his bag and blazer off the passenger seat and closed the car door with a hip swing. Whistling softly, he strolled toward the house. And a pleasant feeling, velvety like the Chianti he'd pour himself soon, filled his heart while his thoughts remained with Mimi.

Chapter 3

Mimi

Stepping out of the maze of alleys and canals, Mimi stopped in the middle of *Ponte degli Scalzi* and moved her eyes in slo-mo from left to right, from the sixteenth-century *San Simeone Piccolo* church with its green cupola, and across the ever-busy Grand Canal to the flat-roofed white Santa Lucia train station.

Did Jake catch his train? she wondered while she watched vaporetti, gondolas and other boats of all sizes weaving in and out in their well-coordinated dance of loading and unloading passengers.

"Jake...Jacob...Giacomo," she quietly repeated how he introduced himself, and let the Italian version of his name roll over her tongue. She always loved playing with words and languages—a side effect of being a fan of literary fiction, especially the old masters.

Mimi descended the pedestrian-friendly flat steps of the bridge and walked toward the train station, emotions overcoming her as she turned one last time and took in the squawking seagulls circling above her head, the masses of people from around the world, and the magical light of the early evening reflected in the rippling water of the Grand Canal.

Venice—what a feast for the senses!

Arrivederci, La Serenissima.

As if in answer, the bells of San Simeone chimed the full hour— and the end of her visit.

Mimi wiped away a trickle of tears and swallowed hard before she followed the stream of travelers into the train station and the hustle and bustle swallowed her. Retrieving her weekend bag from the self-storage locker, she couldn't help wondering whether Jake had also stowed his luggage here. He said he'd been in Venice for work but didn't carry any bags.

Why do you care?

Because she could still feel the heat from his goodbye peck on her lips.

Because she could still picture his long fingers when he held the stem of his wine glass and said, "To a wonderful afternoon in charming company."

Because of the way his eyes sparkled when he watched her while he sipped.

And it didn't bother her to be watched because she'd only seen friendliness in his gaze. And a healthy dose of flirting, which had sent gentle waves of warmth through her belly.

If she was honest—and she hadn't even confessed this to Paloma, her best friend—she missed being in a wholesome, sound relationship. And she didn't miss just the intimacy and sex, but also the familiarity and trust that built slowly over time.

But honesty required confidence, and hers was a little wobbly when it came to men.

After Mimi boarded and found her reserved seat, she stretched her legs and watched fellow travelers pulling out books or electronic devices, but she wanted to soak in every fleeting image she could catch, to store the memories for when she needed something cheerful in the coming weeks and months.

But they weren't moving yet, and stragglers still boarded, so she groped for the cell phone in her purse and scrolled through the newest photos. As always, the superb image quality baffled her. She had a decent digital camera at home, but in a city ripe with pickpockets, she didn't want to tempt fate by carrying expensive equipment when her mobile already did a fantastic job.

At the final photo, her heart jumped and, using two fingers, she enlarged the image. *Talk about tempting fate!*

Jake! Turning at the bottom of the Rialto Bridge and walking toward the café. He really was good-looking. And easy to talk to. And did she mention sexy?

She exhaled slowly, her heart rate returning to normal. With a quick tap, she added the image to her "favorites" folder before slipping the phone back into her purse.

The train lurched and was on its way across the bay toward Verona with stops in Padua and Vicenza, all cities she'd also visited frequently. But Venice held a unique place in her heart—and perhaps more so after today.

Mimi pondered the city's nickname, *La Serenissima*. She knew "The Most Serene" was a Byzantine title bestowed upon the ruling Doge that was eventually extended to the entire Republic of Venice when it was a maritime trading empire.

The history of Venice was as fascinating and colorful as its world-famous masks, now only worn during the annual festival that drew millions of visitors.

But Mimi wasn't one of the mask-wearing festivalgoers. She couldn't stand masks, didn't like how people hid behind them, pretending to be someone else for a day or two, and acting invincible. There were countless stories and books or movies about infidelity and folly during the Carnival season, and she not only didn't care whether they were true or fictional, she had absolutely no desire to play a role in those stories.

Like most people, she loved partying and cutting loose every now and then, but she also believed wholeheartedly in decency and having a moral compass.

And she'd been the victim of someone blurring the lines between fun and offense. And who got away with it—while she was labeled a liar.

Chapter 4

Mimi

ANNA STOPPED DOODLING ON THE NOTEPAD IN FRONT OF HER. "Miss Mimi, will you write to me?"

"You know I will, Anna. Will you write back to me in Italian?" Mimi smiled at the twelve-year-old sitting kitty-corner from her at the table.

"Yes, of course," the girl nodded, then said with a grin, "*Sì, certo.*"

Mimi ruffled Anna's unruly blonde curls. From the day she met the alert girl last December, Anna had been an eager student and a pleasure to work with, and it amazed Mimi how quickly the girl picked up Italian.

For the past five months they'd spent several hours a day, five days a week, in the villa's home office, which included a door that opened into a backyard surrounded by tall cypress hedges for maximum privacy. Anna's mother Belinda, an American A-list actress, was notorious for keeping her personal life—and, foremost, her daughter's—out of the public eye and away from paparazzi.

The private villa Belinda rented for the duration of the movie project was located in Verona's residential but lively *Cittadella* neighborhood, and provided protection yet was also within walking distance of the historic city center.

Mimi checked the time on her phone and placed both hands on the table. "I don't know about you, but I'm ready to eat something. Luciana told me there are plenty of leftovers from last night, and after lunch we can go to the farmer's market and pick up fresh fruit and vegetables."

"Luciana is the best housekeeper we ever had, and her lasagna is my favorite," Anna said with a big smile. "Can we also go to Juliet's house?"

Mimi smiled. Not a week went by without Anna asking to visit the most famous balcony in literature. "I guess we can make a stop there. Especially since I want to go to Fabio's gelateria at *Piazza Erbe*. Which means..."

"...we're right around the corner from *Casa di Giulietta*," Anna clapped her hands while she finished the sentence. "Hmm, what flavor will I try today? I love that they always have something new, like that licorice gelato."

"I THINK FABIO LIKES YOU," ANNA SAID, AS SOON AS THEY LEFT the gelateria an hour later, each holding a sugar cone. "Like...*reeeaaally* likes you."

"Oh, yeah? But what's the difference between liking and *really* liking?" Today wasn't the first time they had this or a similar conversation. For weeks Anna had tried to play matchmaker, hinting that Mimi should go on a date with Fabio.

"He always winks at you and calls you *cara* or *amore*."

"It's what he calls every woman," Mimi said and licked some of her ice cream.

Immediately thinking of Jake, who'd also playfully called her *cara*.

"I think he's giving you more gelato than the other customers."

Anna didn't give up easily, and compared her two scoops with Mimi's. "And don't you think he's hunky?"

Mimi bit the inside of her mouth to keep a neutral face, because, yes, he was hunky, but she also knew Fabio was as straight as the hairpin curves in the Alps, and owned the gelateria with his husband, Giancarlo.

"Listen, I don't think your mom would appreciate you calling Fabio, or any grown man, a hunk. Let's keep that between us."

"Okay, but if you don't want to go out with Fabio, how about Alessandro at *Trattoria La Volta*?"

"I think we need to find something else to talk about," Mimi smiled. "And don't forget, I'm leaving Italy next week." She leaned closer and whispered, "I don't want to leave a trail of broken hearts behind."

They walked through a long stone archway into a walled-in courtyard and joined dozens of tourists, most of whom reverently snapped pictures of the stone balcony protruding from the second story of a gothic-style thirteenth-century house.

Mimi knew Anna wouldn't leave until she peeked at some of the love letters covering part of the wall where the fictitious thirteen-year-old Juliet Capulet supposedly lived.

Licking the fast-melting ice cream before it dribbled down to her wrist, Mimi stood aside and kept an eye on Anna, but also watched tourists waiting in line at Juliet's bronze statue.

She chuckled. If rubbing a hand over Juliet's right breast increased one's chance of finding love, maybe she should get in line...

Licking more of her vanilla ice cream, Mimi shook her head over her fantasy of sharing some with Jake. Now, two weeks later, it seemed so silly. But the memory still sent warm shivers through her, and she had to admit that she'd pulled up his photo more than once.

I wonder how he's doing. She also wondered if he still thought about their meeting. She was pretty sure not one of the men she dated in the past would have. Maybe that was why her relationships never lasted.

Anna sidled up to her and recited, just loud enough for Mimi to hear, *"If I profane with my unworthiest hand This holy shrine, the gentle sin is this: My lips, two blushing pilgrims, ready stand To smooth that rough touch with a tender kiss."*

Mimi wasn't surprised to hear Anna quote the original version, but she was still impressed. There weren't many twelve-year-olds who'd recite Shakespeare instead of some modern pop song lyrics, not even at the private school at home where she taught English.

Especially not there...

"Miss Mimi, do you consider *Romeo and Juliet's* ending a good or a sad one?"

"Hmm... I think, if you look at it as a romantic play, it's a sad ending, because even though they love each other, they don't get to live a long and happy life. But, as some scholars argue, if you consider that the Capulets and the Montagues put their blood feud aside as a result, I'd say it's a positive ending."

Anna glanced up at the balcony where tourists called out mangled versions of *"O Romeo, Romeo! Wherefore art thou Romeo?"*

"I can't decide," the girl said and shrugged.

Mimi finished eating her sugar cone and pulled a package of wet wipes out of her purse. Holding out the package to Anna, she asked, "Did you know that there's no balcony mentioned anywhere in the entire play?"

"Really?" Anna's forehead crinkled.

"Romeo enters the Capulets' orchard and sees Juliet at a window."

"Yes, I remember! '*But, soft! what light through yonder window breaks? It is the east, and Juliet is the sun.*'" Anna's eyes lit up like Romeo's sun.

"The word 'balcone,' spelled b-a-l-c-o-n-e at the time, first appeared in 1618. Actually, the whole concept of a balcony was foreign to Shakespeare and his contemporaries because they didn't have them in England. About fifteen years after *Romeo and Juliet* was first performed, an English writer named Tom Coryat visited Venice and described a 'terrace that jutteth and butteth out from the main building.' He also referred to them as 'little galleries of pleasure.'"

Anna's shoulders slumped. "So, why is the balcony in the play now?"

"That's an excellent question. It's assumed that it sneaked in after Thomas Otway, a seventeenth-century playwright, wrote a play with many blatant parallels to Shakespeare's dialogue, plot, and characters."

"He copied Shakespeare's work?"

"Plagiarism wasn't unusual in those times, and it continued until the 1840s, when Charles Dickens advocated for international copyright laws." Mimi put a hand on Anna's shoulder and gently turned her toward the archway to leave the courtyard. "And as for the balcony on this house, that was constructed in the early twentieth century by adding an old sarcophagus to the outside of the building."

"How do you know all that?"

"I'd be a lousy English teacher if I weren't familiar with Shakespeare. But more importantly, I wanted to learn as much as possible about Verona."

Once they were again strolling through the historic streets and dodging tourist groups, Anna sighed, "I want to fall in love like Juliet one day. But with a happier ending."

You have no idea how much I also long for that happy ending.

Chapter 5

Mimi

AT THE END OF THE FOLLOWING WEEK, MIMI AND BELINDA sipped red wine in the privacy of the backyard while Anna popped the metal cap off her second bottle of *Orangina*.

"Mom, can Miss Mimi be my tutor again when you go to your next location?"

"We'll see. But first we're going home for the summer. Daddy can't wait to see you," Belinda said.

"He could've come visit us more often." The Shakespeare-quoting preteen morphed into a pouting twelve-year-old.

"You know our goal is for one of us to always be at home with you, but circumstances out of his control kept him away longer than expected."

Mimi had met Anna's father twice. Like his wife, Christian Solomon was a sought-after actor—and equally down-to-earth in his private life.

"Stupid Australia. Why does he always have to work there?" Anna pouted.

"Honey, you're not being fair. He's not always there, but people go where their work is, and Daddy's was in Australia this time."

"Why can't Daddy be a teacher like Miss Mimi? Then he wouldn't have to travel."

Belinda raised her shaped eyebrows, "Excuse me? You know Miss Mimi is from Boston and has friends and family there, and you just asked if she could travel with us to the next movie set. Does that make sense?"

Anna scrunched up her face, then jumped out of her chair. "I can't FaceTime with Daddy right now because of the time difference, but I'll send him an email, then he can read it when he wakes up," she said, once again the logical preteen.

"Good idea, honey. Daddy will love it."

After Anna left, Belinda said, "I appreciate everything you did for us. We'll both miss you. Hiring you as Anna's tutor was like finding a needle in a haystack. And so much easier for her than getting used to a new school for only a few months—or staying in the States with her grandparents. I prefer for her to be with my husband or me."

"She's such a smart girl, and it was my pleasure to work with her." Mimi looked around, memorizing every nook of the sheltered garden. "The past months are hard to describe with only a few words or sentences but let me try."

She held up a fist and ticked off fingers, "Living with an international movie star"—her pinkie snapped up—"in a luxury villa in one of the most romantic cities in Italy"—her ring finger snapped up—"meeting some of your co-stars"—the third finger joined the first two—"fabulous food prepared by a housekeeper every day"—the index finger went up—"and all the weekend trips with you and Anna"—all five fingers were up—"yeah, I'd say it's me who should be saying thank you."

Belinda smiled. "You're very welcome. And I would hire you again without hesitation. I haven't finalized my next contract, but my agent pesters me daily." She sighed and sipped her wine. "I told Archie to let me go home first and take a break, but I don't have much time. Would you mind if I contact you if Chris's and my schedules overlap again?"

Mimi hadn't considered working as a tutor in the future, but she'd be silly to burn that bridge. She wanted to think positive, but, as Belinda reminded Anna only a couple of minutes ago, people had to go where the work was, and who knew what awaited her in Boston? Plus, she enjoyed tutoring the artistic, inquisitive Anna.

"What are your next plans?" Belinda asked and chuckled. "Maybe I should've started with that question."

Mimi savored the aroma of the Shiraz and vaguely detected notes of smoke and blackberry. She didn't know much about winemaking, and was no connoisseur, but she did know pinot noir and Shiraz were her favorites.

She sipped slowly, then said, "My sister's getting married in August, and, knowing Nicki, she has lots of stuff planned, so that'll keep me busy for a while. And I have to prepare for the next school year."

"What about seeing your colleague again? The one who..." Belinda left the sentence unfinished.

Mimi took a deep breath. When she initially interviewed for the tutor job, she shared her professional background with Belinda. But once she arrived in Italy, they quickly became friends, and one evening she confided why she'd taken a sabbatical.

"I have to accept and deal with it. Derek still works there, no matter how mad it makes me. I'm not afraid of him, but I'll make sure I'm never alone with him ever again."

"He shouldn't be there anymore," Belinda muttered into her glass. "But, needless to say, I'll write you a glowing recommendation, and please come visit us in Amagansett if you have time."

"Before you jet off to wherever you'll go next," Mimi laughed, then sobered. "Saying goodbye to Anna tomorrow won't be easy, and I'd love to stay in touch."

At ten o'clock the next morning, Mimi fastened the plane's seatbelt in her lap and winced. The metallic *click* was like the door to a chapter of her life snapping shut behind her.

Cold crept along her skin, the shawl around her shoulders no match for it.

As the Embraer 195 departed Verona's Villafranca Airport and smoothly climbed into the cloudless sky, tears puddled in Mimi's eyes.

She glanced back at the rapidly vanishing city, couldn't enjoy the views of the deep-blue Lake Garda or the still snow-capped mountain tops of the Alps or the Rhine River snaking leisurely between Switzerland, Germany, and France on her one-hour flight to Frankfurt to board a larger jet, which would take her farther away from the place where she'd been happy.

She imagined an invisible clock ticking away the minutes—a merciless, unstoppable countdown to her old life.

Chapter 6

Jake

Mɪᴀ ᴀɴᴅ ʜᴇʀ ғɪᴀɴᴄᴇ́, Aɴᴛᴏɴɪᴏ, ᴅʀᴏᴘᴘᴇᴅ Jᴀᴋᴇ ᴏғғ ᴀᴛ ᴛʜᴇ winery after visiting *La Sagra della Ciliegia*, the annual cherry festival in Lari, a small town in the province of Pisa.

He never tired of the historical costumes or the medieval contests like jousting. But his favorites were the colorful parades of the *contradas*, the town's districts, the experience heightened by the authenticity and atmosphere of the ancient Italian towns. In the States he'd never been interested in battle reenactments or Renaissance Fairs, and couldn't imagine them even coming close to the ones he visited here.

"Are you sure you don't want to come with us to Salvatore's party?" Mia asked as she jumped out of Tonio's car and followed Jake into the house. She needed to speed walk to keep up with his long strides, but what she was missing in height she easily made up in spunk.

"Tell him I'm sorry, but you know how crazy this week was. I need a quiet evening."

"You'll break Gianna's heart if you don't show up," his cousin teased him after she grabbed her sweatshirt off a high-backed chair in the foyer and turned to leave again.

One more reason to bail.

"I hear she's telling people you two are an item." Being thirty didn't stop Mia from making silly kissing sounds, especially since she knew it would aggravate Jake.

"We are absolutely not an item, and I hope she isn't spreading rumors."

"Didn't you take her out a few times?" Mia put her hands on her hips.

"We met for drinks twice, but there were other people with us. I never asked her out alone."

Conversations like this one irritated the hell out of him. He knew several of his cousin's friends wouldn't mind a roll or two in the hay, and some were rather transparent about it, like Gianna. But even if he was remotely interested in her—which he was not—he wouldn't do it.

When he was seventeen his father got wind of Jake making out with a seasonal waitress at his family's hotel on Martha's Vineyard, and gave him a thorough tongue-lashing. Since then Jake adhered to three house rules that might as well be written in stone for him and his siblings:

No dating or sleeping or making out with guests.

No dating or sleeping or making out with staff—year-round or seasonal.

No dating or sleeping or making out with his sister's friends.

And when he moved here, Jake automatically transferred those rules to Uncle Fausto's winery, because why would his uncle think any differently?

"What do you want me to say if Gianna asks where you are?" Mia asked.

"Tell her it's none of her business," he grumbled.

Mia's leather sandals clacked on the tile floor as she crossed the entry hall and smacked him on his shoulder. "I will not be rude to a friend because of you."

She grinned up at his 6'3" from her 5'4", undaunted by her height disadvantage. "Maybe I'll tell her you'll give her a call this week. You know, if she's really inconsolable..."

He glared at her. "Mia, if you think you're funny, think again. Do yourself a favor and disabuse Gianna of her silly idea that we have something going. Because it'll be *you* she'll come crying to."

Mia screwed up her face. "Yeah, I guess that's true. Ugh..." She turned and opened the front door. "But... Are you sure you can't meet her just once? A little kissing and holding hands, maybe? You could do something gross, like chewing gum when you're smooching, and maybe she'll think you're an ogre and lose interest."

Jake put a finger to his ear and shook it hard. Did he just hear Mia correctly?

"I'm not going to dignify that insanity with an answer." A car honking in the courtyard saved him from further discussions of his kissing techniques. "Ah, hear that? Don't make Tonio wait." He held up a hand and waved to his cousin as he walked toward the back of the house. "Bye—and have fun. Tell Salvatore I'll catch up with him soon."

Jake entered the farmhouse's large, modern kitchen, about to pour himself some Chianti, but paused, then grabbed the entire bottle and a glass and took both outside. The air was dense with the rich scent of the vineyard's soil, and he took a few deep breaths. He'd never get tired of the rich, and wholesome, smell.

He strolled past the in-ground pool, shivered at the thought of the still-frigid water, and walked through the damp grass toward a small olive grove at the far end of the property.

Neatly tied umbrellas and lounge chairs were scattered all over the lawn, a stark contrast to the straight, orderly rows of vines on his uncle's twenty hectares—roughly fifty acres—of land.

None of the guests were around, and he was grateful for the solitude.

Aunt Francesca's *agriturismo* only included breakfast, and Jake assumed everyone went out for dinner and evening drives through the country-side, especially after the short but furious afternoon rainstorm that had cleansed the air and would reward them with a spectacular sunset.

Jake reached the gnarly olive trees, put the bottle and glass on a low stone wall, and sank into a wooden lounge chair almost as ancient as the trees.

It was one of Jake's favorite spots to relax in the evenings, and he reveled in the picture-perfect views over the vineyard, orchards, and the impressive skyline of the fourteen conserved stone towers of San Gimignano in the distance.

Somewhere a church bell tolled, a sound as familiar as the wind rustling the young leaves of the chestnut trees and the farm equip-ment still humming on neighboring land.

He poured some Chianti and savored the aroma. It was a new blend, and would make a decent house wine. Not every year produced outstanding vintages, and not everybody could afford the prices those vintages would sell for, so they needed to make wines for everybody's taste and wallet.

Jake's attention swept over the rolling hills, then landed on the wild corn poppies, or "Tuscan poppies," growing on the edge of the olive grove. The pretty, hardy agricultural weed had been around for centuries and was still growing all around the globe.

After swirling the wine, Jake sipped and let it sit on his tongue, then rolled it around his mouth before swallowing it. This wasn't a wine tasting, so he didn't need to sip and spit, a practice he found disgusting. Necessary, but no less repellent. And he knew of more than a few wine tasters who chose to forgo it.

In front of him, the glowing sphere of the sun touched the horizon and transformed the sky into a mesmerizing spectacle of luminous shades of yellow, orange, red, and purple.

He reached down to snap off one of the poppies, and held it against the wine glass, liking how the bright red flower comple-mented the burgundy. Jake took out his cell phone and snapped a few pictures. He might use one for an ad or display it on the winery's website.

A woman's laughter flowed through the air, followed by a playful shriek. And it made him think—as he so often did these days—of Mimi.

Meeting her was nothing but happenstance, and he didn't have an ulterior motive when he invited her for a drink. It had simply been a spontaneous act...

Right time—right place.

So why was he still thinking about her so much?

Was it the ease he felt in her company? How he was only aware of that moment—fleeting as it had been—and wished they could've had more time together?

He sipped his wine, letting the velvety liquid caress his throat.

If she was sitting here with him, would they be talking, or enjoying the silence? Or would he reach over to play with her hair...?

The wooden chair was suddenly too hard and uncomfortable. *Mental note, suggest to Aunt Francesca that she should invest in outdoor cushions.*

Jake scooted around, knowing his discomfort had nothing to do with the chair or lack of cushions. His body reminded him—also not for the first time—of a few other things about Mimi that hadn't escaped his attention.

The way her eyes sparkled when she listened intently. How she wasn't embarrassed to burst out in hearty laughter. Her slender body when she rose from her chair. The swell of her breasts when he glanced down before giving her a peck on the lips.

Without thinking, he reached for his phone and typed, I'LL BE IN YOUR AREA NEXT WEEK. CAN I TAKE YOU OUT TO DINNER?

Jake attached the photo of the poppy and the wine—and hit send.

The phone pinged before he shoved the phone back in his pocket. *That was fast.* He smiled while his heart galloped.

But his smile faltered when he read, *MESSAGE UNDELIVER-ABLE. INVALID NUMBER.*

What?

He heard her phone ringing when he texted her his number.

Jake re-sent the message—only to get the same error notification.

He took another sip of his wine. And spit it out.

It tasted sour.

Chapter 7

Mimi

Relaxing in a shady spot under the arched, wisteria-covered trellises in Christopher Columbus Waterfront Park, Mimi sipped her Frappuccino and rested her aching feet after hours of shop-hopping. In front of her, blindingly bright yachts bobbed in the calm water of Boston's Long Wharf.

She watched her sister stroll up and down Harborwalk, her phone pressed to her ear. When Nicki giggled and shrieked, "Ray, stop it!", Mimi slipped off her sandals with a deep sigh—they'd be here awhile.

Mimi looked past the long brick buildings flanking the harbor basin and gazed across the sparkling water to Logan International Airport. She watched the sleek airplanes taking off—like a perpetual ant colony, they followed each other at exactly spaced intervals—and quickly getting smaller until they disappeared on the hazy horizon. Equally quickly, new planes arrived, their landing gear extended and ready to touch down.

Only two weeks ago I was a passenger. She sighed and used the straw in the domed plastic cup to stir her drink.

Returning home had been bittersweet, and she was still adjusting.

It was wonderful being with her family again. If she wanted, she could go out to dinner every evening, but she paced herself, mostly because she didn't want to repeat herself daily about her experience of living in Italy—and as part of a famous movie star's household, the icing on the cake for some of her friends.

But she missed Italy and the leisurely life she had. Belinda gave her carte blanche about Anna's lessons after Mimi devised a lesson plan and curriculum in accordance with New York's homeschool regulations. And while their schedule had included several hours of sit-down instruction, it also allowed for museum visits and immersing themselves in daily life.

Was there a better way to combine English lessons with art or history than by exploring local places of interest? Anna would remember *Villa La Rotonda* in Vicenza when she stood in front of the White House or Thomas Jefferson's Monticello, both buildings designed based on Palladio's architectural style.

"If you continue pursing your lips like that, you'll get wrinkles around your mouth."

Mimi's head snapped sideways at her sister's voice. "What?"

"I've been watching you," Nicki said. "You're moving your lips whenever you think. Like this," she demonstrated a few moves that resembled grimaces. "But don't worry, Ray can inject gel fillers if the lines get too bad. I'll make sure he doesn't charge you."

"Nobody's going to inject anything into my lips, thank you very much. When the time comes, I'll wear my wrinkles proudly." She eyed her sister's face, hoping she was only kidding. "Please tell me you didn't turn into an advocate for enhancers only because your fiancé is a cosmetic dermatologist."

"No...at least not yet." Nicki plopped down next to her and lowered her voice, "But maybe I'll do something here." She put the back of her hand under her breasts and gave them a lift.

Mimi almost dropped her coffee. "Are you shitting me?"

"Well, Ray commented about my girls being on the smaller side."

"And he's only noticing that *now?*" Mimi shook her head and glanced down at her own barely size B chest. "I mean, yeah, we got Mom's genes, but come on..." She squared her shoulders, as if standing firm against an invisible evil.

Mimi had never been a huge fan of her sister's boyfriend. Raymond Lancaster III was spoiled and arrogant—at least in her opinion. But if Nicki was happy with him, it wasn't Mimi's place to say anything.

"You've been dating him for what—six years? And have been engaged for one, and *now* he starts complaining?"

Nicki rolled her eyes. "I didn't say I'll do it. But I wanted to hear your thoughts about it."

"Well, now you have."

"Tanya got hers done."

"She did? Well, I guess that shouldn't surprise me." Mimi knew Ray's sister aspired to a career as a model, but the career hadn't quite taken off yet. "Please, Nic, don't do anything you're not a hundred percent sure about."

"I promise. And don't tell Mom, okay? She'd freak out."

"I have no reason to tell her," Mimi said. "So, what's next on our agenda?" She nodded to the mound of shopping bags next to her. "Seems as if we got everything you wanted. Time to head home?"

"I'd like to go look for one more dress for the bachelorette weekend."

"I thought we'll be wearing tank tops. Didn't you order three sets of party tops for us, a different color for each day?"

"Those are for during the day. I need a few dresses for evenings."

"What about the two summer dresses you bought at the same store where I got the sleeveless maxi dress?"

"Yeah, but..." Nicki batted her eyelashes at Mimi at an impressive speed, and added a pitiful expression for good measure. "Pleeease..."

Mimi laughed and bumped Nicki's shoulder. "Okay. You win. Since it's your weekend, you get to decide! So, where to now?"

"Let's go to Boylston Street," Nicki said while she grabbed her bags. "There are tons of stores, and if I don't find anything within the next hour, we call it a day. We still have two weeks until we head to the Vineyard."

Nicki was her only sibling, but because she'd been away, Mimi hadn't been of much help with any wedding-related planning. It was something that frequently gnawed on her, and while they strolled toward Faneuil Hall she said, "You have to let me know how I can help you. I feel terrible that you had to organize the bachelorette weekend by yourself. It would've been my responsibility as your maid of honor."

Nicki swatted her comment away like a pesky fly.

"Don't waste even one more thought about it. I recruited Tanya. But there really wasn't much to do. We rented a three-bedroom cottage for three nights and booked our flights. Mom paid for yours and mine."

"Oh, that's nice of her. But that's a super-short flight from Logan to the Vineyard. How big are the airplanes?"

"Six to ten passengers."

Mimi froze on the spot, the heat of the hot asphalt immediately seeping through her thin leather soles. "Six...to...ten?" she croaked.

"Yup. Tanya said she flew in one a few weeks ago and they're totally safe."

Mimi cleared her throat. She didn't really trust Tanya's ability to judge the safety of an airplane, but if Martha's Vineyard had an airport and offered daily flights, she'd just hope for the best. And didn't statistics always say flying was much safer than driving a car?

"It's so much easier. We'd waste too much time if we drove ourselves. Not only being on the road, but also waiting for the ferry in Woods Hole and then the ferry ride itself. Plus, we'd need to go in two cars, since there are six of us."

Ever heard of stretch limos or SUVs with a third row? Can't be more expensive than plane tickets for six women. But since she hadn't been around to help with planning the event, she decided it was best to keep her mouth shut.

"You're right. I don't mean to criticize everything, Nic," Mimi hugged her sister. "Just ignore me."

"We'll have so much fun, I can't wait. Party time! Woohoo!" With her shopping bags held up high, Nicki danced a little jig, making bypassers stop and laugh.

An hour later, at the last store Mimi agreed to enter, Nicki poked her head around the curtain into Mimi's dressing room. "Holy shit. I told you that's a killer dress."

Mimi turned her head to look in the side mirrors. Even though she hadn't planned to buy anything, this dress screamed "Try me on" when she spotted it on the rack.

The soft-flowing dress had spaghetti straps and an empire waist. It was flirty without being provocative and the ruching across the chest was very flattering for her body type. But what caught Mimi's eye first was how the tie-dye blended from yellow on top into warm ombre at the above-knee hem.

The colors triggered a memory, and Mimi swallowed hard.

"By the way," Nicki babbled on while she closed the curtain again. "I need to know who you're bringing as your plus-one."

"Nobody. Just me."

Chapter 8

Jake

Booming thunder and the incessant pounding of rain against his windows drowned out every other sound. Jake eyed the wine bottle on the counter of his kitchenette, then the clock on his laptop.

Maybe another half a glass?

Nah, it was already past midnight, and the wine wouldn't help him sleep any better. He slammed his laptop shut and shoved it across the coffee table before getting up to pace around his studio apartment in the annex of his uncle's farmhouse.

His nightly online cruising was becoming an unhealthy fixation that tainted his mood, which was already sorely tested after a series of strong storms prevented him, Fausto, and their helpers from working on the crucial green pruning, a task he normally enjoyed.

And then there was his upcoming trip home—another dark cloud over his head.

In less than a week, he'd be on a plane to America—something most people would look forward to, but which he dreaded, and not just because the vines here needed so much work. Besides, Uncle Fausto had hired a young man who usually helped with harvest in the fall, and Aunt Francesca was adamant about Jake spending two weeks on Martha's Vineyard as planned.

"Your *mamma* hasn't seen you since last Christmas," she'd said at dinner. "Now she turns sixty and should have all her children there." Then—accompanied by a very audible "hmph"—she deposited a heaping bowl of pasta on the massive kitchen table and drizzled her homemade olive oil over it.

Jake grinned while he remembered how Fausto turned away and busied himself with lining up flatware like tin soldiers. Years ago he'd confided to Jake that he learned early in his marriage when to keep his mouth shut and his opinions to himself. "Believe me, the first years of our marriage were explosive," he'd said, then grinned.

From interactions Jake observed between his aunt and uncle over the years, he assumed he wasn't only referring to verbal exchanges. He was pretty sure they kept their romantic flame burning and stoked the fire often. His aunt and uncle had a happy marriage, and so did his parents.

Ignoring his earlier resolve, Jake added two fingers of wine to his glass and propped one butt cheek on the counter.

He could have worse role models than his aunt and uncle—or his parents. And although he was in no rush to plant the seeds of the next generation of Bellinis—in fact, he wouldn't mind if his younger brother or sister beat him to those dubious honors—he ultimately hoped to find the same happiness with a woman who shared his goals and understood his dreams.

A woman who completed him.

But where would he find his happiness? Here or in America? Would he, like his father decades ago, turn his back on his home?

And why was he even having these thoughts?

Muttering a few choice words, he eyed his laptop. Ever since the day his text messages to Mimi bounced back, he'd been obsessed with finding her.

He'd double-checked the phone number she gave him and finally noticed the country code for Italy, 39. Which meant the phone was either a burner or she used a prepaid SIM card to avoid astronomical roaming charges. But why hadn't she just given him her American phone number?

Dude, what did you expect? She told you she was leaving soon. You had one drink together.

Jake argued with his inner voice. *Actually, we both had two.*

One or two, what does it matter? Just accept that she's no longer here and let it go.

But that was the crux of the matter—he couldn't let go.

His next step had been to mentally scroll through what he knew about her—and realized it was close to nothing. Again, no surprise. *Why should she have told you anything about her personal life? And when would she have had time to do it?*

He had no last name and didn't know where she lived in the States—even though he was certain she had a Boston accent.

All he had was her first name. "Mimi. Or Emily. Only Emily."

His online quest had taken him into the abyss of social media; another fruitless experience, since the only search terms he had were "Emily/Mimi" and "Boston." And he didn't need to be Nostradamus to predict the outcome of *that* search. The only thing he gained were a dozen daily friend requests from women in varying degrees of undress.

He downed the last of his wine and put his glass in the sink. Turning off the lights, he racked his brain, trying to figure out what other options he had.

Chapter 9

Mimi

THIS WILL BE THREE DAYS OF TORTURE!

Mimi tried—unsuccessfully—to tune out Huey, Dewey, and Louie's babble during their check-in at Logan Airport.

Her sister's friends didn't just look identical, with their long hair, short skirts, designer sunglasses and purses—they also happened to have eerily similar names: Sally, Ally, and Kelly. Years ago, Mimi had secretly named them after Donald Duck's nephews, and the monikers stuck—at least in her mind. She had never dared call the women those names to their faces. Although she might've referred to them as "the ducklings" in conversation with Nicki...

All three hung on Tanya's Botoxed lips and *oohed* and *aahed* about the tales of her latest photo shoot for some guy who put together a photography portfolio—Mimi presumed the photos were more firefighter-calendar quality than *Vogue* level—but she was impressed by the ducklings' ability to listen and wrap scrunchies around their hair at the same time.

She never understood how her sister became such close friends with those women, but somehow they bonded during orientation of their college freshman year and were almost inseparable since.

Mimi chuckled—as sisters, she and Nicki had a lot in common, but while she was happy with a few very close friends, Nicki was a social butterfly.

Maybe that's why she's happy with Ray?

"Mim? Are you coming?" Nicki called and beckoned to her.

"Yup."

They followed a ramp agent in his yellow-orange reflective vest down the stairs and onto the tarmac, where he guided them to several neatly parked twin Cessnas, their blue tails pointing toward the blemish-free morning sky.

The young man stopped at the first airplane and said, "Please remember there's absolutely no cell phone use allowed during the flight. Cameras are fine."

Huey sidled closer to him and asked, "Is the camera on my phone okay?"

Mimi watched his Adam's apple move up and down, mirroring his eyes that then stopped on Huey's cleavage—very prominently displayed in her "Bridesmaid" tank top— before he said, "No, umm... sorry." And Huey only shrugged.

After the bags were stowed on the small airplane, the luggage guy said, "Ladies, your chariot is ready to board. But we need a volunteer to sit up front with the captain. Would the bride like to take the co-pilot's seat?" he looked at Nicki, easily identifiable because her tank top declared her the "Future Mrs."

"What?" Nicki fluttered her hands in front of her. "Why can't we all sit together?"

"We need to balance the weight on the aircraft, which sometimes requires a second person in the cockpit," he said, and Mimi secretly gave him credit for telling them very diplomatically that they brought too much baggage.

"I'll pass, but thanks for offering," Nicki said.

"Any volunteers?" luggage guy asked.

"I'll do it," Mimi said. "It sounds like fun."

Luggage guy nodded and beckoned for her to board first. She

ducked her head and climbed the two rickety steps of the fold-down stairs. As soon as she set foot in the Cessna, a woman called from the nose of the airplane, "Come right up front."

Mimi joined her in the tiny cockpit. "Hi, I'm Mimi. I'm your new co-pilot."

"Have a seat. I'm Amelia, and I'm your captain on our forty-minute flight to Martha's Vineyard."

Mimi sat down in the co-pilot's seat and snorted. "Please say your last name isn't..." She clapped a hand over her mouth.

"Yeah, I get that reaction frequently. And no, it's not Earhart," Amelia said with a twinkle in her eyes.

"I'm so sorry," Mimi said, "I guess I forgot my filter at check-in."

"Don't worry, you're not the first one, nor will you be the last one," Amelia said good-naturedly. "So, what brings you onboard my flight this morning?"

Mimi pointed to the words "maid of honor" on her tank top. "My sister's bachelorette weekend."

Amelia peeked out the window to her left. "Ah, sounds fun. Your friends are boarding as we speak." Her observation was underscored by flip-flops slapping up the metal stairs.

Mimi pointed to the controls in front of her and asked, "What happens if I accidentally touch any of these?"

"Nothing at all," Amelia said. "They're disabled." She held out at a headphone, identical to hers. "But put these on, and you can listen in on my conversation with the tower during taxing and takeoff."

"Cool."

While Amelia ran through her checklists, Mimi turned sideways and watched Nicki and her friends take their seats—a task that took no more than a couple of minutes with only ten seats to choose from —and soon the door to the small aircraft was secured and Amelia received the marshaller's start-up sign.

Mimi was amazed at how different sitting in the cockpit felt compared to the cabin of a larger plane.

They fell into line behind an Airbus A320, which was behind

another Cessna, which in turn tailed a Boeing 737. Of course she'd seen small and large airplanes waiting in line for takeoff, but this was a totally new and surprisingly exciting experience.

Everything seemed much bigger from where she sat. *Well, you're kind of comparing sitting in a Smart car to sitting in a Humvee.*

She wasn't a passive spectator, either. This front-row seat and being able to watch Amelia command the tiny plane made her feel as if she was also in control.

Fascinated, she listened to Amelia's communication with the tower and fought tears when it was their turn to take off. Takeoffs were her favorite part of flying, and when Amelia advanced the throttles and their little grasshopper lifted off within a few seconds, she watched the skyline of Boston through a thin veil of tears. The panoramic view was otherworldly.

As little as she felt like spending the next three days around Tanya and the ducklings, this, all by itself, made it absolutely worth it.

And while the plane climbed higher, then turned and headed toward Martha's Vineyard, Mimi felt free and at ease, all her emotional baggage left behind on the tarmac.

Which was why she paid only minimal attention when Tanya started to entertain Nicki and the ducklings with stories about someone she called Dick. And after hearing about this guy's connections to sports teams and how great he was in the sack, Mimi focused on the spectacular views in front and below her. Tanya's boy toys were the least of her worries.

Chapter 10

Jake

Jake browsed the impressive, temperature-controlled wine cellar of Bellini's Cliff House hotel after his father asked him to pick out the wine for his mom's birthday celebration tomorrow.

All the bottles were meticulously clean, and ready to be opened and served as soon as guests ordered them, the glass gleaming in the bright overhead light—a stark contrast to his uncle's winery, where some vintages rested peacefully under a thick layer of dust in the farthest corner of the underground cellar.

Jake was surprised to find bottles from Bellini's Winery but wasn't going to poke the dragon by choosing one of them. Even though they'd be perfect for the surf and turf he knew they'd be having for dinner.

His stomach growled in anticipation, despite the hearty breakfast he wolfed down an hour ago. The briny ocean air increased his appetite, or maybe it was because of his hour-long jog along the beach.

Since he arrived on the Vineyard a week ago, he started each day by going for an early-morning run, followed by breakfast, and for the rest of the day he pitched in here and there—wherever he was needed.

Just thinking about a juicy filet mignon with fresh pepper and garlic butter and lobster drizzled with lemon juice made Jake's mouth water. Add farm-fresh corn on the cob and baby potatoes, both lightly seasoned—yeah, this meal had always been a family favorite.

At first he'd assumed dinner would be catered. But his sister, Carla, called him out when he asked about it.

"That was before we had a chef *and* caterer in the family," she said with a challenging frown.

"But don't you want to sit and celebrate with Mom?" he asked.

"Dude, if I didn't enjoy cooking, I wouldn't have chosen the profession," she said and rolled her eyes. "And since I'm the event planner *and* hospitality manager at the hotel, I'm mostly behind a desk and don't get to cook nearly often enough."

He could've countered that he'd become a lawyer and wasn't practicing. But that was a discussion he didn't need to have with his sister. It was one he needed to have with himself...eventually...when he was ready for it.

Jake set several bottles of cabernet sauvignon aside, knowing they'd go well with both the beef and lobster. And while he preferred reds, he knew his mom loved the herbal flavors of a chilled cabernet blanc, so he pulled some of those out too.

After adding several bottles of Champagne, he'd just finished filling two cardboard boxes when his brother, Matt, poked his head around the corner. "Finding anything good?"

"Yeah, this should be enough for the weekend. What are you up to?"

"I'm off to the airport to pick up the bachelorette party staying in the Poppy Cottage."

Phew, glad I dodged that bullet. "Why are you going? Isn't one of the summer interns usually delegated to chauffeuring?"

"Yeah, but the kid called in sick today, and instead of pulling another intern and upsetting the fine-tuned schedules, I'll do it. It's part of running a family business, and I'm betting you do the same at Uncle Fausto's winery."

Jake nodded. It was no different.

"When are you picking up Grandma and Grandpa?" Matt propped a shoulder against the doorjamb, his ankles crossed, in no rush to pick up the girls' group.

"Soon. I've got a reservation for the ten forty-five ferry to Woods Hole and a return reservation on the four o'clock one. That'll give Grandma and Grandpa time to get settled before dinner."

"Grandpa told Mom they could drive themselves to Hyannis and take the high-speed passenger ferry."

Jake shook his head. "I thought he's not supposed to drive because of his vision?"

"You're right, he isn't, and we should probably confiscate his car keys. The retirement home shuttle takes them wherever they want to go on the Cape."

"Good luck with that," Jake laughed. "But I really don't mind doing the driving. It's the least I can do. If I'm around too long I'm afraid Dad will snag me for his habitual 'we need to talk' chat…"

"At least they don't come as a huge surprise to you anymore," Matt laughed with him.

"Mom said Grandpa and Grandma are staying in the Daisy cottage, as usual." Jake picked up one cardboard box and pointed his chin to the second one. "Can you grab that for me?"

Matt picked it up and, on their way up from the wine cellar, said, "It's their preferred away-from-home place to stay, and they don't do it often. They're too busy with bridge club, bocce tournaments, and treasure hunts on the beach."

"Ahhh…the Rose, Poppy, Hollyhock, and Daisy, aka the Cliff House Cottages," Jake recited with a smirk. Growing up, he was often enough tasked with painting the doors, window trims and flower boxes in the respective colors. Shades of pink and red for the first three—yellow for the Daisy. If he closed his eyes, he could probably still recollect the sickening smell of the paint.

"You got it," Matt laughed. "I remember when you asked one year why the Daisy can't be painted pink, too. For a 'more uniform appearance,' as you so cannily added."

"Because then, Jacob, it would need to be renamed Echinacea cottage," Jake mimicked their grandmother's voice and chortled. "All summer that year I searched the island to find a pink daisy to prove Grandma wrong."

"Maybe she set their private cottage apart so Grandpa wouldn't wander into the wrong cottage by accident after dark," Matt laughed. "Can you imagine the headlines in the *Vineyard Gazette*?"

"Oh yeah, I can... 'James Faulkner, reputable businessman and founder of Faulkner's Woodworking and Fine Carpentry, surprised a sleeping guest in one of his wife's cottages,'" Jake improvised and laughed too. "I doubt that would've happened. His eyesight was perfect until a few years ago. For as long as I can remember, he could spot a crooked nail from a mile away."

"That's for sure."

After putting the wine in Jake's car, Matt walked toward a minivan parked beside a multicar garage. Halfway there he stopped and came back.

Running a hand over his hair, he said, "You know, it's nice to have you home. Maybe we can go hang out in Boston for a night before you leave next week."

"I'd like that too," Jake said. "But this being July, it probably isn't the best time to play hooky. Dad would have a fit."

"Since I'm sales manager at the hotel, I could say I have a meeting. But you're right, we never got away with fibbing, and that hasn't changed. Our old man can smell a lie like it's three-day-old fish." Matt man-hugged Jake. "Then we'll make sure to spend a few evenings together. Who knows when you'll be back?"

"I promised Mom to be here between Thanksgiving and Christmas, which is a quiet time at Uncle Fausto's Winery."

Matt nodded, then pulled out his beeping phone. "Gotta go, the bachelorettes are due to land soon."

Jake called after him, "I'd rather sit in bumper-to-bumper traffic on the Cape than having to haul around a group of giggling women in my car."

That was the truth—and part of why he didn't want to come home and take over the management position his father tried to push on him for years. Catering to every whim of overexcited vacationers wasn't how he planned to spend the rest of his life.

His parents had built a very successful hotel business, but it wasn't what Jake envisioned. Which begged the question: what *did* he envision? Until he knew the answer, he'd continue what he was doing—and stay as far away from the flower cottages as possible.

Chapter 11

Mimi

Standing outside the gray-shingled terminal of Martha's Vineyard's airport, Mimi was glad for the filtered shade a white pergola provided. It wasn't even noon but today could be a real scorcher.

When a blue passenger van marked *Bellini's Cliff House* stopped in front of them, she picked up her weekend bag without paying much attention.

And did a double take when a man jumped out from behind the steering wheel and whipped off his Ray-Ban sunglasses.

Her heart raced. *That's impossible.* He looked so familiar, with his dark hair, stubble, and general physique.

"Ladies, welcome to Martha's Vineyard. I'm Matt Bellini." He bowed playfully.

Her joy deflated. *Silly, did you think he was Jake?*

Sliding open the side door of the van before he went to the back, he said, "Let me take care of your luggage while you have a seat." He grinned, "You should have almost as much leg room as you had on your flight."

The ducklings climbed in first, taking up the third row. Nicki and

Tanya scooted into the middle row, piling everyone's purses or back-packs between them and leaving the passenger seat for Mimi. What was it with nobody wanting to sit up front?

During the fifteen-minute ride to the hotel, Nicki and Tanya tossed around ideas about going to the beach first or getting a feel for what else there was to do.

Tanya said, "I vote for going into town and grabbing something to eat. And after lunch we'll play our first game. Then we have the rest of the afternoon to work on our tans."

Mimi didn't ask what games Tanya had in mind. In her limited experience, bachelorette games involved drinking and slightly embarrassing behaviors, preserved for all eternity in videos and photos. The ducklings giggled, obviously knowing what awaited them.

"Matt, are there any 'must-sees' in Oak Bluffs?" Nicki asked.

Mimi was glad she asked, because she hadn't put much effort into googling it prior to this trip.

"Oak Bluffs is a lively town, especially in the summer, and there's always something going on. Starting with Ocean Park, which is popular for kite-flying," he said, eliciting a groan from one of the ducklings.

He glanced in the rearview mirror and continued, "Then there's the Flying Horses Carousel. It was built in 1876 and was originally housed on Coney Island, but was moved to Oak Bluffs in 1884. It's the oldest continuously operated carousel in the United States."

He scratched his chin, and this universal gesture also reminded Mimi of Jake.

If it was true that everyone has a look-alike somewhere in this world, then she just found Jake's. Go figure...

"What you shouldn't miss are the Gingerbread Cottages on the Campground," Matt said. "Have you heard about them?"

One of the ducklings mumbled, "I only know gingerbread houses with gumdrops and lots of frosting." At least Nicki and Tanya said in unison, "Yes."

Mimi briefly wondered what Matt was thinking when she

noticed him biting the inside of his cheek, but figured he must be used to dealing with weird ducks—as fitting as the term was.

"Can you give us a quick rundown?" she asked.

Since they were at a four-way stop intersection with cars in front of them, Matt quickly turned his head to her, his eyes hidden behind his sunglasses, and Mimi itched to get a glimpse of their color.

He said, "They were built in the 1860s and 1870s to replace tents on a year-round Methodist campground that goes back to the 1830s. 318 of the approximately 500 cottages remain, and they're built in a very distinctive style called Carpenter Gothic."

"Like *Rebecca* gothic, all dark and creepy?" asked one of the ducklings, and Mimi jerked upright. How did a duckling know about the Daphne du Maurier book?

"No, quite the opposite," said Matt. "They have arched windows, the trims are painted in bright colors, and fanciful bargeboards highlight the steep roof gables. That style is known as gingerbread."

Mimi knew she couldn't excuse herself from everything that Tanya had planned for the weekend, but she said over her shoulder to Nicki, "We've got to see them."

"It's not far to walk there, but you'll actually get to stay in one," Matt said, making Mimi gasp. "Our cottages are original Gingerbread houses, even though they're not on the Campground. My mother's parents bought the first one after they got married in 1960, then three more, and renovated and rented them out to summer guests."

"Are we still able to use the hotel's facilities?" asked Tanya. "Especially the outdoor pool, gardens, and private beach you advertise."

Matt nodded. "Yes. The cottages are part of Bellini's Cliff House, located directly across the street. They're popular with small groups and couples who are celebrating anniversaries because they allow self-catering. But all resort amenities are yours to use."

Mimi liked Matt's personal tidbit about his grandparents. She had a lot of respect for people who followed their dreams and built something from the ground.

"Actually, my grandparents are staying at their old cottage this weekend. It's the Daisy cottage—you can't miss it, because of the four, it's the only one where the door and window trim aren't some shade of red or pink. If you see them, feel free to ask any questions, but be prepared to get the extended story, in every rosy detail, not just the abbreviated version," Matt laughed and pulled into the circular driveway of a multi-storied building.

"Welcome to Bellini's Cliff House," he said and turned in his seat.

"Our check-in time is 3 p.m., but since you let us know ahead of time about your early arrival, we're working to get the cottage ready for you as soon as possible. If housekeeping isn't finished yet, we'll store your luggage and deliver it to the cottage this afternoon," Matt said, and jumped out of the car.

He rounded the minivan and opened first Mimi's, then the sliding door. "Enjoy your stay with us."

Mimi slid out of the passenger seat and did a slow one-eighty to look from the hotel's main building, covered with the gray cedar shingles so typical for the area, to the beach and the ocean, separated from the hotel property by a two-lane street with cars parked along one side.

She inhaled deeply. And exhaled slowly. And did it again.

The fishy smell was even stronger than at the airport, and her skin felt covered by a thin layer of salty sweat. A breeze ruffled her hair, sending it flying like the colorful kites she saw dancing in the wind.

She hardly noticed Matt piling their bags on a luggage cart or the other women heading toward the hotel's entrance.

"This is gorgeous," she muttered and listened to the deep blast of a ferry horn as it started its trip back across the water.

Even though she'd grown up not far from the ocean, in an affluent suburb of Boston, Mimi felt a million miles away. Something about the water soothed her from the moment she got out of the van. As it did when she visited Venice.

49

"Mimi, are you coming?" Nicki called.

"Yes, sorry," Mimi called back and crossed the short distance to her sister. "I was thinking how beautiful this is and how I can't wait to explore the town. I have a feeling that this will be an unforgettable weekend for you!"

Chapter 12

Jake

JAKE STOOD AT THE BOW OF THE FERRY'S TOP DECK AND SHADED his eyes with his hand against the sun glinting off the water. He could've worn his sunglasses but didn't care for the crusty layer that the salty droplets left on the lenses. Millions of bright sparkles danced across the water, reminding him of raindrops on plump grapes when the sun comes out again after a short shower.

Just before the ferry switched direction and steered toward Woods Hole, he saw Matt pull the van into the hotel's driveway—and breathed out a sigh of relief.

He'd been serious when he said he'd rather be on the road all day between the Vineyard and Brewster on the bay side of the Cape to pick up his grandparents. The idea of spending time around a group of revved-up women wasn't tempting at all—and he didn't really care that his snarky attitude was probably unfair since he knew nothing about these newest arrivals.

In Italy—and other European countries—bachelorette parties were called *hen parties*, a perfect term. Fittingly, the male equivalent was known as a *buck party*, which said it all.

Yet Jake also knew that weddings, and anything related to them, were an essential part of the hotel industry, and Martha's Vineyard was a top location for destination weddings. Which meant a lot of business for Bellini's Cliff House.

But he much preferred the more unobtrusive guests at his aunt's B&B in San Gimignano. They stayed at a farm guest house to avoid turmoil and wild partying, wanting to relax in a peaceful environment after a day of wandering around ancient hill towns.

Jake took a deep breath, relishing the salty taste on his lips.

As much as he loved Tuscany, there was one thing he missed— the ocean. The nearest beaches were in Cecina or Livorno on the Ligurian Sea, but the ninety-minute drive usually wasn't worth it, given how overrun with tourists they were.

Being surrounded by the ocean was one fat checkmark on the plus column for Martha's Vineyard.

And his parents and siblings were here. That was another huge checkmark.

But Uncle Fausto, Aunt Francesca, and Mia were also family. Even when he was growing up, spending summers in Italy when his paternal grandparents were still alive used to be like coming home when he, Matt, and Carla ran into *Nonna's* kitchen—and her wide-open arms—to greet her.

Family was important to Jake, and he knew he was lucky to have always gotten along well with his parents and his brother and sister. Most of the time, at least. Siblings would always be siblings and needle each other occasionally. Just as parents would always try to influence their children's decisions.

Jake was surprised his father hadn't taken him aside yet—as he was wont to do every time he visited. He knew their chat about Jake's future at Bellini's was coming as surely as he knew the imprints on his uncle's wine corks.

The time to decide what to do next was closing in on him—and Jake was fully aware of it. Just as he knew it would be one of the hardest decisions of his life.

Because someone would end up being disappointed. Who it

would be just wasn't clear yet. His father—or Jake himself.

But not for one single day did he regret his spontaneous decision five years ago, when Uncle Fausto suffered a heart attack during Jake's visit and left the winery rudderless.

Jake only returned to the States long enough to quit his job at a law firm in Hyannis and inform his parents he was going to help with the winery his grandfather, Lorenzo Bellini, started as a young man.

But Jake working and living in Italy was the ultimate thorn in his father's side, and he didn't tire of making his opinion clear.

The Woods Hole ferry terminal came into view, and Jake wound his way to his car, his thoughts churning around the winery and winemaking.

He enjoyed learning about viticulture and even took an online certificate program in agriculture. Most people didn't think about how much work went into producing wine when they uncorked a bottle. They didn't realize how many tasks a vintner had to juggle daily. No matter what time of the year, there was always something to do. Even during the dormant season equipment needed to be maintained, repaired, or replaced.

And then there were sales and marketing, maintaining the winery and B&B's website, online sales, etcetera, all of which took up more and more time year-round, but were a necessary evil.

Uncle Fausto had happily delegated sales and marketing to him, but Jake knew that as soon as his uncle and aunt decided to step back —never to retire, but cutting back on hours, as Fausto liked to say— and Mia took over the winery, her fiancé would also work full-time there and be the marketing director of Bellini's Winery.

And Jake was okay with it.

The past five years had been the best of his life, but he knew the end of his time in San Gimignano was inevitable.

But he couldn't imagine being as happy or as contented on Martha's Vineyard.

So where would he end up, then?

And how much was he willing to compromise?

Chapter 13

Mimi

FOLLOWING THE RECEPTIONIST'S DIRECTIONS—PLUS USING A paper map as backup—the six women ambled into the center of Oak Bluffs and were within minutes immersed in a bustling tourist area bursting with restaurants and bars and shops.

"Anybody want Mexican?" asked Kelly, the blonde duckling, while she pointed to a restaurant. "I could eat something."

"Yes! And some margaritas," said Sally, the brunette duckling. "To get us in the mood."

Mimi wasn't sure what mood she was seeking—Sally was already giddy—but wasn't going to out herself as a party pooper. Yet the weekend was just beginning...

"I want nachos," added Ally, the black-haired duckling.

After they were shown to a table in the outdoor seating area, Tanya ordered a pitcher of margaritas, and Nicki asked, "Wanna get several appetizers to share?" Everyone agreed, and they ordered wings, fried shrimp, pork sliders, and nachos.

As soon as the drinks were poured, Tanya called, "Okay, ladies. Are you ready?" She pulled several folded pieces of paper out of her purse. "Our first game of the weekend iiiissss...the photo challenge!"

The ducklings woo-hooed, Nicki pumped a fist in the air, and Tanya beamed proudly.

Mimi waited for more details.

When five pairs of eyes stared at her, she asked, "Oops, did my excitement not show? Yay..." She copied Nicki's fist-pump.

Tanya patted her hand, "We'll teach you. By Sunday evening you'll be a different woman. Much less serious."

Mimi did a mental eye roll. Her and Tanya's definitions of *serious* were probably oceans apart. To smooth the waves, she asked, "So, what's this challenge about?"

Tanya—totally prepared for the question—handed each of them a sheet of paper.

Mimi scanned it—and grinned. It sounded fun and wasn't as raunchy as she'd expected. Sipping more of her margarita, she read the tasks again: 1) find a random guy to serenade the bride, 2) take a photo with a married couple, 3) high-five a cop, 4) photo-bomb another bachelorette party, 5) kiss a bartender, 6) take a picture of someone wearing a white dress, 7) take a selfie with a bald guy, 8) prom-pose with a guy who looks like the groom, 9) take a flaming shot with the bride.

"What do you guys think?" asked Nicki. "Should we work in small teams, like three and three, or as a group?"

The ducklings favored staying together, and Tanya and Mimi agreed.

"Together it is," decided Nicki. "We can always split up if it takes too long, but that takes the fun out of it. Remember, we want to hang out at the beach this afternoon."

Suddenly one of the ducklings jumped up and zigzagged through cars idling at a red light. She slid to a stop in front of the cop watching the intersection, talked to him briefly, then shouted, "Can someone take a picture, please?"

Mimi laughed, pulled out her cell phone, and took several photos as Ally high-fived the cop. She had to admit that it took some spunk to do what Ally just did, but the cop was young and had looked bored, so probably enjoyed the sudden attention.

When Ally rejoined them, she fanned herself with a menu and said, "He's a cutie," making them all laugh.

After lunch they spread the street map and a task sheet out on the table.

"Okay, number three is covered," said Nicki while she checked it off on her paper. "Number five, finding someone who's wearing a white dress, should be the easiest task. Just look around," she flapped her hand around in a semicircle.

Mimi nodded—to check that off, they only had to stand at any street corner and wait. This being New England and July, it wouldn't take long for someone to walk by in a white summer dress. "Should we work on the most difficult task first?" she asked.

"Which one would that be?" asked Kelly.

"Hmm...my guess is the prom-pose with a guy who looks like Ray," Mimi said.

Tanya said, "I think our chances will be better tonight, when we're out for dinner and visit some bars. Same goes for number one. It shouldn't be too hard to convince a guy to serenade Nicki once he's three sheets to the wind."

Mimi laughed, "Maybe that's why karaoke bars are so popular."

"I hear disapproval. Are you saying you don't like karaoke?" asked Tanya.

"Not particularly. I'm not interested in making a fool of myself by singing off-key in front of a mob of strangers."

"Oh, we'll have to loosen you up, girl," said Tanya.

No, thank you.

Mimi whipped her sunglasses off her head and propped them on her nose. Then she rolled her eyes while Nicki giggled at her.

After draining her glass and licking the last of the salt off the rim, Tanya said, "Here's my suggestion. Let's just walk around, keep our eyes open, and set ourselves a time limit. It's one thirty now. What if we give ourselves two hours, then we head back to the hotel, get settled, and go to the beach? We might even find another bachelorette party there to take a picture with."

Mimi flashed her a thumbs-up and finished her own drink, then washed the sour, salty taste down with water. She'd never been a huge fan of margaritas and stuck with one glass with lunch while the other girls shared the rest of the pitcher.

Instead of flagging down the waiter for the bill, she went inside to use the restroom, then paid at the counter. To make bookkeeping simpler, they'd agreed in advance that one person paid for meals and drinks, and they'd square up after the trip.

Three hours later, after browsing stores and stopping for ice cream, checking off tasks of the game, and hanging out, they crossed the crunchy gravel and shell driveway to the hotel entrance.

The same young woman who checked them in earlier smiled and said, "Your luggage is already in your cottage. If you take a right outside the front door, you'll see the cottages across the street." She handed the key to Nicki. "I hope you find everything to your liking. Let us know if you need anything."

They exited the main building and crossed the street to where four houses stood so close to each other that their gutters almost touched. Each house had a small front porch, a tiny balcony on the second floor, and all were covered with grayish, weathered cedar shingles.

The first three houses looked about the same size, whereas the fourth house—its yellow paint giving it away as the Daisy—was slightly bigger.

What set the other three houses apart was the intricate wood-work around the gables and the front porches, and the eye-catching trims in poppy red, raspberry pink, and pale pink. To make things foolproof, each cottage had its name written in iron letters on a porch beam.

Mimi trailed behind Nicki and her friends, itching to take some pictures, but she reminded herself that she had two more days on this island which, she had to admit, made her feel as if she stepped into another world.

Like Villa Villekulla. Mimi suddenly thought of the Astrid Lindgren books she loved as a child. She drew a blank on why she also knew the German name of Pippi Longstocking's house, *Villa Kunterbunt*, which could loosely be translated as Villa Motley, and was a fitting description for the houses in front of her.

She hurried to catch up with the others on the porch of the poppy-red house, where four wooden rocking chairs beckoned her to relax with the book she brought along.

Mimi looked over her shoulder at the beach. Maybe she'd stay here instead of frying in the afternoon sun.

Following the others through the double door that took up half of the front of the house, Mimi stepped into a cozy living room. Two love seats and two chairs were grouped around a coffee table, and there was a moderate-sized TV perched on a low corner bookshelf that also held some board games, books, and magazines.

Mimi grinned at the sight of the kitchenette in the left-hand back corner of the open first floor. The fridge could double as a time machine, the kiwi-green exterior either a witness of its real age—hello, 1960s!—or it was an ultramodern one going for a retro look.

"There's a powder room here, and a small utility room with a washer and dryer," called Ally from behind the kitchen before she stepped over their neatly lined up luggage at the bottom of the stairs.

"I'm not planning to do laundry this weekend," replied Sally, then laughed at her own joke.

"And a full bathroom is up here," called Tanya from the second floor. "But there's not enough counter space for all our cosmetic bags. We'll have to keep them in our rooms."

Nicki opened the refrigerator and said, "Wow, there's bubbly and white wine in here! And a cheese and fruit platter, too." She looked at Mimi. "I wonder if that's included in the price or if they charge us later? Like a mini bar at the hotel."

Mimi smiled as she walked closer. "It's for us. Mom arranged it.

She and Dad assumed we'd be eating out, but they wanted to surprise you. There should also be red wine somewhere. Mom said she ordered two bottles of each."

Looking around, she spotted two bottles of Chianti next to the coffee maker and picked one up. After reading the label, she said, "This one's from Bellini Winery in Tuscany. I wonder if the hotel buys it because of the name."

"I don't think it's important. Are you going to have some of it later?" asked Nicki.

"Yes, I absolutely will." She'd never say no to a Chianti, and maybe, if she closed her eyes, she could pretend she was back in Italy again. She sighed and set the bottle back on the counter.

Nicki hugged Mimi. "I'm so glad you're here with me. Wanna go and check out our room?"

"Sure." Mimi was grateful that sleeping arrangements had been determined in advance. She and Nicki shared one room, Tanya and Ally shared the second bedroom, and Kelly and Sally the third one.

Upstairs she and Nicki found the others already busy unpacking their toiletries and clothes.

Then they walked into their room, which was painted a pale pink and—like the other two bedrooms—barely had enough space for a queen bed, dresser, and two wooden chairs. A fluffy blanket covered the bed, throw pillows with poppies stitched on them invited guests to lie down, and a lace curtain hung on the door to the tiny balcony she'd spotted from below.

"Girls, chop-chop. Let's change into bathing suits and go to the beach," called Tanya, who received a chorus of excited voices in reply.

While Nicki changed, Mimi stepped out on the balcony. The memory of another balcony flashed through her mind, and she couldn't hold back a chuckle.

"What's so funny?" asked Nicki from behind her.

"Standing here reminds me of Juliet's house. I never went out on that balcony because it felt too touristy. Now I kind of regret it."

"Do you miss Italy?" Nicki slathered sunscreen on her arms and legs while they talked.

"Yes, I do. And not because life there was better, but it was more relaxed. I have so many wonderful memories of my time there," Mimi sighed and stepped back inside the room, closing the door behind her. "But I knew from the beginning that it was only temporary and that my life is here in the States."

"We haven't talked about it since you returned, but are you ready for the new school year? How do you feel about being around Derek again?"

"I don't want to go into detail right now. Bottom line is, I can't avoid him because he's also teaching there. But I will not take any bullshit from him, and if he ever so much as touches my shoulder..." Mimi pretended a karate chop before she pulled out her bikini and quickly changed into it without being coy. She and Nicki were used to undressing in front of each other.

"I can't believe the school didn't fire him for assaulting you."

Mimi shrugged while she accepted the sunscreen from Nicki and applied it generously. "Yup... But enough. This weekend is to your last hurrah before you become the respectable Mrs. Raymond Lancaster III, and I won't let even one thought about Derek ruin it."

Chapter 14

Mimi

THE NEXT MORNING AT BREAKFAST TANYA ONE-HANDEDLY carried a tray with six colorful drinks to their table. Mimi was secretly surprised Tanya could manage it because she hadn't thought Tanya ever held a summer job, especially not something requiring real-life skills like waitressing.

"Ooh, where did you find those?" asked Nicki as soon as Tanya sat down.

"Coming back from the loo, I saw a waitress with a tray full of mimosas and snagged three, then asked if we could also have three Bloody Marys," she said cheerily and pointed her chin at the three slouching ducklings.

"At first the girl was hesitant, even though I explained that it's an emergency, but luckily the cutie who picked us up at the airport came by and fixed them himself. But next time one of you gets to do it. I don't want to give the wrong impression."

"There won't be a next time," groaned Kelly.

"Could you turn the volume down a little?" asked Sally.

"I'm dying today," whimpered Ally.

"No, you aren't. Here," Tanya slammed the Bloody Marys in

front of the green-faced women, next to their mostly untouched breakfast plates. "Drink. It'll help. And eat at least some toast and eggs."

Mimi also had only marginal sympathy for the ducklings. The margaritas at lunch yesterday were just the beginning of their drinking spree. But...since she wasn't their chaperone, she kept her thoughts to herself after being laughed at when she suggested they slow down a little.

Tanya handed Mimi and Nicki their mimosas, then took hers. "Cheers!"

After sipping, Tanya asked, "So, are you girls ready for more fun?"

"No," said the ducklings in unison, but dutifully sampled their spiked tomato juices. Ally even sniffed at the celery stick—but decided against eating it.

"What's the plan for today?" asked Nicki while she drizzled maple syrup on her pancakes.

"I'm going back to bed," grumbled Kelly. "Wake me up when you're going to the beach."

"A scavenger hunt first, *then* more beach time this afternoon," said Tanya, sounding like a grand marshal who announced the next maneuver, as if the weekend was written in stone and there wasn't any wiggle room for improvisation.

Mimi took another sip of the mimosa and smacked her lips. *Yumm...*

The acidity of the freshly pressed orange juice and the crisp flavor of the prosecco would perfectly compliment the savory mushroom omelet in front of her that already teased her nose and demanded to be devoured.

The bright yellow of the cocktail and the dark brown cremini mushrooms evoked an image of a sunrise over hills, the grass and soil still moist from early morning dew, releasing an earthy-smelling mist.

She was no painter—her skills barely included drawing stick figures—but she enjoyed photography and had an eye for colors.

Martha's Vineyard wasn't known for hills filled with orchards, but she wished they had time to explore the other side of the island, which was said to have a picturesque coast.

While she took the first bite of her omelet and let the fluffy egg mixture melt on her tongue, her thoughts strayed to last night.

After returning from the beach, they opened the champagne her parents arranged for and munched on cheese, crackers, and fruit while taking turns in the shower. Then, after a delicious seafood dinner at a small restaurant, they went barhopping.

Unlike the ducklings, she and Nicki held back during the drinking games, which earned them plenty of teasing, but also rewarded them with clear—and pain free—heads today. Mimi wasn't quite sure where Tanya fit in—she could either hold her booze or had also stopped drinking in time.

When they finally returned to their cottage close to midnight, Mimi at last was able to open the Chianti and excuse herself to go sit on her balcony. It was a clear night, and she relaxed and gazed out over the water, watching tiny lights on boats bobbing up and down like the fireflies around the hydrangea bushes in her parents' backyard.

Just as she had decided to turn in, a car approached and then a man's baritone voice said, "Sleep well, Grandma. Good night, Grandpa. See you tomorrow."

The voice had sounded so much like she remembered Jake's that just hearing it squeezed Mimi's heart—but then she convinced herself that it must be Matt, because he told her his grandparents would be here. Not wanting to be caught peeking over the balcony railing, she forced herself to stay in her chair, hidden in the darkness broken only by the car's bright headlights, which also meant she probably wouldn't have been able to see anything even if she tried...

Tanya and Nicki's laughter broke Mimi's reverie.

Having no idea what was so funny, she asked, with a glance at the ducklings, "When did you all go to bed last night? I was out cold as soon as my head hit the pillow and didn't even hear you come into our room, Nicki."

"Well," snickered Tanya, "we had to celebrate a little more because we finished all the tasks on our list. And I happened to have a bottle of vodka in my luggage."

"Ugh, can you please not talk about booze?" asked Sally.

"Nobody forced you to drink it," shrugged Tanya.

When Mimi saw Sally's face turn ashen, she focused on Tanya, "What was that about a scavenger hunt today?"

Tanya handed each of them a paper. "It's like yesterday's game. We have to fulfill certain tasks."

Mimi scanned it quickly and said, "It seems as if we already checked off a few. Like taking a selfie with someone who looks like Ray. Even though, Nicki,"—she nodded at her sister—"the guy didn't really have too much in common with him. Maybe we're supposed to keep our eyes open for another one?"

Reading the next item, she chuckled, "But we can definitely cross off dancing on a table. Thanks to you, Kelly, that one's taken care of."

"You're most welcome," said Kelly who, after another sip of her Bloody Mary, bit into her toast. "Umm, guys... Can we go back to the last bar and ask if anyone gave my bra to the bartender?"

Nicki laughed out loud. "Seriously? Isn't that like the walk of shame?"

Kelly shrugged. "I bought the bra in Paris. I want it back."

"Girl, I hate to tell you, but bars like that don't have a Lost and Found box. If you take off your underwear in a bar, consider it gone," snickered Tanya. "Some guy probably took it home as a trophy."

Mimi shook her head, deciding to ignore them and concentrate on her omelet instead. The mushrooms were cooked to perfection and only lightly seasoned with pepper and olive oil.

Before she lived in Italy, she always bought whatever extra-virgin olive oil was on sale. But she learned to differentiate between them when she and Belinda toured a vineyard that also produced olive oil. She vividly remembered the display of bottles in the tasting room and the oils' different colors. Now she made it a game to guess which Italian region an oil came from, knowing the ones from around Lucca were more yellow, and the ones from near Siena more greenish.

An ache spread through her chest and belly. But she couldn't think of a way to go back to Italy any time soon, and the sooner she accepted it, the better for her mental well-being.

Nicki called out, "We can check off buying a shot for the bachelorette and getting a guy to serenade me. The dude last night didn't sing very well, but I think it still counts."

"Wait a second," said Tanya. "He sang 'The Fox,' which is a far cry from a serenade, and the only parts he got right were the strange animal noises."

Nicki laughed, "Did you think we'll find someone to sing 'O Sole Mio'?"

Tanya shook her head and snickered, "Maybe. So, let's say serenading is optional, which means we have five challenges for today. We have to 1) find a man whose name is Ray or Raymond, 2) ask an older couple for marriage advice, 3) get a guy's phone number on a napkin, 4) take a selfie with a bachelor party, and 5) get a condom from a guy."

"Can't we just buy a box at a drug store?" asked Ally.

"And miss all the fun? No, and besides, that one's easy," said Tanya. "Did you pay attention to the other tasks? Except for talking to the older couple and finding another Ray, they're a three-in-one. All we need to find is a bachelor party, and I can guarantee you those guys have a week's supply of rubbers. Getting one of them to write his phone number on a napkin should also be easy-peasy."

Ally mumbled, "I bet they're all still in bed and sound asleep. Where we should be. Why did we have to get up so early?"

"Because the hotel only serves breakfast until ten," Tanya said.

She looked from the ducklings to Mimi. "Unlike Nicki and I, you girls don't have boyfriends. Maybe you can hook up with guys from a bachelor party and have some bonus fun this weekend." She eyed Kelly. "Just make sure to bring your panties and bra home with you."

Kelly wisely didn't take the bait.

"That's a disturbing thought, actually," said Nicki.

Mimi nodded. *Yup.*

"Do you know what Ray and his buddies are up to this weekend? He only told me they were going to take out your dad's boat," Nicki looked at Tanya, who shrugged and said, "No idea. I heard they wanted to go to Provincetown, but they might as well have gone up to Maine."

Nicki said, "People often make fun of what guys do at bachelor parties. I mean, I don't care if Ray's friends are sleeping around," she chewed on the inside of her mouth, "as long as he doesn't..."

Mimi squeezed Nicki's hand. "Ray has never given you reason to mistrust him, right?"

Nicki shook her head. "Not...really."

Mimi heard the hesitation in her sister's voice and glanced at Tanya, willing her to say something to ease Nicki's mind. But Tanya's eyes were glued to her cell phone while her manicured fingers flew over the tiny keys.

Thanks a bunch, missy!

Because—unlike Nicki—Mimi wasn't convinced of Ray's clean-slate personality. She'd seen him being a little too flirty with other women at parties. But Mimi hadn't been around for half a year, and during those six months her sister had accepted Ray's proposal. And if Nicki trusted Ray, who was she to sow doubts?

Chapter 15

Jake

JAKE STROLLED PAST THE HOTEL'S OUTDOOR POOL AREA AND entered the lobby just in time to see the front door slide shut behind a group of six women heading toward the cottages.

He didn't see their faces, but their almost identical outfits of white shorts and teal tank tops made it likely they were members of the bachelorette party.

Through the wide doorway to the restaurant he could see his grandparents sitting at a table in the farthest corner and switched direction to greet them. Besides two other couples, the room was empty. Which didn't surprise him because it was a gorgeous day, with little humidity but plenty of sunshine. This afternoon he planned to jump in the pool at home or go to the beach for an hour himself.

"How come you two are already out and about?" he asked while he pulled up a chair. Before he sat down, he kissed his grandmother's leathery cheek. A young waitress—he couldn't remember her name, but knew she was seasonal staff—materialized next to him and put a clean place setting on the table.

"What do you mean? It's ten o'clock, almost the middle of the day," said his grandfather.

"I dropped you night owls off at the cottage after midnight," Jake laughed. "I assumed you'd sleep in."

"And waste a beautiful day?" his grandfather asked, shaking his head. "We can sleep when we're dead."

"James, don't say that," said his grandmother. She looked around. "Are you joining us for breakfast, Jacob? There's plenty of food left on the buffet."

"No, I ate at the house. I'm here to meet Carla. We're heading to Menemsha to pick up the lobsters for tonight's dinner. I haven't been there in a while, and the drive gives us a chance to chat." He checked the time on the Bulgari leather-and-stainless-steel wristwatch he splurged on three years ago, when he turned thirty.

"Oh, is Carlotta cooking for us this evening?" his grandmother asked, using his sister's full name, just as she had with his. For as long as he could remember, his grandparents switched between both versions for him and his siblings. Jacob/Jake, Matteo/Matt, and Carlotta/Carla. But, just like with his Italian side of the family using his Italianized name, he had long since stopped thinking about it.

"Yeah, she is," Jake nodded and filled his cup from the thermal carafe on the table.

"Then I'll be happy to be her sous-chef."

Jake laughed. "That's between you and Carla. You know how it is with two cooks in the kitchen."

"The least I can do is shuck the corn." His grandmother chuckled and ate a few bites of her croissant. "The baked bruschetta chicken she made last night was delicious."

Jake nodded, "Carla told me she used your recipe, but tweaked it a little. Did she tell you she wants to publish a cookbook featuring your recipes?"

"Oh my, no, she didn't." His grandmother looked up and waved to the slender brunette woman who strode toward them. "Ah, there she is!"

"Are you talking about me?" Carla joined their table and greeted her grandparents, then bumped Jake's shoulder with her elbow.

"Yes, Jacob mentioned your idea of a cookbook. You have to tell me all about it."

"I will. And I want to go through that box of handwritten recipes from your mother with you too. Some are very hard to decipher," Carla said.

"Just tell me when," said their grandmother. "My mom was an excellent cook, but her handwriting was atrocious."

Carla nodded, then looked at Jake, "Ready to go?"

"Yes." Jake gulped down his coffee. Getting up, he asked his grandparents, "What are your plans for today?"

"We're taking a ride with your father to Charles's property in West Tisbury," Jake's grandfather said.

Jake was puzzled. He knew Uncle Charles, his mom's younger brother, bought several parcels of land in the middle of the island before his premature death some years ago. But what could his father have to do with it?

Having grown up on Martha's Vineyard, Jake knew pretty much every turn and curve all the way from Oak Bluffs to Menemsha. The small fishing village on the western coast of the island was roughly thirty minutes away—unless the roads were crowded with traffic, which they weren't yet—and Jake enjoyed the breeze whizzing around their heads while he steered his sister's Audi convertible down the two-lane road. As was typical for the island, the roads were lined by trees and brush, with homes in a variety of sizes and conditions scattered like rolled dice.

"You've got yourself a nice car here, Carla," he said.

"Thank you. We'll see how practical it'll be in the winter," she laughed. "Besides, I just borrow Mom's SUV if I have to go somewhere for work."

"I'm sure she doesn't mind. Hey, do you know anything about what Dad has to do with Uncle Charles's land?"

Stopping at an intersection and checking traffic, he saw Carla shrug a shoulder. "No, I assume it's a brand-new brain fart. You know he never stops plotting. But if it's something that revolves around the hotel, he eventually shares his ideas with Matt and me. Maybe he's thinking about selling it. We have our hands more than full with the hotel and catering business."

Jake winced. He knew her comment wasn't meant as a stab in his direction. Matt and Carla understood his reluctance to return home, and they always assured him that, between them and their parents, the job responsibilities were divvied up perfectly and then commented on how well they worked together. But it nevertheless reminded Jake that they worked their asses off with few or no breaks during the busy season.

Jake and Carla made small talk until the trees on both sides of the street gave way to marshland when they neared Menemsha, where he slowed down to a snail's pace, paying attention to pedestrians and bikers.

The picturesque village was one of Jake's favorite places on the island. The colorful, weathered houses, the water, the boats with masts reaching high in the sky, the stacks of lobster traps—it was simple and breathtakingly beautiful.

Like the vineyard in Tuscany.

If only the two could be combined.

It wasn't the first time the thought crossed his mind, but today the truth of it hit him with extra force.

As he slowly wound his way toward a parking lot, he asked, "Mind if I take a quick walk to the harbor basin?"

"Of course not. Do you want a few minutes to yourself?" Carla asked.

Yes.

"No." He parked the car and jumped out, took a deep breath, and savored the potent smell of fish. Like the slightly sickening smell of fermenting grapes, it wasn't the most pleasant odor, but it was nature's perfume, pure and undiluted.

"Well, I know how much you like spending time there." Carla grabbed a wide-rimmed sunhat and her purse from behind the passenger seat, then joined him as they strolled along the docks. Fishing boats and small charter vessels bobbed in the water, and fishermen unloaded their catch while calling out to tourists and locals, occasionally tossing a small fish to the circling swarms of seagulls.

Jake took in the water and blue sky as far as his eyes could see—and for a moment the world was limitless.

Chapter 16

Mimi

"My feet hurt," complained Nicki while she kicked off her flip-flops.

"My head hurts," moaned Ally, holding an icy water bottle against her left temple.

"My shoulders hurt," lamented Tanya, and eyed the angry red skin. She marched straight to the fridge and took out a container of yogurt she'd snatched from the breakfast buffet.

Mimi plopped down on the nearest chair. It felt good to sit for a spell after hours of walking in the hot sun with only short reprieves when they went into a store or café.

To her surprise, everyone had agreed to explore the famous Campground with its sprawling iron and stained-glass Tabernacle, and they were surprised to learn that the 1879 landmark was one of the last remaining wrought iron structures of its time—along with the Eiffel Tower in Paris.

Afterward, while strolling around the whimsical Gingerbread cottages of which no two were alike, the women couldn't stop taking photos and quickly made a game out of comparing the picturesque Victorian buildings. Mimi thought it was easy to see why they were such a tourist magnet, and she was also glad that they had found something to do other than bachelorette games.

Now back at the cottage, the six women slouched on chairs like rag dolls.

"Who wants to go to the beach in a little bit?" asked Tanya while she smeared yogurt across her shoulders.

"What are you doing?" asked Ally.

"The lactic acid in Greek yogurt has anti-inflammatory benefits and is very soothing. Plus it's a great moisturizer," said Tanya.

"Says the daughter and sister of dermatologists," mocked Kelly.

"Yeah, well, Dad and Ray would yell at me for not reapplying sunscreen. But they're not here," she shrugged—and winced.

"Do you really want to show up at the beach covered with yogurt?" asked Nicki. She held out her hand for the container. "Is there any left? I could try and rub it between my toes. Maybe it would help where the flip-flops rubbed my skin sore." She scooped out a good amount and sighed while she dabbed it between her toes.

Mimi laughed. "Look at you guys. Any other boo-boos to take care of?"

THIRTY MINUTES LATER, ARMED WITH TWO BEACH UMBRELLAS and some folding chairs they found behind the house, they paraded to the beach across from the hotel. Tanya, white-shouldered from enormous amounts of sunscreen but otherwise scantily dressed, immediately settled under an umbrella, typing away on her cell phone.

The ducklings bravely tested the water temperature by dipping in their toes, but shrieked and raced back to the beach whenever it lapped above their ankles.

Nicki flipped the pages of a women's magazine and Mimi tried to concentrate on the book about historic Oak Bluffs she'd bought at a local bookstore. When she caught herself going over the same paragraph for the fifth time, she gave up and resigned herself to looking at the vintage pictures and reading the captions.

She hadn't known that in the late 1800s and early 1900s, the Martha's Vineyard Summer Institute offered summer courses for teachers. More than 700 educators from across the country came to spend five weeks in Cottage City, as Oak Bluffs was known then.

Her eyes landed on a circa 1904 image of Summer Institute participants standing shoulder to shoulder on the wide stairs and a porch of a multi-level house. The women all wore long, heavy skirts and white lace blouses neatly buttoned up to their chins, the men in proper three-piece suits, some with hats in their hands.

They must've been incredibly uncomfortable without air-conditioning, sea breeze or no sea breeze.

She could imagine participating in a program like this one. A few weeks off after school got out in June, then go to an interesting summer camp at a nice location for five weeks of continuing education, then having another couple of weeks off before the school year started again...

A chill ran through her.

Mimi didn't want to think about the upcoming school year and—for the first time in her career as a teacher—she wasn't looking forward to it.

She shooed the thoughts away like a pesky fly. September was months away.

Sharp whistling from the street behind them interrupted her thoughts—or, even better, nightmarish daydreaming.

She ignored it, until more whistling cut through the air, followed by Tanya's shrill squeak. "Hey! Look who's here!"

Mimi turned to look and saw five men headed their way with long, cocky strides, all wearing khaki shorts, boat shoes, and short-sleeved shirts—the New England elite's standard summer outfit.

And then she looked again. *This better be a dream.*

She looked at Nicki, but her sister was already racing across the hot sand to fling herself at Ray, wrapping her arms and legs around him like an octopus.

Tanya was on Nicki's heels, greeting another man in a very similar manner.

And Mimi's stomach nearly heaved.

Chapter 17

Mimi

What the hell was Derek doing here? And why was Tanya clinging to him like a bug on a strip of old-fashioned sticky flypaper?

"Emily, Ally, Kelly, Sally," Ray said in his nasally Bostonian accent, "what an unexpected surprise to run into you ladies!" He snickered at his own lame joke.

Unexpected surprise?

Mimi's stomach cramped. If she had to put her finger on it, she'd guess Tanya spilled the beans about where they could be found. She'd tapped on the phone often enough today.

After Ray and his company greeted the ducklings with obligatory hugs and air-kisses, Derek stopped in front of Mimi. "Emily, what a small world!" he said.

His smirk sickened her anew.

"What are *you* doing here?" she hissed—and didn't give a hoot about the ducklings gawking at her.

Derek pulled Tanya closer, his fingertips grazing the side of her breast that threatened to spill out of its skimpy triangle while he continued to grin at Mimi. "Since my new ladylove is the groom's sister, Ray invited me to come along on his men's weekend."

I bet you and Ray are getting along very well. Two peas in a pot full of filthy water.

Mimi harrumphed and speed-scrolled through her memories of Tanya's comments about her newest boyfriend. Hadn't she said on the plane that his name was Dick?

A mental forehead slap later—and agonizingly slowly—the pieces clicked into place. And she wanted to barf. Dick was Derek.

Mimi noticed Nicki's frozen expression. It was obvious that her sister was just as blindsided as she was.

Mimi didn't even bother trying to be polite, instead stomping off to her beach chair and burying her face in her book. Her nightmarish daydream just became a prime time horror show.

The men made themselves comfortable on the towels they brought, took off their shirts and shorts, under which they all wore matching swim trunks that boasted, "Groomed for you," and owned the beach like David Hasselhoff in his *Baywatch* heyday.

For a while Mimi tried to read, but eventually put her book aside. Her prying eyes concealed by sunglasses, she watched Ally and Kelly swarm around Ray's groomsmen—Ronald, Charles, and Humphrey.

Because not all the groomsmen and bridesmaids had met before, Nicki and Ray decided to have a cookout at the new house they'd move into in two weeks, using the housewarming party as a "meet & greet" for the wedding participants.

Mimi, of course, had her own name for the dreaded event—the "scratch-and-sniff" party—and when she saw Ally lean playfully against Humphrey, she knew it fit.

And she wondered for the umpteenth time how Nicki could stand being around these superficial people, who didn't seem to ever grow up. The underlying question, though, was whether they couldn't or wouldn't.

Mimi looked around. Tanya and Derek were nowhere to be seen, which was fine with her. And she didn't see Ray either. Shouldn't he be with Nicki, since apparently he couldn't let her out of his sight for even a weekend?

Tossing her book and towel in her beach bag, Mimi said to Nicki, "I'm going to the house to read. Do you mind?"

"No, why should I? I don't think we'll be at the beach much longer either," her sister said without looking up from her towel, where she tanned her back. "It's going to take a while until we're all showered and dressed for dinner."

"Is the house key in your bag?" Mimi automatically reached for Nicki's as she bent down for hers.

"Sally took it. She needed to use the bathroom."

"Oh, okay. Then the door should be unlocked. See ya in a bit."

Making her way across the hot sand, but still relishing the feeling of it between her toes in spite of the unwelcome intrusion of the guys, Mimi hoped the men would at least have the decency to disappear as magically as they showed up and let the women enjoy their last evening on the island without their interference.

At the cottage, she returned the beach chair to the back of the house, climbed the stairs to the second floor and turned toward the room she shared with Nicki when she heard voices coming from one of the other bedrooms.

"I said no."

"Come on, Sal, I'll be quick."

Mimi's foot froze midair. This day was turning from a shitshow into an effing disaster faster than a mosquito went after blood.

"Ray, take your grabby paws off me right now and I'll forget this happened," Sally said.

"You'll like it. I'll make you come fast."

"I told you I'm not interested in doing it with you. Even if you weren't Nicki's fiancé," Sally's voice was low but left no doubt about how serious she was.

"But I'm so hot for you, Sal," he whined.

Mimi's blood started boiling. This was frickin' déjà vu. *What a scumbag.*

She couldn't just stand there any longer and was about to make herself known when Sally spit out, "Then go jerk off, but without me."

Mimi discovered newfound respect for Sally. It took pluck to stay as calm as she seemed to be.

"Now get out of my way, or I'll give you something to whine about that might not be easy to explain to Nicki."

Hearing the slapping of flip-flops on the hardwood floor, Mimi knew Sally had walked safely away from Ray. Mimi raced down the stairs and out the front door, but stalled on the street. If Sally didn't emerge from the cottage in a moment or two she'd go back in for her.

But what was she going to do now?

She didn't want to tell Nicki about Ray and Sally, and needed time to think this through.

Wrong, not Ray *and* Sally—Sally hadn't done anything wrong.

Letting several cars pass in both directions before she crossed the street, Mimi spotted Derek and Tanya meandering along the side of the road, pausing every few steps to kiss and hug.

Something close to envy churned inside her.

Her last relationship ended over a year ago, and she missed the comfort of being with someone. And she also missed the physical side.

Because, contrary to what Derek threw at her last fall—"Do you always close up like mimosa leaves when someone touches you?"— she had no problem with sex, as long as it was with the right man.

A car's angry-sounding honks brought her back to the present. Right now she knew only one thing for sure. She wouldn't let anyone ruin this weekend for her sister. Mimi had no way of predicting what Nicki's reaction would be once she heard about Ray's infidelity, especially after she said this morning that she had no reason to mistrust him.

But telling her about Ray had to wait until they were at home. And she needed a solid strategy for that conversation. Because she doubted there were online guides for how to tell one's sister shortly before her wedding that her intended was a scoundrel.

On second thought, Jane Austen or the Brontë sisters might have the answer to that dilemma...

Then there was the unpleasant issue of Derek being here.

Mimi's willingness to be agreeable and peaceful ended with Derek, and she hoped Nicki would understand if she made herself scarce for as long as the guys—and that one jerk in particular—hung around.

She crossed the street, and by the time she reached Nicki her sister had already shaken out her towel and said, "I've got sand in places where it doesn't belong."

"Umm, Nicki..." Mimi began to say when Ray called from not far behind her, "Nic, I saw there's an outdoor shower at your cottage. I'll help you wash off the sand where you can't reach," to which Nicki chuckled and agreed.

Ray's arrogant grin irked Mimi, and she almost lost it when he called to his friends, "Hey guys, meet me in fifteen minutes." He illustrated his intentions with a pumping hand. "I need a private moment with my bride."

Like well-trained puppies, the guys grabbed their own packages and cheered him on, while Mimi watched with disgust as Ray high-fived Derek in passing before he and Nicki crossed the street and disappeared into the cottage moments later.

What does Nicki see in that jerk?

When Tanya came to stand near Mimi, she grinned and said, "Dick told me the guys suggested that we could grab takeout and go for a sunset cruise around the island together. They have wine and beer on the yacht. Sounds fun, don't you think?"

No, I'd rather personally pluck out each individual hair on my entire body.

"It sounds amazing, but I think I'll stay put," Mimi said. "Something's not sitting well with me, so I'd rather not be on a boat."

"Are you sure?" Tanya asked, and Mimi thought she detected honest concern.

"Yes, I'll catch up with you girls when you get back," she said, then added lamely, "Your curfew is midnight."

Back at the house, Mimi went to her room and sat on the balcony while she waited for Nicki. Loud laughter and banter drifted up the stairs, and she heard the bathroom and bedroom doors being opened and closed. The little cottage was a beehive of activity and felt as if it was bursting at its seams.

No wonder. There are eleven people in a tiny house that's built for six.

As soon as Nicki entered the bedroom, wrapped in a large towel, she asked, "Did you hear what we're doing tonight? Ray and the guys are taking us out on his dad's yacht."

"Tanya told me, but I'm not going."

"Oh. Why?"

"You know why. Obviously, Derek is dating Tanya, which I still can't wrap my mind around. But I'm not about to spend more time in his company than I absolutely must. And since they barged in on us and threw our plans overboard, I consider tonight optional."

"I didn't know she was dating him, Mimi. She always refers to him as Dick," Nicki said quietly while she slipped on underwear, then a pair of shorts and a regular tank top—not one declaring her a bride. "Ray said inviting Derek was a spur-of-the-moment decision when Christopher, his best man, dropped out of this weekend because of some family emergency."

Mimi nodded. "Let's not discuss this now. I want you to enjoy this weekend."

Even if you have no clue what's going on behind your back.

"But you're my sister, and I feel terrible, Mim." Nicki pulled a comb through her wet hair, then twisted it in a loose knot on top of her head.

Mimi smiled. When they were children, Mimi often fixed Nicki's hair, and even then, she'd asked for that exact style.

"Don't worry about me. Seriously. I'll go to the hotel restaurant to eat and have a glass or two of wine while I relax on the balcony. I'm okay. Really."

Nicki threw a light sweater on top of her purse, then hugged Mimi. "I'll talk to Ray when we're at home. When I tell him that Derek is the man who assaulted you last year, he'll uninvite him from the wedding."

That remains to be seen. I'm not holding my breath.

"Nic, are you coming?" Ray's voice boomed through the little house.

"Be right there," Nicki called back and hugged Mimi again. "Love you, sis."

"Right back atcha."

When she finally heard the front door bang shut, Mimi went downstairs and poured herself a glass of the Bellini wine, then sat on the porch, listening to the many sounds of the busy tourist town. She raised her glass until the sunlight shone through it and illuminated the ruby liquid. It reminded her of the glass studios in Murano, where she watched the glassblowers turn a hot glob of liquid glass into a beautiful and unique piece of art.

Maybe she'd go sit in the park after dinner. Sitting there by herself wouldn't be overly romantic, but just thinking about Ray's inexcusable behavior—and the pain it would cause her sister—made Mimi glad she didn't have to worry about infidelity or relationships in general.

Ray was such a louse. Judging by what she overheard this afternoon, he had already tried something with Sally at least once, and who knows what else he'd done behind Nicki's back. Maybe instead of talking to her sister as soon as they returned home tomorrow, she'd have a chat with Sally to brainstorm how to approach the topic with Nicki. Since Sally was one of Nicki's best friends, she might know things Mimi wasn't aware of.

Knowing she'd ruin her sister's happiness broke her heart. But unless Nicki was already aware of Ray's escapades and chose to ignore them—which Mimi highly doubted—Mimi would be damned if she'd let her sister marry the scoundrel without being warned.

Mimi sipped the wine and savored the full flavor and smoothness as it went down her throat.

"I think you and I have a date tonight, Mr. Bellini," she said and brought the glass to her lips, not caring how stupid she sounded to any passerby, talking to the wine.

"Mimi?"

Chapter 18

Jake

"Bye, Jeremy, I'm heading out." Jake waved to the reception desk employee and left the hotel to meet his grandparents and accompany them to his parents' house.

They had vehemently declined his offer to pick them up with a car, saying they weren't too old for a ten-minute walk. And Jake had to bite his tongue to resist pointing out that it was a ten-minute walk for *him*, not his eightyish grandparents, who seemed to need their canes more than he remembered. But he also admired them for their determination to be independent, so he compromised and insisted on walking with them, also knowing there was no doubt about how they would be returned to their cottage later tonight—by car!

As soon as the glass door closed behind him, Jake walked down the gravel driveway and stopped at the white picket fence surrounding the property. He closed his eyes, let the warm, late-afternoon sun kiss his face, and inhaled the humid sea breeze while he listened to the sharp cries of the seagulls.

Since Saturdays were turnaround days, and the hotel was fully booked plus hosting several events, one of his parents was usually on-site. But this being his mom's birthday, Jake didn't mind manning the office after he returned from Menemsha, and the afternoon passed without any hiccups. At least none that required him to get involved.

Hanging out at the office had also provided him with plenty of time to rack his brain about what his dad showed his grandparents that he hadn't shared with anybody else.

So Jake did what everybody else with an ounce of curiosity would do and snooped. And didn't feel too bad about flipping through his father's file cabinet—his dad wanted him to be involved in the hotel, didn't he? He found folders for intended renovations of two of the cottages, and another one with estimates to redo the four-season room that was popular in the colder season for weddings and anniversary celebrations—and it pleased him to see that his father planned to consult Damian, Jake's lifelong friend.

But his search for hints about Uncle Charles's land came up empty.

Maybe Carla was right and their dad was considering selling it. Jake instantly hoped it wouldn't go to some developer who'd build more gigantic vacation homes that sat empty half the year.

He sighed and took another deep breath. Now his curiosity was piqued, he wanted answers, so, instead of waiting for his dad to graciously share his ideas, he'd ask him directly before he left at the end of next week.

Jake's mind still revolved around his dad's secrecy, when he crossed the street to his grandparents' cottage and heard, "I think you and I have a date tonight, Mr. Bellini."

His head snapped up.

His eyes ping-ponged around, but he didn't see anybody until a movement caught his attention, and Jake's heart did an Axel jump at triple speed.

He blinked, then squinted, then felt his eyes widen.

"Mimi?"

He watched, speechless, while she sloshed wine over her fingers, set the glass on the wooden banister and looked up.

"Jake?"

In two long strides, he met her on the porch stairs. He'd thought of her so often, his arms reached out so naturally, as if they'd embraced her countless times before. As he had wanted to do at the Rialto *vaporetti* stop.

His fingertips sizzled when his hands touched her bare shoulders.

"What... What are you doing here?" he stammered.

"What are *you* doing here?" she asked at the same time.

Their resulting laughter broke the dam, and he breathed a kiss on her flushed cheeks.

"*Ciao, bella,*" he whispered before his lips moved to hers on their own accord. Just as they did in Venice.

"Ahem." The throat-clearing startled Jake, and he jumped back, pulling Mimi off the porch. His arm came around her waist when she stumbled, and he pressed her into his side. Where she fit perfectly.

"Umm, is there a problem with the cottage?" asked Matt with a giant grin.

"No, but..." started Mimi from the safety of Jake's embrace, while he searched for a reasonable thing to say.

"Well, Jake, Mom sent out the troops," Matt pointed to himself. "She needed something from the hotel and called Jeremy to have you bring it. But you'd already left." Matt's grin widened even more. "Did you get lost on the way to pick up Grandma and Grandpa?"

Yeah, I got lost in a pair of gorgeous eyes.

"I'm coming. But why the hurry? There's plenty of time until dinner," Jake said, refusing to take Matt's bait.

"Well, like I said, she forgot something at the hotel. And, man, am I glad she sent me to pick it up." Matt eyeballed Mimi with unveiled curiosity.

Jake inhaled and exhaled deeply through his nose, then said, "Mimi, this is my brother, Matt. Matt, this is Mimi."

"We met yesterday," Matt said. "How's the bachelorette party going?"

"It took an unexpected turn," said Mimi.

"Are you getting married?" Jake asked and dropped his arm.

"No," she shook her head, her cheek brushing against his chest because she was still standing so close to him that he could smell her shampoo. "My sister is."

He sighed inwardly—and stopped his arm before it sneaked around her again. Not only because of Cheshire-Cat-Matt.

But because a huge yellow flag fluttered in front of his mind—reminding him to slow down, like a Formula 1 race car driver on a dangerous track.

Which he was...

He knew nothing about Mimi—choosing to ignore that he'd been about to kiss her before Matt's rather ill-timed appearance—she could have a boyfriend at home, or...or...he didn't know.

Mimi was short-circuiting his ability to think.

"I better go and grab Mom's stuff before she sends Dad out to bring home his wayward sons," said Matt. "Bye, Mimi."

After Matt left, Jake took a step back and said, "I'm sorry, but I also need to run. We have a family gathering for my mom's birthday. But, umm..." he ran a hand around the back of his neck. "Can I see you later?"

"Won't she be disappointed if you leave her party early?"

Why hadn't he noticed the cute mole on her right cheek in Venice? It almost disappeared into the dimple underneath it when she smiled.

"Not if it's after dessert." He silently begged her to agree. After searching for her for weeks, he couldn't let her slip away again before they had a chance to talk. Although at this point he had no idea what he wanted to say.

"Please. Meet me at the gazebo at the park at, let's say, ten?"

Relief washed over him when she nodded. He shoved his hands in the front pockets of his pants and grinned—probably as wide as Matt's smirk earlier, but for different reasons.

"Seems as if you're getting your date with Mr. Bellini."

"Huh?" It took a moment for her to understand, then she laughed, "Oh, yeah, I guess I am, aren't I?"

"See you later, Mimi."

Chapter 19

Mimi

THE SUN SET MORE THAN AN HOUR AGO. THE "REAL" SHOW WAS on the other side of the island, where Nicki was right now, but Mimi enjoyed the spectacle of the sky turning into magnificent colors from the cottage's upper balcony, her favorite spot in the little house.

She'd taken dozens of photos with her phone, and now double-checked to make sure she had time to change into a nice dress before heading to the park—a two-minute walk from the cottage—to meet Jake.

She did a mental eye-roll—a habit she'd better shake off again. Soon. Besides, what good did it do if nobody saw it?

And why should she even bother changing? It would be almost dark by the time Jake arrived for their date. Which, as she reminded herself (not for the first time), it wasn't. It was just a... *Good question, what is it?*

"Who cares?" she said—and applauded herself when she managed not to roll her eyes. "And it beats sitting around all evening by myself." Which, of course, was her own fault. She could've joined Nicki and the others on Ray's family yacht.

Fat chance!

89

In the bedroom, she took off her shorts and slipped into the tie-dye dress she bought in Boston. The silky fabric cooled her flushed skin—or maybe it was the breeze coming in through the open balcony door. After running a brush through her hair and opting to leave it down, she slipped into sandals, snagged her purse off the bed, then skipped out of the house, strolled down the street, and turned toward the park.

Because she'd checked out the park before dinner, she knew there were benches scattered around, but none at the bandstand. Short of dragging one of the cottage beach chairs with her, she hoped to settle on the closest bench to keep an eye out for Jake. Otherwise she'd walk around the gazebo until he found her.

Nearing the illuminated gazebo, she saw people scattered across the vast lawn, lounging on folding chairs or picnic blankets. Children played catch or chased balls, groups of teenagers and young adults hurled frisbees, couples wandered around as if lost—and maybe they were lost...in each other, Mimi mused, with just a hint of jealousy.

When she spotted a family vacating a bench, she made a dash for it. Since she didn't know from which direction Jake came, she simply sat and let her eyes and mind wander.

Throughout the evening she'd replayed the moment when he appeared at the cottage out of nowhere. Like a jinni, only instead of rubbing an oil lamp, she had summoned him by talking to a glass of wine. Naturally her curiosity about Bellini winery increased, so over dinner at the hotel restaurant she googled the name.

Another few clicks later she found the winery's website and, after fine-combing through the picture gallery—aka enlarging the photos to their maximum size—spotted Jake in several. And in every one of them he looked happy and relaxed.

Why did he live in Italy when his family obviously ran a successful family business here on the Vineyard?

But then she thought about how she and Nicki veered off the family path by becoming teachers instead of going into medicine like her father—a dentist—or indirectly their mother, who handled the administrative side of the dental office. Their parents had always supported her and Nicki in their endeavors and never pressured them to follow in their footsteps.

Bottom line, she had no idea what Jake's story was. Maybe she'd have a chance to ask him.

Or maybe you should just worry about yourself instead of nosing around in his business.

It wasn't as if she didn't have enough on her plate, between dealing with Derek's sudden appearance in her personal life—which gave her an even worse case of the creeps than when he assaulted her —and how to mention Ray's infidelity to Nicki.

But one thing was as clear to her as the bright stars glimmering above. When Jake put his arm around her to keep her from tumbling down the stoop, she felt safe and protected, and longed to stay snuggled close to him.

"There you are, *bella*," he said as he rounded the bench and sat next to her. "Have you been waiting long?" His eyes gleamed in the last glow of twilight.

Would he try to kiss her?

"No, I got here a few minutes ago." She noticed that he had changed from shorts to a pair of khakis and a polo shirt. "How was your mom's party?"

"It was only a family dinner." He grinned at her. "I can't say much about how the food tasted, because I was too busy counting the seconds until I could excuse myself—but don't tell my sister or she'll get mad."

Mimi pretended to turn the key that locked her lips.

Sadly, he didn't make any effort to greet her with a cheek kiss or any other kind of kiss, but in all fairness, sitting side by side made a kiss an awkward challenge.

"What did you do this evening?" He stretched out his legs and draped one arm across the back of the bench.

"I had dinner at the hotel, which was delicious, and then I went back to the cottage and had a glass of wine while I watched the sunset from the balcony." His forearm brushed lightly against her bare shoulder, as if by accident, triggering goose bumps.

"Are you cold?"

"No." *Amazing how observant he is!*

"Did you get dessert with dinner?" Now his thumb drew circles on her upper arm, replacing the goose bumps with pleasant tingles.

"No, I'm not a big dessert eater," she said. "Except for gelato. Show me gelato and I drop everything else."

"Ha!" Jake jumped up and held out a hand that she automatically accepted, finding herself only inches away from him when he tugged her closer.

"And by the way..." The darkness couldn't conceal his smile when he kissed her cheeks. "Thank you for meeting me."

He lightly touched his lips to hers, making her lips—heck, the rest of her, too—scream for more, but he broke away and said, "Come with me."

She licked her lips, savoring the teasing taste of him while he led her across the lawn without letting go of her hand. "Where are we going?"

Jake squeezed her hand, "It's a surprise. Do you trust me?"

She nodded, then realized he couldn't see it because he was looking straight ahead, so she said, "Yup."

After all, he would hardly drag her into a dark alley. Not with the hundreds of tourists out and about town on this Saturday night.

Chapter 20

Jake

Jake didn't let go of Mimi's hand while they walked toward the neatly lined up Victorian houses on Ocean Avenue. He wasn't afraid she'd disappear at the stroke of midnight, but as soon as she entwined her fingers with his—as if they'd done this countless times before—his heart swelled.

When was the last time he'd strolled with a woman like this, knowing that the evening wouldn't end with the rhetorical question, "Your place or mine?" He never invited his casual acquaintances to the winery, so it was usually their place. Which also simplified his exit strategy.

When he rounded a corner and guided Mimi into the dimly lit area behind a row of stores, she stalled, tugged on his hand and asked, "Where are we?"

"Almost there. See those people?" He raised their clasped hands and pointed two houses down, where several people were gathered around an open, brightly lit door.

"What's the delicious smell?" she sniffed the air like a puppy following an irresistible scent.

"This is where we get our dessert."

When they reached the door, Mimi took a deep, savoring breath. "Mmm..." With the light behind her, his eyes were drawn to the curves of her breasts, fueling his lust.

Attempting to wrestle his libido to submission, he cleared his throat and said, "This bakery has been selling fresh donuts out of their back door for decades. Since they're open until midnight, I thought we could grab a few and take them to the beach." He pointed to the propped-up blackboard with the available choices. "Pick anything you want."

Within minutes of ordering, they received two paper bags of donuts plus two coffees and wound their way back to Seaview Avenue.

Immediately, Jake could've kicked himself for adding a coffee, since carrying the bags in one hand and his coffee in the other meant he couldn't reach for Mimi's hand again.

Once they reached Inkwell Beach, he asked, "Wanna sit on one of the benches along the sidewalk or on the beach?"

"A bench is easier with the coffees." She steered toward one and set her cup down while Jake set the donuts bags between them and ripped them open.

She ogled the two donuts. In the glow of the streetlight, he saw her licking her lips. "Can we split them in half?"

Jake laughed, "Sure, but why didn't you just order one of each?"

"Because I don't want two," she reached for her donut with sprinkles and broke it in half. "Take it or leave it, but I'll definitely take a bite out of yours."

And with that, she bit into his cinnamon donut. With anyone else he would've told them to keep it. But with her he could only chuckle. Mimi was refreshingly normal and—cute.

He took a long sip of his iced coffee, willing it to cool him off and give his hands something to do for at least a few minutes. Sitting here with her was surreal, and he had to glance at her frequently to make sure he wasn't dreaming.

Her moan after she swallowed the first bite was almost his undoing, and he had to force himself to remain where he was. The other options were to kiss her senseless or do wonderful things to her and elicit lots more moans.

"I tried to call you," he said after clearing his throat several times.

"Oh? When?" she asked before her darn tongue sneaked out and licked the sugar off her lips. "Today?"

"After Venice. But your number wasn't in service."

Don't sound so damn pathetic, Bellini. Tell her you couldn't stop thinking about her.

"I'm so sorry. Because I was about to leave Italy, I saw no reason to give you my other phone number. I didn't think you'd have any use for it."

"Well, I could've reached you." *Stop whining and ask for her number, idiot.* "Would you mind giving me your number again? The real one this time?"

"The other one was real too." She wiped her fingers on a paper napkin and pulled out her phone. "Here, why don't you add your contact info while you're at it?"

He did as she asked and sent himself a message from her phone. As soon as his phone vibrated in his pocket, he checked. "Done. Got it. Thank you."

Jake finally reached for his donut and broke off half of it, then quickly ate the piece with the bite taken out. After washing everything down with more iced coffee, he asked, "How long are you going to be on the island?"

"We're flying back to Boston tomorrow." Mimi took a few deep breaths and tilted her head back.

Following her lead, Jake also looked up at the sky and marveled at the dense carpet of stars. Together with the gentle slap of waves rolling onto the beach, it was such a peaceful moment that he wanted to remember it forever.

"You mentioned this afternoon that you're here for your sister's bachelorette weekend. Where is she now?"

"Her fiancé, Ray, and his groomsmen showed up unexpectedly.

They were supposed to cruise around the Cape on his father's yacht, but apparently changed their plans." He heard the hesitation in Mimi's voice but waited for her to offer more.

"Ray suggested we all spend the evening together on the boat, but I just couldn't." She looked at him. "And something happened earlier today that I'm still trying to figure out how to handle."

Without knowing what she meant, his protective antenna went up. "Did anything happen to you?"

"No, but I overheard him coming on to one of Nicki's bridesmaids." Even in the darkness, he saw her shudder. "I don't know how to tell my sister. And I most definitely don't want to be around him right now, having to pretend everything's fine."

"That's a tough situation. Do you think she's okay on the boat with him?"

"Yeah, he's not a physical threat to her. But if my suspicion that he's a lying cheater is true, it'll break Nicki's heart when she finds out." She shrugged, "Better before the wedding than afterward, right?"

"I guess so." He sipped more coffee to give himself time to regroup.

"Jake?" her voice was hardly any louder than the gentle waves hitting the beach.

"Hmm?"

"You said you tried to contact me in Italy. Why?"

"I wanted to see you again. When I had to go to Vicenza to meet with a distributor, I thought I'd ask you out for dinner." There. Short, sweet, and the truth.

"I've been thinking about you too. At first I thought it was you when Matt picked us up at the airport yesterday," she said. "But then I told myself I was being silly, and to stop looking for you, because why would you be here when I know you live in Italy?"

"Well, Matt and I do look alike. And although I'm living on my uncle's vineyard for the time being, here is where I grew up."

His mind circled back to what she just said. *I've been thinking about you. I told myself to stop looking for you.*

What were the chances that their surprise meeting in May had left them both wanting more? "You said you're flying back to Boston tomorrow. Is that where you live?"

"Yes, in Waltham. My father has a dentistry practice there, and I'm teaching English at a private school."

Finally! Something he could store away for later. Feeling lighter than he had in weeks, he prodded, "Since we exchanged phone numbers—again—and now know where we each live, do you think you could also tell me your last name, or should I look it up on the hotel reservation? In case the phone number you gave me doesn't work..."

Mimi laughed, "The other one worked too...at the time. But no, this number is in service, so there's no need for you to dig through reservation files. But you're not allowed to laugh when I tell you my name."

He was puzzled, but promised, "I won't, and why would I?"

"Because I've had enough people make fun of it to last a lifetime." Then she leaned so close her breath tickled his face. "It's Albizia."

An image of the beautiful, hardy plant with its pink or yellow flowers and sensitive leaves materialized in his mind. "The Persian silk tree, named after Italian nobleman Filippo degli Albizzi. Also known as Mimosa tree." The name suited her perfectly.

"Wow, I'm impressed."

"I like Italian history, and the Albizzi family happens to be from Florence, a city I love," he said and before he knew it, reached over to touch her face. "Plus I work with plants."

"Should I ever go back to Florence, I'll take you up on the offer you made in Venice. Do you remember it?"

"I remember, and I'd like nothing better than to show you around. I stand by my word. Always."

His thumb caressed her cheek, and when she leaned into the

palm of his hand, he was a goner. He wanted to kiss her so badly, but was afraid to jostle their delicate connection.

Minutes went by in comfortable silence. He didn't know what time it was, but he'd be damned if he would let go of her to check it.

"Will your sister worry about where you are?" he asked eventually.

Mimi shrugged, squeezing his hand between her cheek and her shoulder. "I don't think so, but I should probably go back."

"Can I see you again before I fly back to Florence at the end of the week?" The cruel reminder that he wasn't staying here chilled him to the bone.

He felt her swallow and willed her to agree. "I was planning to go to Providence to visit my friend for a day or two, but Paloma and I haven't decided on the exact day yet. When were you thinking?"

"I'm flexible." Should he offer to meet her in Providence? It was an easy day trip with the high-speed ferry.

Mimi pulled back and got up, so he did too. She rubbed both hands over her upper arms, and Jake instinctively stepped closer and enfolded her in his arms.

"Think about it, okay?" he pleaded. "I don't mind driving to Boston, or to Providence, or anywhere in between. But I just found you again..." he trailed off and brought one hand to the back of her head, the other around her slim waist.

She nodded and looked up at him, her face mere inches away. "I'd like to see you again, too."

Was it the moonlight that reflected in her eyes, or was she glowing from within? It was as if he got sucked into two whirlpools of bottomless water, and he lowered his mouth to hers.

The slow, gentle kiss quickly became more intense. Cute moans escaped her, and he regretted that they were on a public town beach with no privacy at all instead of somewhere more secluded. On the other hand, he prided himself on having at least some class and wasn't the "ravish-a-woman-behind-the-rocks" type.

She stood close enough to feel his body's reaction to her, but he didn't try to hide it by taking a step back—a stupid rookie move, anyway—and he wasn't ashamed of being aroused by her.

Jake broke the kiss and said, "I can't..."

Mimi smirked at him, "Your body says otherwise," which made him iron-hard. That she didn't shy away from what was happening between them thrilled him.

"*Cara*, I'm not worried about performing. With any other woman I might not hold back, but you're special. And you're a hotel guest, which is one of my father's golden rules I won't break."

She drove him crazy when she pressed her curves against his chest, put her mouth close to his ear, and asked, "Do you want me to go check out right this moment?"

Jake laughed, grateful that she defused the situation without making it awkward. He wanted her and was now certain it was mutual. But this wasn't the time or place. Did such a time or place even exist for them? He was determined to find out.

After one more kiss he said, "Let me know about next week, just tell me when and where."

He didn't let go of her hand until they reached the cottage, where he felt a pang of disappointment that it was brightly lit with lively female voices drifting out the windows.

Mimi turned to him. "Thank you for tonight. It was perfect."

"*Arrivederci, bella.*" He kissed her again, then watched her disappear into the house. *Yes, tonight was perfect.*

Chapter 21

Jake

"Are you gonna spill the beans now or later?" Matt trumpeted while he handed Jake a mug of hot coffee, poured one for himself, and slumped down at the breakfast table, smirking at Jake.

How about never? Jake eyed the croissants his mom or Carla left in a woven basket on the table and selected one. He bit into it, loving the flaky consistency and buttery taste. "Do we have Nutella?"

Matt got up and took a jar out of a cabinet, setting it directly under Jake's nose. "Would you like me to spread it on your croissant, or are you able to handle that yourself?"

"Asshole." Jake stretched his arm and got a knife out of the drawer behind him, then sliced the croissant lengthwise.

"Got up on the wrong side of the bed?" Matt's smirk was back.

"Nope."

"I wasn't aware that you'd gotten yourself a little vacation fling," Matt said, his eyebrows going up when Jake shot up and towered over the table.

"Mimi is *not* a fling," he snapped.

"Whoa, hold your horses." Matt threw up his hands in playful surrender, the corners of his mouth twitching while he struggled to maintain a straight face. "And you better get your temper under control before you meet with Dad. Because he wants to see you in his office in," he consulted his wristwatch, "half an hour."

"Would've been nice if he'd let me know himself," Jake grumbled and sat down again. Being summoned like that made him feel like he was twelve again.

He knew he overreacted to Matt's teasing, but memories of Mimi's body pressed against his, and his lips on hers, had ensured a pretty uncomfortable night. So instead of sleeping, he scoured social media for information about her, now he knew her last name, but came up almost as empty-handed as previously. He found a few older photos from events in Boston that showed her with her parents, but no personal Facebook, Instagram, or Twitter accounts.

Who doesn't have at least one of those nowadays?

When he finally did fall asleep, the sun woke him up way too soon by sending her rays like spears of light through the curtains.

"Dad told Carla to tell you, but she had an errand to run, so she told me, and now I have relayed the message. Mission accomplished..." Matt rubbed his hands together with a grin.

"What does he want?"

"No clue." Matt helped himself to a croissant and spread Nutella on it. "Probably the come-to-Jesus talk."

"I'm so sick of those," Jake muttered.

Responsibility and *step up* and *for the family* were Jake's least favorite words, especially when they came out of his dad's mouth. Not that they were a bad thing—he considered himself a responsible person who put family above everything else, isn't that why he was in Italy with Uncle Fausto?—but because they were regular features of his father's tirades.

All Jake was interested in right now was how to get ahold of Mimi before she left. He *had* to see her, even if only briefly.

"Do you know when the bachelorette party is leaving?" He realized his mistake as soon as the words were out of his mouth.

"Well, checkout time is eleven o'clock, and they didn't ask for an extension. But I'm not chauffeuring the airport shuttle today, so I don't know what the arrangements are."

Then Matt grinned and held up his phone. "Would you like me to find out? And don't think I haven't noticed that you didn't answer my question about...what's her name?"

You jerk. You know darn well it's Mimi.

Jake wanted to tell Matt to wipe that smirk off his face. How was he going to explain his connection to Mimi? Why did he have to explain himself to begin with?

Because you were always brothers and buddies.

"Not that it's any of your damn business, but Mimi and I actually met in a café in Venice in May. A stupid kid tried to act smart with her and I sent him packing. Then Mimi and I had a drink and that was it."

"And?"

"And then I saw her again yesterday and said hello."

"Oooo-kay."

"What else do you want to know?"

"I'm sensing there's more to the story, but I'll let it go. For now." Matt moaned dramatically after he took a bite out of his croissant while still managing to keep his eyes on Jake.

Please tell me you didn't see us at the beach.

It was entirely possible that Matt had been out and about last night, too. Carla mentioned that Matt was casually seeing a musician or dancer participating in an artist-in-residency program in Chilmark. But what were the chances that he walked by, without making himself known, just when Mimi moaned while she ate the donut? *Shit, the chances were pretty good. And Matt wouldn't be one to let it slide.*

Jake bit down a snarky remark and gulped his coffee. "I'd love to continue with this inquisition, but I gotta run." *Out of the frying pan and into the fire.*

"M-hm."

"What's that supposed to mean?"

"Nothing. But I love how squirmy you are, and I doubt it has anything to do with Dad."

Jake ignored Matt's remark and pocketed his car keys, wallet, and phone. "I might head out for a drive, but text if you need me for anything."

A few minutes later, he parked his car at the hotel and snuck a peek at the Poppy cottage, where two young, laughing women sat on the porch. To his disappointment, they weren't the one he hoped to see.

In the lobby, he jokingly saluted the front desk staff, then made his way to his father's office. Although he didn't hear anyone talking through the half-open door, Jake knocked before he entered.

"Morning, Dad," he spotted his father standing in front of a file cabinet with his back to the door.

"Jacob, come in," Robert Bellini turned around with a smile. "Did you have a nice evening last night?"

Why is everybody making it their business? "Yes, thank you. I ran into a friend."

His dad nodded but refrained from commenting further. "Thank you for coming."

Jake scoffed, "Not that I had much choice, Dad, after receiving the summons. What's up?" He prepared himself for the customary "it's time to come home" speech, or the other version of "when will you stop stomping around in the grapes?"

"I want to run a business idea by you."

Whoa, that's a new one.

His dad put an ominous-looking rolled-up map and a thick folder on the oval conference table, and Jake's suspicions increased when his dad asked, "Do you want some coffee?" *Since when do we sip coffee while having* The Talk?

His father wasn't hostile or Godfatherish when he voiced his opinions about Jake's decision to work for his uncle, but there was always an unmistakable undertone about family responsibilities. If

103

this were a movie, they'd probably sip whiskey, making the situation appear relaxed, but no less serious.

"Your grandfather should be here any minute."

That's a new one too. "Grandpa is joining us?" Jake tried very hard to keep his poker face in place.

"Yes." His dad picked up the desk phone and hit a button. "Danielle, will you have someone bring coffee for three to my office, please? Yes, some biscotti would be great. Thank you."

Coffee and *biscotti? What's going on here?*

Raspy laughter from the short hallway between the front desk and the administrative offices announced his grandfather before he entered the room. "Ah, to be young again," he chuckled. "Those kids are always a delight to talk with."

Jake refrained from mentioning that he better not call the interns "kids" to their faces. But his grandfather grew up at a time when things were not as tense, and his generation hadn't had corporate etiquette drilled into them as was habitual today.

"Jacob, did you enjoy your invigorating evening walk?" Grandpa asked, and Jake almost blew a fuse.

"Yes, I did," he ground out. What was *wrong* with his family? Not even Mia was so inquisitive about what he was doing—perhaps because nothing escaped her and Aunt Francesca's attention to begin with.

"So, unless we're waiting for more people, what's up?" Jake asked, trying to keep his voice neutral.

"Are you in a hurry?" his dad asked.

Possibly. "No. Just curious."

"Let's have a seat." His father tapped his finger on the map and got straight to the point. "Yesterday your grandparents and I had a look at Charles's property."

A knock at the door interrupted them and a waitress entered with a tray. "You can just leave it on the table, thank you," said his father.

After the young woman closed the door, he unrolled a town property map and pointed to farmland north of the Vineyard's small airport. "This is Charles's land. And I want to build an inn there."

A slap on his face couldn't have slammed Jake's head back any harder than his father's announcement.

"Did you just say you're building another hotel?" Jake asked and shook his head. He must've misheard.

His father looked at Jake's grandfather, "James, would you like to continue?"

"Yes, of course." Jake's grandfather wiped under his eyes and said, "A while back your grandmother and I discovered a folder with information Charles had collected. He envisioned a combination of an inn and cabins. The inn would offer only breakfast."

"In other words, a B&B," Jake said and looked at his grandfather. "And the cabins you mentioned?"

"Charles had something family-oriented in mind. Comfortable and practical two-bedroom mini cottages with kitchenettes and a communal outdoor barbeque area. There's a hand-drawn sketch in which the cabins are arranged in a half-circle on a large meadow, giving the illusion of a village center."

Jake didn't want to offend his grandfather or disrespect his late uncle, but what he heard so far sounded mostly like something that would attract groups of aging hippies looking for a place where they could relive Woodstock, let their junk hang out all day, and smoke pot in peace—not the best premise for the backyard of a B&B.

"Is this pond part of the property?" Jake pointed to a kidney-shaped pond on the edge of the property.

"We have direct access, yes, which is an advantage, because the nearest ocean beach is twenty minutes away. Clearing off a few trees will provide enough space and make it perfect for swimming and kayaking," said his grandfather.

Great—the stoned, beer-bellied hippies can go skinny-dipping, scaring away minnows and ducks and everything else that doesn't run fast enough.

"Do Mom and Grandma know about this?"

"Yes, they do," was all his father said—to Jake's mounting annoyance.

"And what do Matt and Carla think of your idea?"

"We haven't shared it with them yet."

"Why not?"

His dad's eyes never wavered from Jake's face. "Because Charles was your godfather. We're hoping you'll be at the helm of Faulkner's Inn."

Jake almost bounced up out of his chair. Had they lost their minds? He wasn't going to flip pancakes or fry bacon for the rest of his life, any more than he was going to hand out bottles of calamine lotion to idiotic guests who traipsed through the woods and ended up with poison ivy in unmentionable places.

"I can't run a bed and breakfast." *And that's the polite version of what I really think.*

"Why not?" his father leaned back and folded his arms across his chest. A gesture that pretty much told Jake this wasn't up for discussion.

Was this the take-it-or-break-it moment he'd been dreading for years?

"I'm a lawyer," Jake said—and winced when he realized his mistake.

"You haven't seen the inside of a courtroom since you went to work with Fausto," his father volleyed back without missing a beat. "What are you still doing there after five years? I need you here."

Jake wasn't going to have *that* discussion with his dad, either. "Maybe Matt or Carla want to take on this new opportunity?"

"They'll have their hands full with the hotel when your mother and I retire."

"You're retiring?"

His dad shrugged. "Eventually. I promised your mother we'd travel more once she turns sixty, and that was yesterday."

Time to change the trajectory of this little chat, because Jake wasn't too keen for what usually came next—the other thorn in his side: when was he going to settle down?

Jake couldn't wait to get out of his father's office and out of Oak Bluffs. He didn't care where he went—just out!

"So, just out of curiosity, when is this all supposed to happen?" he asked.

"We're hoping to get started soon," his grandpa said. "Your grand-mother and I aren't getting younger and would love to see Charles's vision fulfilled."

Realizing there was nothing he could say that wouldn't be either insensitive or insanely rude, Jake bit his tongue. But he wasn't going to agree to something of this scope just because they ganged up on him. As much as he loved his parents and grandparents, he wasn't about to let them dictate his future.

His grandfather slowly rose from his chair. "I think everything's said, so I'll go meet my Cora for breakfast." He patted Jake's shoulder in passing. "Think about it, Jacob."

"Yes, sir," Jake said tersely.

"Is there anything else?" he bit out as soon as his grandfather left.

"Not for now. I'll see you later." His dad effectively dismissed him and rolled up the map with a calm Jake envied.

Liquid lava boiled in his veins while he stormed out of his father's office, ready to change his return flight to Italy and leave on the next plane.

Then he saw Mimi at the front desk.

Chapter 22

Mimi

Mimi didn't know whether to cry or scream or throw an Oscar-worthy hissy fit. And it was a tossup who she was madder at: Ray and Derek—because what just happened looked like the successful collaboration of two unrepentant assholes—or Tanya, for convincing Nicki to agree to the stupid idea.

"Oh, won't it be so much fun to return to Boston on Dad's yacht instead of that rickety tin airplane?" Tanya had whined after Ray suggested they all spend the day together.

Unfortunately, after some back-and-forth, Nicki conceded, and only then pulled Mimi aside and asked, "Are you sure you don't want to come with us? Doesn't a day on the boat sound fun?"

To which Mimi had replied, "Not on that boat. Nic, I'm sorry. But don't worry about me, I'll catch up with you at home, okay?" Then they hugged and Mimi went to have breakfast—and plan how to kill time until she would happily board the rickety tin airplane that was beneath Tanya's standards.

Shaking her head and keeping further opinions to herself, she watched her sister and entourage—Tanya and Nicki in the lead, the ducklings dutifully in a single line behind them—drag their luggage across Ocean Park to meet the guys at the Dockside Marina. It didn't surprise Mimi that the men hadn't offered to come and carry the luggage—she was actually grateful for it, because she had no desire to lay eyes on either of those handsy morons.

In the hotel lobby, Mimi made a beeline for the front desk. "Hi, my friends and I arranged for a shuttle to take us to the airport this afternoon, but something came up and I only need transportation for one." She pointed at herself. "Me. Will that be a problem?"

The young woman behind the desk said, "No, I'll make a note..." when a deep voice asked, "What happened?"

Mimi turned around and found herself less than six feet away from Jake. "Oh, hi! Umm, it's a long story, but bottom line is that Nicki and her friends left with Ray on the boat. I wanted to let the hotel know that it's only me for the airport run and they don't need to send the big van."

"I can take you."

Mimi had spent most of her night replaying every minute from the moment Jake discovered her at the cottage until he kissed her good night—and he seemed earnest about his offer. "Won't I be taking you away from something else?"

"You won't. When does your flight leave?" His eyes traveled from her eyes to her mouth, making her lips tingle. *Yes, I want to kiss you, too.*

"At five. If you're sure..."

"One hundred percent sure." Jake said to the desk employee, "Danielle, you can cancel the shuttle. I've got this covered."

"Thanks, Jake," Danielle said and turned her attention to the next guest.

Jake asked Mimi, "Did you already eat breakfast?"

"No."

"Why don't we check out the buffet and decide how to spend the day?"

"Are you really su..." Mimi began, but he put a finger over her lips and said, "*Bella*, I was up all night wondering how to catch you

109

before you're leaving. Spending several hours with you is a dream come true."

His words went down like ambrosia. "Okay, but I insist on buying your breakfast." When he opened his mouth, she said, "No, you bought dessert last night. Now it's my turn."

His smirk made her nerves tingle. This unexpected bonus time with him was the best gift ever, especially since she'd promised herself to find a way to see him again before he flew back to Italy.

But she'd also asked herself why she couldn't have met someone who lived closer to her. Why was she starting to fall for someone who lived almost four thousand miles away? And, okay, maybe she had looked up the distance between Boston and Tuscany.

"Fine," he said and rested his scorching hand on her lower back. "Let's go find a table."

Which wasn't easy, because the breakfast room was a beehive of activity and Mimi didn't see any empty tables. She was about to suggest grabbing a coffee, bagel, and banana to go, when an elderly woman called, "Jacob, come join us."

And then Jake surprised Mimi with the most adorable reaction.

He ran a hand over his hair and down his neck—and blushed. "Umm... Are you ready to meet my grandparents?"

Mimi pressed her lips together, but the chuckle still snuck out. "I guess it's too late now. As a matter of fact, I'd love to talk to your grandma. It impressed me when Matt told us the story Friday of how she rented out the cottages in the 60s."

Jake rested his hand on Mimi's back again. "Then we don't need to worry about how we're going to spend the next few hours, because Grandma looooves to talk about it."

Even with the cotton fabric of her T-shirt covering her skin, Mimi was surprised by her powerful reaction to his touch, and by how much she craved the physical connection.

"Good morning, Grandma." Jake kissed his grandmother's cheek, then clapped his grandfather's shoulder. "Grandpa, long time no see." He lightly put his arm around Mimi's shoulder and said, "This is Mimi." He smirked, "Or Emily."

Mimi already held out her hand to Jake's grandmother when she remembered too late that she didn't know their last name. "It's a pleasure to meet you, Mrs..."

Jake's grandmother shook it and said, "I'm Cora Faulkner. Nice to meet you too, my dear."

And Jake's grandfather said, "You can call me James. The only people who call me Mr. Faulkner are my urologist and my investment advisor. Please, have a seat."

"Thank you."

The table was for set for six, with James sitting on a short end and Cora to his left, where she had an eagle's eye view of the comings and goings in the restaurant. Mimi wondered if it was a habit she acquired during her decades of caring for guests and their well-being.

Jake pulled out the chair to his grandfather's left, opposite his grandmother, for Mimi, and then sat down next to her.

She itched to reach for his hand under the cover of the tablecloth, but the gesture felt too assuming, or intimate, so she folded her hands in her lap. When a waitress arrived, Jake smiled at Mimi and asked, "Would you like a mimosa, *bella*?"

Mimi saw that Cora and James already had theirs and laughed, "Sure, why not? And today you don't even have to catch a train."

Jake said to the waitress, "Two mimosas, and we'll help ourselves to the buffet. Thank you." Then he did what Mimi hadn't dared. He covered her hand with his and said, "You're right, I don't have a train to catch. Instead I'll have to watch *you* walk away from *me*."

Mimi tried to clear the congestion in her throat but, before she could reply, noticed Jake's grandmother's unabashed interest in their conversation. Then the old woman nodded and winked at her.

"How long have you two known each other?" Cora asked.

Mimi found the question a little forward, but then was reminded of her own grandmothers. Whatever was on their minds came right out of their mouths.

Guess advanced age gives them that right.

"For about four hours," she said at the same time as Jake said, "since May."

Cora cackled, "Oh my, you two need to make up your minds."

"Actually, we're both correct. We met in May and spent a little over an hour together, then we ran into each other yesterday and hung out for a few hours." Mimi smiled at Jake.

"I see... Will you be here for the dance tonight?" asked Cora, her inquisitive eyes going back and forth between Mimi and Jake. "The hotel has local musicians performing on summer weekends." Now the woman's eyes sparkled, making Mimi wonder whether it was because she was recalling fond memories or if she was plotting something.

"Unfortunately I have to leave later this afternoon," Mimi said, hoping to deflect any further questions.

After a waitress served their mimosas, Jake touched his glass to Mimi's, "To memories, old and new."

Mimi knew she was already going home with a boatload of new memories.

Chapter 23

Jake

JAKE ONLY WANTED TO SIT BACK AND WATCH HIS GRANDPARENTS chat with Mimi.

No, false. What he *really* wanted was to be alone with Mimi and kiss her like last night at the beach. And he wanted to tell his grandmother—it didn't escape Jake's notice that his grandfather didn't say a word but was eagerly following the conversation—to stop nagging Mimi.

But when he glanced at Mimi, she didn't seem bothered by the questions.

He scratched his chin and eyed the breakfast buffet. "Wanna grab something to eat?"

"Sure. I'm starving." Mimi said to his grandparents, "Please excuse us."

"Of course, my dear." Jake watched his grandfather rise halfway and smile at Mimi. *The geezer is going all old-school.* If Jake didn't know better, he'd say Grandpa was flirting with Mimi.

Jake took possession of Mimi's hand again while they walked to the buffet. It was so endearing when she insisted that she should pay

113

for breakfast. Over the years he'd come across plenty of women who gladly let him pay, assuming his wallet was always padded.

What Mimi didn't know was that his grandparents were sitting at the table permanently reserved for their family, and every family member always ate for free—which included her as his guest. But he'd ease her conscience and let her leave a tip for the staff.

"Oh yummy, look at all these delicacies," Mimi gushed. "Hmm... I'll start with a gravlax bagel and fruit salad, and then I'll go back for seconds and have... I don't know." She leaned closer to him, and he lost all interest in the smorgasbord. All he wanted was to wrap his arms around her.

She took a step away and surveyed the buffet more closely. "On second thought, maybe I'll leave some room. You said the donut bakery is open daily except Tuesdays, right? I mean, this all looks amazing, but they were..."

"Hey, Mimi, come here," he pulled on her arm until she stood only inches away. Just remembering how she took a bite out of his donut made him crave more carnal things.

"We can do anything you want, *bella*." His eyes wandered to her mouth, then back to her gorgeous eyes, more hazel than brown right now, then to the dimple on her cheek.

And then he remembered his grandmother mentioning the concert later. Could he convince Mimi to stay another night and take her to dinner, enjoy the music, dance, have a few drinks...

Could he get one night with her? He didn't know when he'd see her again, so why not make the best out of the present? But Mimi deserved more.

"I rely on you to show me the island's best spots," her voice brought him back from daydreaming some pretty explicit fantasies. "All I have to do after breakfast is to check out and make sure to catch my flight later," she said with a shrug and the sweetest smile.

After breakfast, while Mimi was still fully engaged in one of his grandma's tales about the good old times, he excused himself and went to Carla's office.

"Hey, I have a question," he knocked perfunctorily on the open door and entered the room. "What are you doing today?"

"Good morning to you, too. I'm glad to see you survived your chat with Dad," his sister said while she barely glanced at him, her attention on her laptop. Then her head shot up. "You want something! I recognize that shit-eating grin."

"What are your plans for today?" he asked, rephrasing his earlier question while he plopped down in one of the two chairs in front of the desk.

"No plans. I'm here for another hour or so to scan and print some of Grandma's old recipes, then I'll go home. She's coming over to help me decipher some of the handwritten notes." She leaned back in her chair and narrowed her eyes. "Spill it. I know you're not here so say hi."

"Can I borrow your car?"

Raucous laughter greeted his question. "Would that have anything to do with the girl you've been seen with?"

"What the fu..." he hissed, then restrained himself. "Why does everybody keep asking me about Mimi?"

"Is that her name? Ah..."

"What's *that* supposed to mean?"

Carla only shrugged.

Jake ran a hand over his hair. "Yes, her name's Emily, or Mimi, and I wish you guys would keep your noses out of my relationship. You're not the first person today to comment."

"You're in a relationship?" Carla's short, manicured fingernails tapped on her elbows.

"Drop it. So, can I borrow your car or not? You can drive my rental instead." Jake got up, needing to get back to Mimi to protect her from his overly nosy grandparents. Although he had a feeling Mimi didn't need rescuing. She seemed to be holding her own pretty well.

"Sure, since you've asked so nicely," Carla dug through her purse and tossed the car fob to him. "You owe me."

"Add it to my tab." He dreaded the day when she called in the favors she'd done him over the years, like fibbing to their parents about his whereabouts, curfews, and a few other misdemeanors.

"Treat her well."

"That's why I asked to take your car."

"I *mean* my car."

He smirked, dropped the key fob of his rental car on her desk, then pocketed hers. "See you later, sis."

"M-hmm..."

———

After Mimi checked out, he dropped her weekend bag in the trunk of his sister's Audi, self-stored the retractable top, and revved the engine.

"Where are we going?" Mimi asked as he drove out of Oak Bluffs and away from prying eyes.

"I thought we'd drive to Menemsha. It's one of my favorite spots on the island."

"Sounds good." Out of the corner of his eye, he saw how she wiggled deeper into the sports car seat, then pulled a scrunchie off her wrist and tied her hair into a loose ponytail.

A pang of disappointment shot through him. Her hair should be unfettered, flowing over her shoulders and over her chest, tickling her breasts...

Wrong train of thought, Bellini.

They didn't talk much for a while, except when Jake pointed out occasional scenic points. Instead of driving to Menemsha as he planned, he made a last-minute change and drove toward Aquinnah, the Vineyard's westernmost town.

"Jake?"

He snuck a peek at her and almost slammed on the brakes when he saw her head resting against the headrest with her eyes closed. She was so damn cute and sexy. Why couldn't he have found her months ago? Why couldn't she still live in Italy?

He cleared this throat, "Yeah?"

"Yesterday, when you first saw me, I was drinking a glass of Bellini wine. I googled the winery and saw you in a few pictures. Is that where you live and work?"

"Yes, it's my uncle's winery in San Gimignano."

"How long have you been living there?"

"For about five years. My uncle had a heart attack while I was visiting. It was a busy time, and they were short of people. I always loved the science and the groundedness—" Before she could call him out, he added, "yeah, I made that word up, but it fits. Anyhow, I love the craft behind winemaking, its connection to nature, so I made the spur-of-the-moment decision to stay."

Jake parked the car at Aquinnah Cliffs Overlook and cut the engine. Fluffy cumulus clouds drifted lazily across the blue sky, and the sparkling conjunction of Vineyard Sound, Buzzards Bay, and Block Island Sound stretched out in front of them. As much as he loved the Tuscan landscape, these beach-rose-covered dunes and the expanse of the Atlantic Ocean dotted with vessels of various sizes, were equally showstopping.

Again, he thought if he could just combine the two, he'd have found his paradise.

"Wow, this is beautiful." Mimi shifted in her seat and turned sideways as much as the seat belt allowed.

Facing him, she asked, "Was it hard to leave all this," she waved her arm through the air, "and your family behind when you decided to stay in Italy?"

She managed to ask the one question that had been on his mind for years. How often had he wondered in the twilight hours of the day whether courage or stupidity, ignorance or selfishness, had prompted his decision.

Jake unbuckled his seat belt and reached into a lunch-box size cooler behind the passenger seat. He pulled out two bottles of water and offered one to Mimi, who accepted it with a smile and took a long sip.

"Want to go to the lighthouse?" Jake asked—conveniently avoiding Mimi's question for now—and gestured toward the Gay Head Lighthouse behind them. He would answer her, but it helped him to be in motion when he discussed iffy topics.

As if she sensed his reluctance, she asked as soon as they started walking, "What do you know about the lighthouse?"

"Aquinnah was originally called Gay Head. Out there," Jake swung out a hand and pointed over the water, "is an area with strong tidal currents and huge underwater boulders called Devil's Bridge, and to facilitate safe passage for ships, the first Gay Head Lighthouse was built in 1799. But prior to English colonists, the Wampanoag tribe inhabited the island. They were whalers, and used small boats and harpoons to harvest them long before whaling became an important maritime industry in the nineteenth century."

"Oh, yes! Of course!" Mimi's eyes lit up. "Tashtego, Herman Melville's character in *Moby Dick*, is a harpooner from Aquinnah."

"I read the story long ago, but didn't remember that detail."

They reached the lighthouse and walked to the edge of an overlook offering unobstructed views of the clay cliffs. Mimi leaned against the rough wooden railing, taking a few photos with her phone while stray strands of hair fluttered around her face.

Then she turned around, and Jake's breath hitched. The natural beauty of the white and ochre cliffs behind her stood no chance against the brilliance of her smile. After pretty much sitting on his hands all morning, he couldn't stop himself from reaching out to her.

He slid a hand behind her head and guided her to him. Or maybe he met her halfway—he couldn't remember later—and looked deep into her eyes.

Soul-searching.

But whose soul? Hers or his?

The tip of her tongue peeked out between her lips, and he closed the distance and kissed her. Nibbling on her lower lip, he beseeched her to give him more, and the moment she opened to him he deepened the kiss.

As soon as her arms went around his neck and her soft curves pressed against him, the screeching seagulls, jabbering tourists, caressing wind, and clashing waves quieted down.

Nothing else mattered, and nothing else existed, only the two of them.

When breathing became difficult, he pressed his lips to her forehead and whispered, "You asked me if it was hard to leave everything behind to go to Italy. It was nothing compared to having to say goodbye to you this afternoon, *cara.*"

Chapter 24

Mimi

MIMI WANTED TO CLING TO JAKE AND BEG HIM TO NEVER LET her go. For once in her life, she wanted to be spontaneous instead of planning every move. She wanted to go to the dance at the hotel. Wanted to spend more time with Jake.

But she wasn't the clingy type, and she didn't beg. Being impulsive was amazing in theory, but it still had to be doable. She had nowhere to stay, and another flight reminder had popped up when she got her phone out to take photos.

Tears burned behind her eyelids, and she turned away from Jake. Swallowing several times, Mimi relished the comforting breeze on her face.

Her body hummed when she was near him, and she had solid proof how affected he was too. What was it that pulled her to him? What did they have in common? What did she really know about him?

The first thing that came to mind was that he turned his back on his old life on a whim and stayed in Italy to support his uncle—what was the term he'd used for why he liked it there so much?

Groundedness.

And wasn't that what she'd done? Maybe not on a whim, but she fled to Italy to ground herself, only for the foundation to tremble now with unprecedented intensity.

Where would she go this time to steady herself?

Because there was no doubt in her mind that it wasn't going to be a smooth passage when they parted ways, no matter how tender and green their connection was. And running away wasn't an option.

"Where are you, *bella*?" Jake's breath tickled her neck as he stood behind her, his arms wrapped loosely around her waist.

"Right here," she laughed and wiggled her shoulders, effectively snuggling closer.

"No, you were far away." He turned her around but didn't kiss her, his earlier hungry look replaced by worry and genuine curiosity. "Wanna talk about it?" He stroked her cheek with the backs of his fingers.

Not particularly.

"Can we sit down somewhere?" she asked instead of a simple yes or no.

"I know just the place if you don't mind a fifteen-minute drive."

She nodded and, holding hands, they strolled back to the car without talking.

There's so much comfort in silence.

She settled in the car seat and let the sun and wind kiss her face. The drive would give her time to regroup and consider how much she was going to tell him. Tainting this gorgeous day with ugly memories was so wrong, but the past already played Whack-A-Mole with her by throwing Derek into her personal life.

And since she was sick and tired of being the mole, it was about time to be the mallet!

Jake parked the car in a fishing village after a short drive, during which she paid no attention to the scenery.

"Welcome to Menemsha." He led her to a jetty built into the harbor basin, sat down at the far end, and patted the boulder next to him.

Mimi took a few deep breaths and *grounded* herself in the here and now by watching the fishermen unload their catch, tossing the occasional small fish to the waiting seagulls.

The gulls of course reminded her of Venice, where they were nowadays considered a bigger nuisance than the pigeons, who were mostly to be found around *Piazza San Marco*.

"I want to tell you why I went to Italy last year," she said. "Not all the gory details, but the basics."

"You can tell me as much or as little as you feel comfortable sharing."

"Okay," she nodded and looked straight ahead over the softly surging water. "I mentioned yesterday that I'm an English teacher..."

"Yes."

"I work at a private school outside of Boston. Last fall one of my co-workers hosted a Halloween party, and during the evening one of the athletic trainers assaulted me."

Out of the corner of her eye, Mimi noticed Jake sitting up straighter.

"He'd been making stupid comments for some time, acting as if he was the catch of the day, but I never paid much attention."

"What kind of comments?"

"It started with 'What did you do for fun this weekend?' or 'Have you been to this-or-that new restaurant?' The usual mindless small talk co-workers often make, but his sudden interest felt...off. We never had much interaction before, aside from staff meetings."

Mimi paused and stared across the water before she continued, "Then he got handsier and constantly bumped elbows or shoulders, wanted to know if I was seeing someone, until he began to enlighten me with me his opinions about the benefits of open versus committed relationships."

She caught herself wringing her hands and paused for a deep breath.

"What a weird topic among colleagues. Who is doing that?" Jake asked.

She shrugged. "Apparently Derek does."

"Was all that before or after the Halloween party?"

"Before. He'd approach me in the staff room or in the school cafeteria. Sometimes I wondered if he was watching me. He showed up too conveniently, and too often, for it to be a coincidence."

"That's already harassment right there." Jake's voice had a sharp undertone.

"I know, but I didn't want to make a big deal out of it. Then at that Halloween party, when everybody was handing out candy in the driveway, he waited for me after I used the bathroom, pushed me against the wall, and began to feel me up." Mimi looked at Jake, curious about his reaction.

"What?" Jake's eyes shot daggers. "Did you..."

Please, not you, too.

She couldn't take it if he also said it was her fault and that she should've put Derek in his place sooner.

"I told him to leave me alone and tried to push his hands away. But he continued groping me and pressing me against the wall, and with his leg between mine I couldn't get away."

Jake flexed his hands, then balled them into fists.

"He said stuff like, 'I know you need it too,' and, 'Let me unclench you, Miss Mimosa.'" Mimi almost gagged at the memory of Derek's sick idea of being witty—and decided against telling Jake how Derek then begun to push her toward the nearest bedroom.

"It was disgusting. Luckily a few other guests entered the house and startled him, so I was able to sneak away. The next day I reported it to the school's administration and was informed that they couldn't do anything because it allegedly," she made air quotes, "happened at a private party and it was my own decision to go there."

"That does not fly," Jake boomed, startling a few seagulls and ducks who'd been cleaning their feathers not far from them.

She shrugged, "It was my word against his, and he's the athletic director of the boys' varsity hockey team. He's the big fish, and I guess the school wasn't going to explain to Boston's rich and famous why they fired their sons' revered coach in the middle of the school year. I couldn't stand it any longer and took a leave of absence and went to Italy. I think they were glad to be rid of me for half a year."

"Wait a minute. That's not same school you're going back to in the fall?"

"Yes, it is. And I'm staying as far away from Derek as possible and will never, ever be alone with him in a room."

"Mimi..."

She held up a hand. "Let me finish, please. Unfortunately, my plans were blown to smithereens yesterday when Ray showed up with his entourage, and Derek was one of them."

"What?" Jake growled.

"Yup. Turns out he's the newest boytoy of my sister's future sister-in-law." Mimi held out her arms in a what-are-ya-gonna-do gesture. "And now you know why I refused to spend last night with the bridal party, and why I didn't accept the 'oh-so-tempting' offer to return to Boston on Ray's father's yacht."

She grimaced. "You might've figured by now that Ray's loaded and thinks he can do whatever he wants to do. He and Derek are both scum who think every woman should be putty in their hands."

Jake jumped up and paced within six feet of where Mimi sat. "You have to report it to the school's board of trustees. You can't let him get away with that behavior. Since I'm a lawyer, I'll help you write a letter."

"You're a lawyer?" She hadn't known Jake long enough to be up to date with his background, other than that his parents obviously owned a fancy hotel on Martha's Vineyard and his uncle a winery in Tuscany.

"Yes, I'm a member of the Massachusetts Bar Association, but I hated working for my slimeball of a boss—who could be Ray and Derek's role model." He combed his fingers through his hair, mussing it even more, and ran a hand over his stubbled jaw.

So he also ran away from something he despised?

Jake's pacing made Mimi antsy, so she stood up. "Thank you for your offer to help me with a letter, but I'm not going to pursue it. Derek already got away with it, and I don't see how any other outcome is possible, even if I try again. Honestly, I have bigger fish to fry right now."

"Like what?" His eyes almost bulged out of their sockets.

"Like how to tell my sister that I caught Ray pulling 'a Derek' on one of her best friends."

"And I think Ray shouldn't get away with it any more than Derek should," Jake growled and placed both hands on her waist. "You can't go back to that school, *bella*. It's not safe."

She chuckled, even though there wasn't anything remotely funny about the situation. "What do you want me to do? It's my job, and I told you I plan to make sure to never be alone with Derek."

"I don't know, Mimi. I don't have a good feeling about this." His forehead touched hers. "But who am I to tell you what to do?"

She raised a hand to his face, mirroring what he did last night at the beach. Her thumb caressed his cheek and his arm tightened around her waist.

"Promise me you'll think about my offer to help you with a letter to the board. It's not too late."

"I just don't know what I should do anymore," she whispered.

Chapter 25

Jake

"I just don't know what I should do anymore."

Mimi's words played in an endless loop in Jake's mind while he drove back to Oak Bluffs. She'd melted into his arms after that statement and cried and cried until her sobs became hiccups and finally subsided.

And all he could do was hold her. Eventually they sat down on the jetty again, and he shielded her from nosy looks.

Before he drove her to the airport they went to a hole-in-the-wall eatery for lobster rolls, and then she was gone.

Watching Mimi disappear into the one-story airport terminal was the hardest thing Jake had ever done. At least he had her promise that they'd see each other before he also left at the end of the week.

But seeing her only once wasn't enough. He wanted more time with her. And he needed to know she was okay. Assholes like Ray and Derek didn't simply give up. They were like predators, lurking to strike again.

He pulled over at the side of the road, took out his cell phone, and opened a text message window. And closed it.

She'd already promised to be in touch as soon as she landed and when she arrived at home. He'd barely refrained from begging her to text him when she went to bed...

Jake wrung his hands.

This wasn't going to cut it. He wasn't about to sit around and wait. Tomorrow he'd drive to Boston.

But why wait? Why not drive there now?

And how, Casanova, are you going to get there? Do you have a ferry reservation?

He smacked the steering wheel. Even if he had a reservation—which of course he didn't, and during high season it was delusional to think he could get one by just showing up—he was supposed to take his grandparents back to Brewster in the morning.

Yes! From there, he would follow Route 6, then Route 3, and then drive I-95 straight to Waltham... To Mimi.

With a tentative plan in place—he'd worry about the details later—Jake put the car in drive again and circled the airport road—hoping to catch a last glimpse of one particular brunette boarding a Cessna.

Almost blindly, he followed random roads until he found himself on what looked at first glance like fallow farmland with a main house and some ramshackle maintenance buildings. There was even a dilapidated red tractor on the side of a barnlike structure.

With a pang he realized where he was—on Uncle Charles's property.

Jake got out of the car and strolled down dirt paths, some barely wide enough for a tractor. He didn't know how long ago the farm was abandoned, but to his surprise he could still make out some resilient, untamed plants like squash, potatoes, and other low- or below-ground vegetables that didn't care if no one harvested them. Eventually deer and other wildlife would feast on them.

He walked through a thicket of trees and underbrush and came to the pond he'd seen on the map in his father's office. On the opposite end, people were kayaking and children's laughter carried across the calm water.

But when he scanned the area, Jake instantly pictured a brand-new dock and colorful Adirondack chairs close to the currently untreated waterline. *A few truckloads of sand would make a huge difference. Probably more than a few...*

Making his way back to the car, he followed another path that wound up a gentle slope. More than a mound, but not quite a hill. He pulled out his phone to take snapshots when his heart skipped a beat.

No more than eight or ten feet away stood a row of vines. Neglected, untamed, and barely able to breathe under the chokehold of climbing weeds, but still producing clusters of small grapes. He automatically patted his pants for his pruning shears, but of course didn't have any with him.

"Mimi, come look what I found," he called, then smacked his forehead just as the low, rhythmic whir of a turboprop plane announced its presence before it flew over the treetops and climbed into the sky. He shaded his eyes and watched with a heavy heart as it disappeared. Was Mimi on it?

Jake turned his attention back to the land around him. Turning this acreage into Charles's dream would be a hell of a lot of work, and he could only imagine what the zoning commission, historical committees, and who-knew-who-else had to say to his father's and grandfather's plans.

His study of the land ended at the red-roofed Victorian main house with its slightly sagging front porch and a broken window on the second floor.

A money pit if he ever saw one.

On second thought, though, it wasn't too difficult to visualize the house brought back to life after it got architectural—and most likely structural—facelifts. A large patio with views of the pond maybe, including some integral protection against sun and wind...

Bees buzzing around returned Jake's attention to the vines in front of him. Their discovery stoked his curiosity, and he squatted down and picked up a handful of soil.

He knew the last wine-producing vineyard on the island closed in 2008. Interestingly though—or better, ironically enough—Massachusetts was now considered a rising star in the world of winemaking. That in combination with deep-rooted New England traditions of farming and handicrafts, held lots of potential for business ideas, and terms like "farm-to-table" and "pick-yourself" tumbled through his mind.

This property could easily accommodate a main building and some cabins, plus provide plenty of space to grow vegetables, as well as fruit orchards, different kinds of berry fields, and flowers to sell or to attract bees.

"It would've been nice if you'd shared your visions with someone, Uncle Charles," Jake said into vastness around him, "instead of secretly cooking up a storm." And mentally apologized. It wasn't his uncle's fault that he died in a boating accident about ten years ago.

But Jake was no more a vegetable farmer than an innkeeper, and he had no intention of becoming either one. And, not for the first time, he wondered what possessed his father and grandfather to consider him for such a dubious honor—the godfather/godson explanation didn't fly with him.

Halfway back to his sister's car, he turned around and gave the slope with the vines another long look.

He rubbed the soil still in his hand between his fingers and palm and thought of rows of healthy vines. What would it take to revive the half-forgotten tiny vineyard that thrived here long ago?

But more importantly—why did he even ask himself that question?

Chapter 26

Mimi

Mimi fought the urge to look back when she entered the air-conditioned building that served as combined arrival, departure, and waiting area, with an ambiance like a bus station.

After checking in she found a rocking chair half-hidden behind a potted yucca plant and pulled out her tablet. And slid it right back into her bag. Reading was out of the question. Like a hummingbird chasing other hummers away from its precious sugar water, her mind was flitting back and forth to Jake.

She reached for her cell phone. Why not get in touch with Paloma to pin down the date for their get-together? Then she could let Jake know and make plans with him.

She scrolled through her contacts and stopped at Jake's.

Should she send him a message? *Thank you for showing me the island and for letting me cover your T-shirt in tears and snot.*

Man, what had possessed her to tell him everything and then completely lose it?

But it was a very soft T-shirt, and he filled it out so very nicely. She very much enjoyed when she stood pressed against him, and had trouble not sliding her hands under the shirt and exploring his abs and chest. She wanted to stay cocooned in his strong arms while he held her with a tenderness that made her yearn for so much more.

Mimi's head dropped against the high-back rocking chair, a fist-sized pit roiled in her stomach, and she stared at the steepled ceiling. Her entire being was revolting at the thought of leaving.

For as long as she could remember she'd played by the rules, even finished college in the top ten percent of her class and secured a good position at a respected school.

Hmph...

And despite her initial objections to this weekend, she played along, not wanting to hurt her sister's feelings. Yet Nicki...or more accurately, Tanya...didn't think twice about changing the course of the weekend in the blink of an eye.

At least you said no to the new trajectory.

It startled Mimi to realize that she'd never done anything spur-of-the-moment. Even going to Italy had been meticulously organized.

And nothing she'd ever done gave her the joy and satisfaction of the past six hours with Jake.

Suddenly, the Miss-Goody-Two-Shoes no longer fit.

When her flight was announced, she sighed and grabbed her bag and purse.

And stepped outside into the warm afternoon and stood under the same shade-providing trellis where she stood only two days ago, pulled out her cell phone and typed, ANY CHANCE YOU CAN COME BACK TO THE AIRPORT?

Mimi willed the three little dots to appear and indicate that Jake was typing a reply. When they remained eerily still and silent, she fought for composure and looked over her shoulder to the terminal entrance. The plane hadn't left yet. She could still change her mind.

Her phone vibrated in her hand. I'LL BE THERE IN A FEW. DON'T MOVE.

Vampire Edward couldn't have arrived any faster than Jake did. The tires didn't screech, and he didn't jump over the driver's side door, but she was in his arms before she made it to the curb. He crushed his lips to hers and dug his hands in her hair.

"Is everything okay?" he asked between kisses.

"Yes, I...I..." She nodded and took a deep breath...or maybe she sucked in his oxygen. "I just couldn't get on that plane."

In reply, Jake took her mouth again before he panted, "I wanted to drive to Boston to meet you at the airport. But there was no way for me to get off this damn island."

"Well," she laughed, feeling free and unencumbered, and pointed to a random spot behind her, "there are a few available seats on a plane that's leaving soon." Rhythmic whirring of propellers filtered through the air, underlining her statement.

"I didn't think that far." His hands roamed over her shoulders and back.

"Jake?" she asked in a low voice.

"Hmm?" He nuzzled her neck.

"I didn't plan this, and I don't have anywhere to stay tonight."

"We'll figure something out."

"Okay." She wiggled against him. "Can we go to the dance tonight?"

"*Bella*, we can do anything you want to do." His lips touched her ear when he whispered, "And maybe we can improvise as the evening progresses."

"I hope so..." she smiled. And knew she'd made the right decision.

After she put her weekend bag in the convertible and climbed in, Jake exited the airport and took the same route Matt did on Friday.

Mimi knew they'd be back at the hotel in approximately twenty minutes, so she asked, "Seriously, now my flight has left, where am I going to stay? I don't assume the cottage is available for another night. But my mini rebellion of being spontaneous doesn't include sleeping on a park bench."

"Yeah, sleeping on park benches is frowned upon and would

cause gossip. And since I'm not planning to leave your side, I don't know what's a worse offense, a Bellini son sleeping in the park, or being caught doing it with an outsider," Jake laughed and squeezed her hand. "Don't worry. We have a guest room at home..."

She interrupted him, "No, Jake, I can't impose on your parents. Especially because it's your mom's birthday weekend and your grandparents are here. Plus, don't forget, nobody knows who I am."

"Not true! You met my grandparents and Matt. And my parents and sister have eyes and ears everywhere, and already know more than you think. The way I see it, you have three choices. You sleep in our guest room, you sleep in my room," he grinned, "or you bunk with my grandparents at the Daisy cottage."

"I should've thought this through before I texted you." She scratched her cheek, "But then it wouldn't have been spontaneous anymore, huh?"

He pulled to the side of the road brought the car to a stop. "Why, exactly, did you text me, *bella?*"

Mimi didn't avert her eyes when she said quietly, "I couldn't stand the thought of leaving. Walking into the airport building was so hard, my feet felt like lead. I can't explain it." She smirked, "Maybe I just want to find out how good a dancer you are?"

She half-expected another chuckle from him, not that she thought what she said was hilarious, but he surprised her when he—very softly—caressed her cheek with his thumb. "I also wasn't ready to say goodbye and while it won't get easier, I want to spend as much time with you as I can. We won't do anything that makes you uncomfortable."

The sincerity in his look made the butterflies in her belly flutter.

"And believe it or not, for the first time in five years I'm not looking forward to going back to Italy."

Chapter 27

Jake

ONCE THEY PULLED UP IN FRONT OF JAKE'S TWO-STORY childhood home and exited the car, he saw Mimi fidgeting with her purse straps and said, "No need to be nervous, *bella*." He took her hand. "But to be totally honest, I'm also on unfamiliar ground."

"Didn't you grow up here?"

"I mean us. I don't know what we are yet, and we don't know where this is going. All I know is I can't think of anything but you."

"I agree. This is happening awfully fast, but I want to be with you."

"You do?" he grinned, knowing what he wanted. He'd imagined her naked body so many times, he couldn't wait to explore it for real. But he promised her they'd do things at a pace she was comfortable with, and he would keep his word. "In what sense?"

Mimi blushed—and he adored her for it. She was a refreshing combination of bashful and forward. "Do you really want me to say it out loud?"

He pulled her against him, fully aware that his parents could see them. *That should take care of explanations!*

"Okay, here goes... I want to be in your arms—"

"You are."

"I want you to kiss me—"

He pecked her lips.

"And I want to make crazy love with you," she said, the blush creeping from her cheeks to her chest while his eyes happily followed.

Whoa! She offered the full buffet, and his body sprang to attention, signaling total and eager compliance.

"Well," he cleared his throat, "to avoid a public spectacle, we'll save that last part for later."

She snuggled closer into his arms and smiled, "Don't ask if you can't live with the answer."

"Oh, *bella*, I can live with it," he croaked while he held her so tight that he worried she'd complain any minute about bruised ribs. "So let me get this straight. If we go in there and my family assumes you're my girlfriend, you okay with that?"

She nodded and looked up at him. "I don't know what we are, or where this is going," she repeated his own words. With her voice steady and solemn, it sounded like a song lyric—or a private vow. "But when I let a guy kiss me and hold me the way you do, I want to think we have something special going."

Jake didn't have a reply ready—which happened alarmingly often when Mimi was involved—so he kissed her. It seemed to be his new *modus operandi*.

Everything was new, but he was willing to put on the skates and step out on the ice for a spin. Desperately hoping he wasn't going to end up on his butt.

Inside the house, Jake wound his way past the gourmet kitchen, through the dining and living rooms, and was relieved when they found his parents and grandparents together in the sunken sunroom. His grandmother called out, "Oh, Jacob, you brought Emily!"

At the mention of Mimi's name, his parents' heads snapped around and two pairs of eyes zeroed in on them. Jake pulled Mimi to his side, "Mom, Dad, this is Emily. Mimi, you've already met my grandparents, and these are my parents, Roberto and Anne Bellini."

Before his parents got up from the sofa, Matt barreled into the room, "Oh, hi, Mimi. See you around later?" He nodded at Jake and disappeared, the slam of the front door the only sign that he'd been there.

Jake was about to say something when Carla strolled in from the backyard wrapped in an oversized pool towel, and leaned against the doorjamb. Her smirk gave away her awareness of Mimi's presence before she joined them. "Did you have an enjoyable drive?"

He wasn't about to take the bait, and instead tossed Carla the key ring, "Thanks again for the loan."

His parents rounded the sofa, and his mom held out her hands, "It's so nice to meet you, Emily. Or do you prefer Mimi?"

"Either one is fine," Mimi shook Jake's mother's hand, then smiled up at him, "Jake calls me Mimi."

"Or *bella*," he winked at her.

"Then, welcome, Mimi," his mom said, and his father added, "Pleasure to meet you, Emily."

"Mom, Mimi kind of missed her flight home today. I'm driving her to Boston tomorrow after I," he looked at Mimi, and couldn't suppress a smirk, "after *we* take Grandpa and Grandma back to Brewster. Do you mind if she stays in the guest room tonight?"

Jake of course hoped that the guest room would remain untouched, but it wasn't something to mention now.

"Of course I don't mind, nobody's using it," his mom said.

"Thank you so much. I hope I'm not a bother," Mimi said. "Oh, and belated happy birthday, Mrs. Bellini."

"It's Anne, please. Jake, why don't you get Mimi settled, and then we'll have a glass of wine together? I was just going to grab some left-over appetizers from yesterday."

Jake suppressed a grin. *Mom code for "We'd like to get a few more details out of you two."*

"Do you have plans for the evening?" his mom continued.

"We want to go to the dance," said Mimi and smiled at Jake's grandma. "Thank you for mentioning it earlier."

"Dinner somewhere nice," said Jake at the same time.

"One doesn't exclude the other," piped up his grandmother. "Have dinner at the hotel and stay for the dance."

"Why thank you, Grandma. It never occurred to me," huffed Jake.

"We'll be there too," his grandma said.

"Wonderful." He really didn't want his grandmother to chaperone his first real date with Mimi.

"Let's all go to the hotel for dinner," said Jake's mom. "Bob, would you mind calling and telling them to add a few chairs to our table?"

A family outing was most definitely not what Jake had envisioned, but he also knew getting a table at any of the fancier restaurants in Oak Bluffs without advance reservations was impossible in the middle of the summer.

To ask Mimi in private what she wanted to do without the pressure of being polite in front of everyone, he said, "I'll show Mimi the guest room, and we'll discuss our dinner plans. We'll let you guys know."

They collected Mimi's luggage from the foyer, and Jake led the way up a winding staircase to the second floor, where he stopped on the landing. "Matt and Carla's rooms are to the left," he pointed down one short hallway. He wiggled his eyebrows, "My room, as well as the guest room, are conveniently on the other side, far away from everybody else."

"And your parents?"

"Their private rooms are in an annex off the first floor. When they renovated this house top to bottom about ten years ago, they declared they wanted more privacy, built the addition, and turned the existing bedrooms into master suites for Matt, Carla, and me."

He walked past a small sitting area with a reading chair and a glass-paned cabinet filled with neatly folded teal towels, then opened the door to a breezy room at the end of the corridor. "Here we are. The guest room."

Mimi set her purse on the bed. "This is very pretty." She stepped up to the window and looked out, then said, "If this room is facing the backyard and pool, yours must be facing the street?"

Jake wished he'd grabbed a bottle of water from downstairs. The air was suddenly too dry in the climate-controlled house. "Why don't you go check it out?"

"You bet I will," her eyes sparkled with mischief.

Entering his room across the hallway, he scanned it anxiously. What did she see? Discarded clothes strewn across the floor? Nope. Thank goodness he wasn't in the habit of dropping everything right where he stood.

Was there anything obscure, or insensitive, or discriminating, or anything else that would give her a wrong impression? There shouldn't be, but it was for Mimi to decide.

Jake couldn't believe how nervous he was. After a disastrous relationship while he was in law school, he'd never brought a woman home to meet the family. Until now.

But Mimi put his fears to rest when she did a brief one-eighty, scanned the view from both windows, then wrapped her arms around his waist. "Your parents seem very nice. And I understand that they're curious about us. I don't mind if we all have dinner together. What do you think?"

"Hmm?" He wasn't thinking at all, at least not with the gray matter between his ears. With Mimi smiling up at him with her hazel eyes, and his bed conveniently right behind them, he was nothing more than a brainless marionette in thrall to his yearning for her.

Jake kissed Mimi, lowered her onto the thick mattress, and hovered over her. But kissing wasn't enough. His hand sneaked under her T-shirt, and he had a hard time—a painfully hard time—not shredding her clothes.

He hissed when her fingers touched his skin and trailed up and down his back. This kind of getting to know a new partner's body was such a special moment. With the women he slept with in the past years, he was attentive, but never let his guard down, and they all knew they were only having a one-time encounter or, at the most, a short-lived fling.

But Mimi was different. In every possible way. With her he needed to take his time, to remember every detail of this moment in years to come as their sacred first time—when they became one.

He wanted to lavish every inch of her body with his attention, but forced himself to go slowly, no matter how much he wanted to get lost in her arms.

He cupped her breast—firm but soft, and it filled his hand perfectly. He imagined suckling her like a baby, exploring her even more intimate spots with his fingers, making her writhe and squirm and beg for release. When her breath hitched and her nipples responded to his touch, he was suddenly dangerously close to an orgasm himself.

Dear Bacchus, God of wine and ecstasy...

He *had* to see her naked, he *had* to kiss her everywhere...and he wanted her hands touching him, stroking him. If he came prematurely, which was an embarrassing possibility given how hot he was for her, at least he'd come in her hand.

Jake shuddered at the thought. He was NOT going to ejaculate in her hand during their first time. They'd reserve that for when... well, for some other time.

"*Bella*," he huffed, "we better stop here."

He stroked her cheek and put one leg between her thighs, letting her feel what was waiting for her, should they continue this later.

"Okay," she laughed. "But I want to go on record that I didn't want this to end."

"My, my, you sound like a lawyer," he teased, and damn, but it made him go even harder and thicker than he already was. This boner would take a while to bring down.

"Oh, I'm not a stuffy lawyer, but if that's your kind of pillow talk, I can google some legal jargon so I'll be prepared," she trailed her fingers over his back. Up and down, up and down, in a slow, teasing, and very intimate move.

"Stuffy? Did you just say stuffy?" he laughed. Then he kissed her nose, her lips, her chin, her neck, and was about to push up her T-shirt so he would finally get to see her, when exaggerated throat-clearing from the hallway reminded Jake that it was only afternoon—and that the door to his room was wide open.

Stupid rookie mistake.

Carla chirped, "Knock, knock, knock. Are you two joining us downstairs for appetizers?" His sister's voice deflated his erection at record speed.

Jake dropped his head and nuzzled Mimi's neck. "Tell her to go away."

She whispered, "If we spend time with your family now, we won't be disturbed later."

He jumped up, "Good thinking! I'm glad you're better than I am at putting things into perspective. Let's go."

Before they left his room, he pulled her to him again. "You do know you don't have to sleep in the guest room tonight, right?"

She put her lips to his ear, "I think I'll let that be a surprise for later..."

Chapter 28

Mimi

WALKING INTO THE SAME RESTAURANT WHERE SHE'D ALREADY enjoyed several meals felt...odd. Jake's family didn't exactly get a red carpet rolled out, but staff greeted them left and right, and guests looked on as if celebrities had entered the room.

Jake's father excused himself before they even sat down. "An inevitable side effect," he said to Mimi after an employee approached and quietly relayed a message to him. She didn't think he needed to explain himself to her, but it was a polite gesture.

The restaurant was almost full, the voices muffled by carpeting and background music, and more people sat outside with drinks. If Mimi had to guess the average age in the room, she'd say around sixty, but there were also couples with kids, and seniors, quite a few of whom waved to Jake's grandparents.

She looked around more attentively than she had in the past two days. The tables were tastefully set with burgundy tablecloths and glass candleholders, while artwork—mostly beach scenes—adorned the walls.

Mom would enjoy this. Maybe she and Nicki could give their parents a gift certificate for a weekend getaway as a thank-you for everything they did for them. Mimi smiled when she remembered her mom's response to her message about staying another day on the island, HAVE FUN, HONEY. SEE YOU TOMORROW.

Nicki's reply had been, WOWZA. I WANT DETAILS. TOMOR-ROW. DINNER. YOU AND ME.

That worked for Mimi, and maybe they'd get to address the Ray issue as well.

Jake's arm rested on the back of her chair, his fingers branding her where they touched her bare skin.

"You're quiet. I'd ask what you're thinking, but that's such a lame question," he said softly, never ceasing his caresses of her shoulder.

"And yet you asked it," she smiled. "I thought about getting a gift certificate for my parents for a weekend here in the fall. They so seldom do something for themselves. And with Nicki's wedding coming up, even less."

She winced, "Aaannnd who knows what'll happen after I talk to Nicki. I see the storm of the century blowing in our faces."

"I'll get you a gift certificate for them."

"No, you won't. If Nicki agrees, we'll buy one. Why would you just give me one?"

He leaned in as much as he could, "Because you're my girlfriend, remember?"

"In that case, remind me to give you a gift certificate for a..." she tapped a finger on her chin and pretended to think really hard, "how about a free dental cleaning at my dad's office?"

Jake laughed out loud and tugged on her hair. "Touché."

Dinner was pleasant and easygoing. Her dish of lobster ravioli was delicious and the conversation was light and thankfully didn't revolve around her and Jake. They already entertained his family with the story of how they first found each other in Venice, and then here.

It didn't escape Mimi's notice, though, how Jake's parents and grandparents exchanged curious looks or almost invisible head shakes at the mention of Italy, especially when Mimi mentioned how much she loved it.

And every now and then she got the sense of underlying tension or unresolved issues being swept under the infamous rug, maybe because of her being here.

She briefly wondered if some math nerd had ever tried to calculate what size that rug had to be if every person on Earth shoved something under it at least once in their lifetime.

Chatting with Carla felt as if she'd known her forever, and when it turned out that Carla had eaten at Paloma's artisan café once and praised her food, Mimi suggested that they should have a girls' weekend in Providence soon.

"Yes!" Carla agreed.

"Isn't it a no-brainer?" Mimi asked. "My best friend is a chef, you're a chef, and I'm lucky if my pasta turns out al dente instead of mushy, so I'll let you two concoct something yummy while I sit back and relax. No, wait. I'll provide the wine." She looked at Jake. "I need to figure out how to order some from your uncle's winery. Maybe you can ship a case to me. I'll pay for it, of course."

"Of course," he grinned, "or maybe I'll hand-deliver it next time I'm stateside."

For a moment she had completely forgotten about the four thousand miles that would soon separate them, and it hit her like a two-by-four smack across her heart that it was uncertain when they'd see each other again. *Not a good foundation for a budding relationship.*

"Do you already know when that'll be?"

"I usually come home between Thanksgiving and New Year's." Mimi didn't miss his glance in his father's direction. "But from now until end of October or early November the winery needs all hands on deck for the harvest, and it's almost impossible to leave."

This elicited another long look between Jake and Bob, and Mimi knew she'd stumbled onto a hornet's nest—and refrained from digging deeper. Maybe he'd share the background with her another time.

Then she reminded herself that Jake didn't owe her any explanations.

Throughout the day they'd talked about many things, but nothing too serious, except for her confession about Derek and the ensuing meltdown. And they kissed—a lot—and they fondled—not enough—and now she'd met his family.

But she really didn't know what kind of relationship they were going to have once Jake left. The odds usually weren't favorable for long-distance romances.

Jake asked, "Wanna go down to the beach for a bit before we grab a glass of wine and listen to the band?"

Beach, wine, music—and Jake! Mimi pushed all self-doubting thoughts away. Why let the uncertainty of the future ruin the now?

At the beach, Mimi took off her sandals, dug her feet into the still-warm sand and relished the soft grains between her toes. She loved the ocean and had a lot of respect for its power and strength. It was unpredictable, sometimes fickle, often gentle. But there was a rhythm to it, and the promise that, even if it was rough and angry for a few days, it would eventually be calm again.

Mimi didn't like uncertainty and murkiness, couldn't live with vagueness and doubt. She needed to know the path she was on, and working toward a goal helped her stay on that path—but lately the goal had been missing, and the path obscured.

Is being with Jake my goal? Should a person even be the goal?

She could hear Paloma calling her out and asking, "Geez, Mim, what's up with this philosophical stuff? Enjoy the moment, for crying out loud."

A flock of seagulls circled above them and cried into the evening. Mimi eyed them cautiously. With her luck, one of them was going to dump one on her next, and the romantic mood would be shot.

She chuckled. Being pooped on by a bird was said to bring good luck...

"What's so funny?" Jake's chin rested on her head while he stood behind her.

"I was thinking of bird poop landing on my head."

"Gross," he kissed her hair. "But don't worry, *bella,* if you stay very close to me, it will hit me first."

"Oh, you're a real knight, aren't you? Taking a shit for me," she couldn't stop herself from teasing him, and with that, her annoying gloom evaporated.

He reached for her hand, "Come with me," and they walked toward the ferry terminal that was still a hive of activity.

Stopping at a cluster of large boulders, Jake leaned against one and pulled her to stand between his legs. "You got very quiet when I said earlier that I won't be back until Thanksgiving. And I think you picked up on some tension with my dad whenever Italy was mentioned. I want to tell you about that."

Wow, his gift to read her emotions was spot on.

She nodded, "It wasn't very obvious, but I'm pretty good at reading between the lines and can sense omissions. A helpful trait as a teacher..."

He rested his hands on her waist and brought her close until their lower bodies touched. Feeling his semi-arousal heightened Mimi's anticipation of what the evening promised for them.

"My father and I respect and love each other, but he wholeheartedly disagrees with my decision to live and work on his brother's vineyard. Dad thinks I should work as a lawyer or at the hotel. We have this discussion every time I visit, and I've never responded the way he wants me to."

"Doesn't he want you to do what makes you happy?" She put her hands on his shoulders and lightly massaged them while her eyes traveled over him.

Men with full beards didn't appeal to her, but his neat three-day stubble was so erotic, and she loved to run her hands over it. Trimmed dark hair peeked out from the unbuttoned top of his shirt, and she was itching to find out if it also covered his chest and abs. He definitely had the perfect amount on his forearms—

"I'm losing you, *bella.*"

145

"What?" she shook off her daydreams.

"I just answered your question, but you didn't respond." His smirk was too sexy.

"What question?"

"About being happy."

Ah! "I'm sorry, I thought about...umm, about..." Her eyes trailed over him again.

"Did you picture me naked?" His cocky grin made her insides go gooey.

"Wha...no...well, maybe..."

"Okay, I'm flattered, but back to what I meant to tell you," Jake wrapped his arms around her waist, bringing her even closer, which didn't help her struggle with the gooeyness.

"When I moved to Tuscany, I knew it wasn't permanent, but I had no idea how long I would need to be there. And until now I had no reason to think about it. My dad's constant nagging is more counterproductive to his cause than he realizes, because it makes me dig my heels in even deeper. I refuse to come back just because he summoned me.

"Meeting you made me start thinking about the future. Immediately, you got under my skin like no one else. There's so much we don't know about each other yet, and we're already running out of time. But I'm serious about you and want to give us a chance, and I wouldn't sleep with you if I weren't."

"We haven't done it yet," she reminded him.

"But I really hope we will," he whispered.

A laugh bubbled out of her.

"What's so funny?" Jake kissed her neck, making her shiver.

"Our conversation. It sounds so...orderly. If this was a romance novel, some readers would scream, 'Get it on, already,' or 'Just do it, don't talk.'"

"But we're not in a romance novel." His mouth moved dangerously close to the swell of her breasts.

"Thank goodness. I prefer having the real you instead of a fictional one."

"You're saying the sweetest things, *bella*," Jake said and looked up from where his lips hovered over her cleavage. "How about a glass of wine and some dancing?"

She nodded. She wanted to dance with him. But to their own tune. And finding their own rhythm.

Chapter 29

Jake

THE BAND'S MIX OF 1990S AND EARLY 2000S SONGS WAS A heady combination of danceable music, and Mimi had more than once jumped up and pulled Jake out on the makeshift dance area.

His grandparents left shortly after he and Mimi returned from the beach, and his grandfather had whispered to Jake, "Don't let her slip away."

Jake had no intention of letting her go. What he told Mimi on the beach was the truth, and he already hated the idea of not being able to see her until Thanksgiving. It would be four excruciatingly long months.

When he noticed Mimi trying to hide yet another yawn, he asked, "One more dance and then we'll call it a night?"

"Yes, I think that's a good idea." She snuggled up against him as soon as his arms went around her waist.

"The next song is by Bruce Springsteen," the band's front man announced. "It's called, 'I'll Work for Your Love.'"

Although he would've preferred a slower song, Jake swirled Mimi through it, knowing she'd end up in his arms after each spin under the starlit sky. It was a perfect end to their evening—in public. He didn't need an audience for the way they would spend the rest of the night.

The house was dark and quiet except for customary nightlights scattered around—a habit from when he, Matt, and Carla were teenagers and got home late—and the hum of the refrigerator and whoosh of water tumbling inside the dishwasher.

Jake grinned when Mimi tiptoed through the foyer. "You can walk normally."

"I don't want to wake your parents," she whispered.

"I told you, their room is off to the side of the house, so they don't hear a thing. And once their heads hit the pillow, they're out cold." He wasn't so sure about that, actually, but what they did behind their bedroom door wasn't his concern.

At the end of the hallway, he reached for the doorknob to his room, when Mimi turned away. "Where are you going?" he asked and pulled her back.

"To the bathroom." She played with a shirt button. "What did you think?"

"I stopped thinking a while ago." *When we danced to the last song, to be exact.*

"Yeah, I noticed how your focus, umm, shifted." She pushed the button through the buttonhole, the tip of her tongue mirroring the action, then her fingers went to the next one. He wanted to rip off his shirt to give her more access, but it was also exquisitely sensual to let her play with him. His skin burned where her fingertips touched him.

"Want me come kiss you good night in a few?" she asked with a coy peek through her eyelashes.

"I hope so..."

"Okay, give me a couple of minutes."

After she went into the guest room, Jake raced to his bathroom, splashed water on his face, and ran a toothbrush over his teeth. Just as he emerged, Mimi appeared in the doorway, wearing a spaghetti-strap nightgown that stopped mid-thigh, showcasing her long, slender legs and slim figure.

He pulled her to him and closed the door firmly. "You changed... and in record time." Her hair cascaded loosely over her shoulders, the way he liked it best, and he let it glide through his fingers.

"One of the many conveniences of summer dresses. You just wiggle out of them."

"I wouldn't have minded lending a helping hand," he mumbled and touched his lips to hers.

"Jake?" she whispered.

"Hmm?" he nuzzled her neck, her intoxicating fragrance of body lotion, shampoo, and a hint of perfume making him a bit lightheaded.

"I'm a little uncomfortable..."

"With me?" Every muscle in his body tensed up. Had he missed or misread something?

Taking her hand, he walked to his bed and pulled her to sit down on the edge of the mattress. The only other option, two chairs in front of the windows, were too far away.

"No, of course not with you. I wouldn't be here if I were. But... your family knows we've only just met, and here I am in your room..." she let the open-ended sentence dangle.

Indescribable relief washed through him, and he reached for her hands, stroking them with his thumbs. "Mimi, you are such a sweetling. Believe me, my mom would've conjured up one last room at the hotel if she wasn't okay with you staying in the house. And my parents are savvy enough to understand that we might have sex tonight."

He cupped her face and looked deep into her eyes. "But if you have any doubts, just say the word and this won't go beyond cuddling."

She shook her head. "I have no doubts." As if to prove it, she put a hand behind his head and pulled him closer, then planted a featherlight kiss on his lips.

As soon as their lips touched, their hands developed minds of their own, tugging and pulling on clothes and caressing bare skin.

Jake slid one spaghetti strap down her shoulder, exposing part of her breast and then cupping it, loving the firm weight of it in his hand while he teased her nipple with his thumb. The little sounds she made were almost more than he could take, and he marveled at how responsive she was.

"I want you so much, *bella*." He slipped the other strap off her shoulder so the nightie puddled around her waist.

Kissing her again, he lay her back on the mattress. Propped up on his forearm, he trailed a fingertip between her breasts to her belly button while pushing the nightgown out of his way.

Wanting to touch and taste her, he started with her breasts. Circled her erect nipple with his tongue, pulled it into his mouth, while his hand slid over her hips, found the smooth inside of her thighs, and teased her through the thin fabric of her panties.

Mimi sucked in her breath, stiffened, and squeezed her legs together.

Sensing she was already close to where he wanted her to be, he found her sweet spot and mimicked the circling of his tongue on her nipple with his thumb.

"Oh...my...yes...p-please...now..." she panted and pushed herself against his hand.

He could make her come with a flick of his thumb but wanted to prolong the moment and build up more anticipation until she cried out his name. When he glanced up, her eyes were closed, and both fists bunching his flat sheet. She was so damn sexy with her hair fanning out over his pillow, the image burned itself into his mind and soul.

His erection strained painfully against his pants, eager for some attention. "What do you need, *bella?*" He hooked a finger into her panties and pulled them down.

"You..." she opened her eyes and smiled. "No...wait..."

She wiggled away and pushed him down on his back, quickly finished unbuttoning his shirt, and straddled him. Then the minx sat down smack over his erection and made herself at home there, torturing him more than she could possibly imagine.

How did she turn the tables within a few seconds, and how did she walk away from her first climax as if it was nothing?

But his mind shut down when she trailed her fingers over his chest and down to his abs, following them with her mouth, dotting kisses everywhere while she slid down on him. When her lips were alarmingly close to the waistband of his pants—where his throbbing head already peeked out, fully engorged as he was—Jake hissed, "Stop."

"Why?" Mimi asked while she unzipped his pants and his manhood sprang free.

"I'm...not...ready...yet..." he panted when she wrapped her hand around him.

"I beg to differ," she smirked and stroked him sensually while she brought him dangerously close to coming.

He couldn't remember later how he shed his clothes in spite of Mimi's possessive hold of him, only that he was being mercilessly stroked in her firm grip, which didn't help his plan to last awhile.

As much as he had planned to take things slowly, getting to know and worship her stunning body before they tangoed, he just couldn't wait. A hair away from climaxing, he gritted his teeth, unclasped her grip—choked out a curse when his sensitive head slid through her fist —and, summoning the last bit of self-control he could manage, rolled her onto her back.

Jake slid his hand over her breast, to her hip, and down between her legs. Her moans turned demanding, and she whimpered, "Jake..."

She fisted his thickness as he gripped the back of her head and kissed her. He was a pawn in her hand when she wiggled under him and guided his moist head to her entrance.

"Con...dom," he managed to croak.

She shook her head and whispered, "Pill."

He entered her slowly, the sensations almost overwhelming him. His first time ever skin-on-skin, nothing separating him and the woman he was making love to. "Mim...wait," he tried to say, but wasn't sure he actually managed to get it out.

She wrapped a leg around his waist, opening wider for him, and he inched in deeper while his erection swelled until it was thicker and harder than ever.

Somewhere in the murkiest twists of his brain he knew he should pull out and sheathe himself, but when he touched Mimi's innermost wall, all he could do was hold his breath and wait for her to adjust to his size. Then he murmured, "Give me everything you've got, *bella.*"

He lifted her hips and drove and withdrew, encouraged by her sighs and gasps, until she tightened around him. "Don't hold back," he rasped, and, after one more deep thrust, felt her coming apart, squeezing him most intimately.

His own orgasm zigzagged through him like a bolt of lightning ramming into a metal rod, and he kept pumping to extend the sensation.

He sucked in sharply when Mimi wiggled under him and reached down to massage his tight balls, panting, "Don't stop. Again."

And he gladly complied.

Finally Jake collapsed and rolled to his side, taking her with him. "What are you doing to me?"

"You said to give you everything I have," she said, her expression sated and perhaps a teeny bit smug.

He finger-combed her hair, "And did you?"

"I let you be the judge next time..." she trailed a finger through his chest hair.

"How long do you give me to recover?"

"How long do you need?"

Jake stopped her hand and brought it to his lips. "I'll let you know."

She snuggled into his arm. "Jake?"

"Hmm?" He traced spirals over her smooth back and firm butt.

"I'm glad I stayed."

"Me too, *bella.*"

At this moment he had no intention of ever letting her go again. But he also knew he had no other choice.

Chapter 30

Mimi

MIMI WOKE UP TO THE SOUND OF A BIRD CHIRPING CHEERFULLY in the tree outside Jake's bedroom window—and exploring hands. She stretched and rolled onto her back, aware she was giving him an eyeful, but her usual shyness about being naked was nowhere to be found.

As soon as she saw the two empty flutes on the nightstand, a gush of wonderful memories swamped her.

After a quick shower last night, Jake had gone to the kitchen and returned with two mimosas, and they leaned against his headboard and snuggled.

He'd said, with a cocky wink, "I have a feeling I'm gonna need the carbs in this orange juice."

Now, several hours later, he was propped up on one elbow cupping her breast while brushing it with his thumb. "Good morning, *bella*," he kissed her, and she wrapped her arms around his neck and shimmied closer. She'd put her panties back on after the shower, but not her nightgown, and her nipples responded to the sensual friction of his chest hair. Which, as she had predicted, was neatly trimmed, and tapered off very nicely into a dark line down his abs.

She was falling fast for Jake, and it scared her. How was she going to say goodbye after their rock-my-world night?

"What's going through that cute head of yours?" he asked, his blue eyes piercing her while his deep, resonant voice set off a tingling buzz in her belly.

"I'm not telling."

"You weren't holding back last night. No need to act shy now, sweetheart." *Ugh...* Did he have to point out how brazen she'd been?

She rolled her eyes and smirked. "Which surprised the heck out of me. I've never been so...responsive before." Mimi's breath hitched when he eased her legs apart and slid a finger inside her panties.

"Will you tell me when I make you come again?" he asked, and began tender ministrations that made her squirm more. "Or do I need to be inside you so I can feel it?"

She nodded.

"Which one? I asked an either-or-question." He withdrew his hand, tugged down her panties, tossed them over his shoulder, and settled between her legs.

"Inside me," she said quietly.

His tip touched but didn't enter her, just waited, poised at her entrance, while Jake watched her reaction. If he waited much longer, she'd come just because he was watching her. She always considered the term *eye-fucking* vulgar, but boy, oh boy, it was exactly what he was doing—on an expert level.

Jake didn't waste time when he entered her, making Mimi gasp and revel in his instinct for giving her exactly what she needed.

"Start talking, sweetheart," he said and began to thrust. "What were you thinking of?"

"I thought...of...your...six-pack," she puffed out while he toyed with her breast.

"That's all?" he asked, without stopping what he was doing or losing eye contact.

She nodded, feeling her climax build up at astonishing speed.

Her body was like a firecracker, ready to explode at the slightest touch.

He increased the intensity of his thrusts. "Are you sure there's nothing else you want to tell me?"

How was he able to speak in full sentences when she barely managed half a thought and a weak croak? "I...don't..."

He pulled halfway out.

"...want...to..."

He thrust in, his eyes turning darker while they challenged her to finish what she was saying.

"...go...back..."

He pulled completely out.

"...to..."

He raised one challenging eyebrow and guided his head along her folds in excruciating slo-mo. How was he so in control? How did he stay so calm?

"...Boston."

"Then come to Italy with me," he whispered and entered her again, mere seconds before his explosive release set off her own orgasm.

———

An hour later, freshly showered, dressed, and her hands around a mug of steaming coffee, Mimi was glad Jake's family wasn't around, so they could speak freely.

She watched him plop two bagels in the toaster before he set plates and silverware on the table in the breakfast nook. "Would you rather sit on the patio?" he asked.

"No," she shook her head. "I think today's going to be a scorcher, and we'll spend enough time outside when we're taking your grandparents to Brewster."

"What do you like on your bagel?"

"I'm not picky. Cream cheese is fine if you have any."

"Anything with it?" he opened the fridge and peeked inside. "There's salmon."

"Ooh, yes, please." It reminded her of yesterday's breakfast. So much had happened in twenty-four hours, it was mind-boggling.

But what kept her mind busy for the past hour was Jake's whispered comment. *Then come to Italy with me.* It was sooo tempting to drop everything and just do it.

The bagels popped out of the toaster and Jake put them in a small basket, their scrumptious smell making Mimi's mouth water. He brought them with a plate of smoked salmon, artfully arranged with thin slices of tomatoes, rings of red onions, and even some capers sprinkled over it, to the table.

"This is wonderful." It baffled her that someone—either Jake's mom or sister—took the time to arrange a platter so lovingly for a regular family breakfast. She knew of plenty of people who just wolfed down a few bites of toast before hurrying to work.

After Jake sat down and sliced his bagel to let it cool, he said, "About today..."

"Yeah, what time do you need to pick up your grandparents?"

"In about an hour, but I was going to say something else." He spread cream cheese on his bagel and topped it with a large dollop of hot red pepper jelly.

"That's an interesting combination," Mimi said while she fixed her own salmon bagel.

"I like sweet and spicy. Maybe it's what attracted me to you," he grinned.

"Ooh, you're such a smooth talker." She bit into her bagel and moaned when the mild salmon flavor combined with the salty capers hit her tongue.

He choked on his coffee. "Shit, Mimi, don't do that. Now I'll never be able to eat a bagel without getting a hard-on because I'll always hear you moan."

"Sorry...I guess," she smirked. "Or not."

He grinned at her, bit into his bagel, and, after chewing, said,

"Anyhow, about today. The plan was to drop my grandparents off in Brewster, then take you home."

"Yup."

"But I'd like to spend more time with you. What are your plans for this week besides meeting your friend?"

"Not much. And nothing's written in stone, so Paloma and I can just as easily meet next week. But Nicki wants to go to dinner tonight and weasel out of me why I stayed here. And Saturday is a house-warming party at her and Ray's new house." She chewed another bite, reminding herself just in time to not moan again, then asked. "And you?"

"I'm mostly at the hotel to give my folks a chance to take a few hours off while I'm around. My flight leaves from Logan on Saturday evening." He spread more jelly over his cream cheese. "So, I was thinking..."

She leaned back in her chair, curious to hear what was coming.

"Why don't we drive to Boston as planned, so you can pick up clothes and other items you need, and come back here tomorrow to hang out for the rest of the week? If you decide you want to meet with Paloma, you can jump on the ferry to Providence—even though I might have to come with you to make sure you're safe in that rowdy college town."

"It's the middle of summer and most students are on vacation." Six more days with Jake sounded much better than parting ways today.

Dinner with Nicki could get interesting, though. If Jake came along, Nicki might bring Ray, and he was the next-to-last person she wanted to see after Derek. On the other hand, she was anxious for Nicki to meet Jake, but wasn't so sure about Jake's reaction to Ray. Ugh, what a mess...

But wait! When they found out they'd be meeting Jake, her parents would most likely insist on taking them all out to dinner—just like Jake's parents had—and then her dinner with Nicki would be postponed until next week.

"What do you think?" Jake asked, his eyes begging her to agree.

"Are you sure me being here won't bother your parents?" she asked.

"Mimi, sweetheart, I tried to tell you last night that my parents are easygoing...most of the time, at least. They'll enjoy getting to know you better." His raunchy grin said more than words. "As do I."

"What do you expect to discover?" she batted her eyelashes at him.

"Oh, I'm sure you have hidden secrets or places to be explored..."

"Aha! Now we're getting closer to the real reason." She finished her bagel and coffee. "But I like your plan. I'll text my mom to let her know we're coming and will stay for a night. But prepare yourself for a Q&A, since they've never heard your name before and suddenly you'll be sitting at the dinner table." *Or sleeping in my bed.*

"That's only fair since you went through the same thing with my parents yesterday."

Chapter 31

Mimi

Mimi watched while Jake disappeared into the hotel, then shrieked when Paloma came to stand between their pool lounge chairs and shook her head like a wet dog.

"Hey, shake your hair out somewhere else," Mimi laughed when the cold water droplets hit her sun-heated skin. It was barely noon and promised to be another sizzler.

"Nope, sorry. You should've been in the pool with me instead of locking lips with your hot boyfriend." Paloma dried off and straightened the spare towel on her lounge.

"Did you just call Jake hot?"

"Yeah, well, I'm sure you've noticed that too," Paloma doused herself with sunscreen, then dropped onto the lounge and donned a pair of oversized sunglasses. Only to slide them down to the tip of her nose a second later and look at Mimi. "Umm... Does he by any chance have an equally hot cousin who's up for grabs?"

"I haven't heard about a cousin, but he has a brother. Even though Matt is rumored to have a girlfriend."

"Shucks." Paloma shoved her sunglasses up again and leaned back. "Ahhhh, this is the life, Mim."

"I know, Pickle, and I can't believe we're actually lounging here as if we belong," Mimi said, using the nickname Paloma wouldn't allow anybody else to use.

"What do you mean?" Paloma wrinkled her nose and added, "We *do* belong like everyone else. We fit right in."

"Yeah, but we're not hotel guests, is what I mean." Mimi tapped her finger on her cheek. "Although, I actually was one until a few days ago. But still, if I wasn't dating Jake, we wouldn't be here today." She smirked. "It feels strange saying it out loud. The part about dating..."

"But you *are* dating him, so you should take advantage of it. And I'm benefitting by being your best friend evaah! Woohoo!" Paloma pumped both arms high in the air, oblivious to the stares—and even a few whistles from a group of young men in the pool.

Mimi knew those reactions didn't bother Paloma, who frequently acknowledged that kind of thing with an extra hip swing or wink. Thanks to genes inherited from a German father and a Jamaican-American mother, she was tall and slender, had a mane of long, curly, but soft dark hair, tan skin, and curves that had caused more than one distracted man to walk into a streetlamp post.

"How did your parents react to your news about a boyfriend?" Paloma asked.

"They were great, as I expected. By the time we got home last Monday, Dad was done for the day, and we had drinks, then went to the country club for dinner, and it was as if Mom, Dad, and Jake had known each other for years. Nicki was cool too. But she still wants more background details."

"Did Dr. Slimeball grace you with his presence?"

Mimi chortled. Paloma's bullshit antenna got calibrated daily in her dealings with customers and their quirks, but Ray held the place of honor on her list of undesirable persons.

"No, Nicki said Ray was held up at the office," Mimi shrugged. "But who knows what he really did? We didn't go to dinner until after seven, but I was glad he was a no-show."

"The jerk probably greased his tool with the assistance of a side-kick," Paloma muttered, confirming Mimi's suspicion.

She already filled Paloma in about everything that happened since Friday, from flying in the Cessna to how the guys wrecked the weekend. And how she ran into Jake and what it led to...

Mimi stopped a waitress and ordered a virgin mojito, and Paloma said, "For me a not-so-virgin one, please."

After the waitress left, Paloma said, "I know I told you already, but I'm really glad I took today off to meet you here. When was the last time we got to hang out at the pool in a resort on a Wednesday afternoon?"

Mimi shrugged, "Never? But you said Gregory gave you a hard time about the short notice. Maybe I should've gone to Providence instead."

"Are you nuts? Gregory should be veeery quiet. He might be my ex-boyfriend and we're running the café together, but I'm not about to put up with any of his bullshit. Plus I haven't taken a day off in months. At least I made sure someone's filling in for me. Which can't be said for when he calls last minute to tell me he's indisposed." Paloma made air quotes and snorted. "And we know what that means... He had a sleepover guest..."

She slid a hand down her arm and grinned, "I'm planning to enjoy every minute of today. After all, it's a special occasion."

"Why?" Mimi asked, and nodded thanks to the waitress who returned with their drinks. She reached for her wallet, but the waitress waved it off with a smile and said, "Thank you, but Jake took care of it, including the tip. He said whatever you order is on him."

"Okay, thank you," Mimi said. "I'll square it with him later."

"Ooh, good-looking and gallant! You've got yourself a keeper," Paloma said and held out her cocktail. "Cheers. I'm happy for you, Mim. You deserve it."

"If only I knew how to make it last," Mimi said after she clinked her glass to Paloma's and tasted her refreshing drink.

She smacked her lips before she said, "When Jake leaves on

162

Saturday, he'll be gone until Thanksgiving. That's more than four months. I don't want him to go. But there's no way around it. And I can't just fly there to visit him for a long weekend. It's not practical."

"We'll think of something," Paloma reached for Mimi's hand and gave it a reassuring squeeze.

Chapter 32

Jake

"I'll see you for lunch," Jake gave Mimi a quick kiss and then stood back to let his eyes roam over her bikini-clad body, the teal blue accentuating her tanned skin. She looked delectable lounging at the hotel's pool, and he couldn't wait to have her in his arms later. And he wasn't ashamed of his urges—after all, a guy could only resist so much.

She must've read his mind, because her eyes sparkled and she mouthed, "Need a bucket of ice?"

He whispered in her ear, "You look so hot, the ice would melt instantly."

"Go! Don't make your father wait," she swatted him away with a rolled-up magazine.

"Jake, let's go," Matt called from across the pool and strode toward the hotel's main building. "You know Dad has a strict be-on-time policy, and he said eleven, not eleven-oh-two."

"Coming," Jake called back and said to Mimi, "Have fun with Paloma. I'm sure you two have lots to talk about. It's great that she came for the day."

He saw Mimi's friend emerge from under the water and hoist

herself out of the pool in one fluid move. If he hadn't already met Paloma, he'd have been tempted to bet a bottle of Chianti Classico *Gran Selezione* that a thirty-year-old Halle Berry just rose from the hotel pool in a perfect reenactment of the classic, and iconic, James Bond scene.

He breathed another quick kiss on Mimi's lips before catching up with Matt, who at that moment did a double take, his eyes riveted on Paloma.

"Hey, Matteo, close your mouth. If you're nice to me at our meeting with Dad, I'll introduce you to Paloma later," he elbowed his brother.

"You know her?" Matt's Adam's apple bobbed and he ran a hand over his head in a typical Bellini brothers gesture.

Jake shrugged one shoulder and said matter-of-factly, "Of course I do, she's Mimi's BFF. But what do you care? I thought you're happily dating what's-her-name?"

"I'm not *dating* Sharon. We're keeping company, nothing more." Matt glanced over his shoulder again and shook his head before they entered the air-conditioned lobby.

"Does she know that?" Jake asked. He only met Sharon once in the ten days he'd been here, but got the impression she believed there was more between her and Matt.

It was Matt's turn to shrug. "Like you, I make it clear to the women I'm hanging out with that it's casual. Which brings up the question..." he lowered his voice as they rounded the front desk, "is Mimi casual, or more?"

"There's nothing casual about Mimi and me," Jake said and scratched his chin. "Not sure how to make this long-distance shit work, though. Damn, I even miss her when she leaves the room for just a minute."

"Ask her to come to Italy."

"I did, but it was at an...umm...inopportune moment, and I haven't brought it up again yet."

"Dude, don't tell me you asked her in bed? You were the one who told me to never bring up important topics when you can't think straight." Matt fist-bumped Jake's shoulder. "It's great seeing you in love."

"Oh, yeah," Carla made kissing noises while she met them at the door to their dad's office. "I like Mimi, and am glad you found a nice, down-to-earth girl, not one of this one's," she flipped her thumb at Matt, "artsy-fartsy starlets."

"Carlotta, when you're done telling your brothers what you like or dislike about their girlfriends, we can start our meeting. I have things to attend to," their father said from behind his desk as he got to his feet. "Why don't we all sit at the conference table."

"What's more important than having all three of your children with you, *paparino*?" Carla kissed their dad's cheek, and a big smile spread over his face. Jake marveled about how Carla managed to defuse the situation so effortlessly. Where he was tempted to tell his dad to stop treating them like subordinates, Carla played snake charmer.

Jake snatched one of the water bottles off the conference table and asked, "So, what's up?" His attitude wasn't much better than his father's, but a summons like this always raised the hair on the back of his neck, plus he wanted to get back to Mimi.

Then he reminded himself to let Mimi and Paloma have some girl time without him hovering. Which meant he'd hang out in Matt's office or rearrange wine bottles in the cellar just for shits and giggles until he took the ladies to the late lunch he promised.

With a sinking feeling, he watched his father bring the now-familiar folder and rolled-up map to the table. His father made fleeting eye contact with him before he patted the folder and looked at Matt and Carla. "This contains ideas your Uncle Charles pursued before he passed away. Your grandparents came across this folder just recently and approached me with an idea."

Jake was impressed with how calmly his siblings listened to what Jake already heard before: Charles's legacy, inn, business opportunity... They nodded, pursed their lips, sipped water, but didn't utter a peep.

"It's your grandparents' wish to get started soon," their dad said, after he finished describing the vision and preliminary idea, "and we've asked Jacob to manage it. Do you have any questions so far?"

Matt and Carla's heads snapped up and they stared at him, more surprised than annoyed—to his relief.

Jake held up a hand. "You neglected to mention that I haven't agreed yet. In fact, we haven't talked about it at all since you and Grandpa sprang this on me Sunday morning."

"Jacob, why are you being so obstinate?" his father asked, adding a third pair of eyes staring at him. "I told you your mom and I want to step down and let you kids take over the business."

"You're stepping back?" Carla yelped and jumped up. "Since when?"

"You're doing what?" Matt wheezed.

Jake let out the breath he hadn't been aware he was holding. Ah, so he wasn't the only one being steamrolled. Not that it made a difference. He wasn't going to let his father strongarm him into doing anything he didn't want to do.

"We're not planning to drop everything in your laps immediately and leave, but over the next few months we intend to discuss and plan the transfer of power," Bob said. "Because you, Matteo and Carlotta, are already established in the management of our hotel, your mother and I assume you'll continue here. It makes sense for Jacob to be the driving force behind the new project."

"Matt and I can't just add your responsibilities to the ones we already have," Carla said, scowling. "It's not as if we're downsizing. Quite the opposite, in fact. May I remind you that we added catering services only recently? At your insistence."

"Your mother and I aren't stepping down cold turkey, but we're cutting back a little. We've spent forty years making this hotel what it is today. As you and Matteo take over more of our daily tasks, we'll hire staff to assist you in your current positions." Jake couldn't shake off the feeling that his parents had given this more thought than his dad let on—which was so typical.

"I don't know..." Carla fumed as she sat back down with her arms folded.

"It seems you've given this a lot of thought, and apparently all behind closed doors," said Matt, giving Jake's beliefs a voice. "Has it ever occurred to you that we might not want to do this for the rest of our lives? Maybe Carla and I would like to pursue other interests, like Jake does." Matt looked at Jake, "No offense."

"None taken."

"What are you saying?" asked their father, his face pale. "Are you...are you thinking of leaving?"

"No, but what if Carla and I have ideas for the future of the hotel that require a change in our responsibilities? When do you think we're old enough to be included in your brainstorming, instead of sat down and merely informed of decisions made without our input?"

Jake watched the color return to his father's face and secretly gave Matt's shoulder a squeeze. Their old man needed to be reminded that he wasn't *Don* Bellini but *Dad* Bellini. *Paparino*—as Carla lovingly called him—not *padre*.

"I was out there on Sunday afternoon—" Jake started, only to be interrupted by his dad's excited, "You were?"

"Actually, I ended up there without meaning to and looked around. I think a lot of what you mentioned would work, even though a landscape engineer and architect would have to be consulted. But there's sufficient space for the cabins, and it looks easy enough to incorporate the lake for recreation or just for a nicer view," Jake said, to smooth the waves. "If I was a guest there, I'd rather look at the water than an overgrowth of trees and shrubbery."

"I knew you'd come around, Jacob." Delight—and satisfaction—gleamed on his father's face.

"I haven't said yes," Jake said as he got up to pace the room. *And I still don't know why I should do it.*

While he paced, he rubbed a hand over his jaw, and took a few deep breaths. Through his father's office window, he caught a glimpse of the pool area. Too bad Mimi's side wasn't visible from here. Her smile had a calming effect on him—even after only three days of knowing her.

"Then what are you talking about?" boomed his father, his temper flaring. "You drove there but aren't interested in it?" He threw his hands in the air.

"I told you I ended up there by accident."

If Jake didn't tread carefully now, he might as well jump headfirst into a muddy, bottomless sinkhole, never to see the sunlight again.

He took a deep breath, "First of all, you can't expect me to make a decision of that significance without knowing every angle. And second, what makes you think I'll turn my back on Uncle Fausto?"

Ask the question that's been bugging you awhile.

"And while we're at it, would you ask the same of me if I still worked at the law firm in Hyannis?"

"That's not the same..." started his father.

"It wouldn't be any different. If I hadn't quit five years ago, I'd likely be a partner by now." He mentally thanked the combined deities in the universe for saving him from that fate, because he'd only have made it there by sucking up to his former law-bending, rotten weasel of a boss.

"No, because being a successful lawyer is different from breaking your back by digging in the dirt and stomping barefoot in grape barrels." His father swiveled around in his chair, solely focused on Jake.

Here we go again...

Behind their father's back, Carla flashed him two crossed fingers while she and Matt left the room. And Jake didn't blame them. They didn't need to be spectators during this long-overdue conversation. It was strictly between him and his dad. As soon as they closed the door, the second question he'd been dying to ask for years burst out of him.

"How can you talk about your own parents' vineyard—their

169

livelihood and legacy—so contemptuously?" He balled his hands into fists instead of grabbing the folder next to his father and tossing it against the wall—or into the cold fireplace. His anger was hot enough to light a fire. "Are you forgetting that their labor paved the path for you to start all this?" He flung his hands in the air.

"Do you think I don't know that? I grew up watching my parents live and breathe those acres of land, always at the mercy of the weather or the soil conditions. Yes, they catapulted it into a very successful business, but at what cost? They were hardly able to take time for themselves because there was always something to do. And when it quieted down in the winter, they were too exhausted. Or too busy with marketing and advertising. They were like hamsters in a wheel."

"Would you say they were happy?" Jake asked quietly. He remembered his grandparents fondly.

"Yes, I think they were. Until they almost lost everything at an age when they should've enjoyed their golden years." His father's tone was firm, but low. Not his usual booming voice, his English more accented when he was agitated.

"One more reason you should be thankful to Fausto for turning it around after two consecutive years of weather catastrophes and no income."

"But at what cost!? My brother had a heart attack when he was fifty-eight." Jake's father got up and walked to where Jake stood. "That damn vineyard almost ruined my family twice, and now it's coming between you and me."

He ran a hand over his eyes. "As the firstborn, I was supposed to inherit the winery, even though I never wanted it. But Fausto *wanted* it. I didn't want to get the business degree my father insisted on either, but I did. And I wasn't happy."

He took a photo of Jake's mom from his desk and ran a finger across her face. "Then I met your mother, and she gave me the courage to leave everything behind, even though I knew it wasn't easy for your *nonna* and *nonno* to watch me go. I left for love."

"Which is why I offered to help Uncle Fausto. He had no one except Mia, who was only twenty-five and barely out of university. It wasn't love for a woman, but love and admiration for the land and the grapes that made me stay in Italy. *Nonno's* winery is also part of my legacy."

Jake avoided his father's stare by looking around the room and noticing several small mementoes that had most likely been there forever, but which he never noticed till now: a picture of this dad and Fausto with their wives and parents standing behind a huge barrel of grapes, with a young Jake, Matt, Carla, and Mia stomping inside it. Four sample glasses with the Bellini winery logo on the bookshelf behind his dad's desk. Several delicate linen and lace doilies like the ones his *nonna* had been so fond of.

And then there was the extensive collection of Bellini wines in the wine cellar. Understanding hit Jake with a force that almost brought him to his knees.

You can take the man out of Tuscany, but you can't take Tuscany out of the man...

His father's epicenter might be here—by his own choice—but a sliver of his heart would always be in San Gimignano.

Jake fought back tears when his dad pulled him into a bear hug and said in a trembling voice, "Look deep into your heart, Jacob. Think about what you really want. That's all I'm asking you today."

Another glance out the window rewarded Jake with the sight of Mimi sitting at the edge of the pool, her legs dangling in the water. She looked so relaxed, his heart clenched tight. When she looked up and waved, he hoped it was for his benefit, but then Carla walked up and crouched down next to Mimi.

He couldn't hear what they said, but seeing them laugh together soothed him. Mimi radiated happiness.

Look deep into your heart, Jacob. Think about what you really want.

"When do you need my answer about the inn?" Jake turned and looked at his father.

"By Thanksgiving. I'd like to get started with drawing plans this fall, but we need to know who's on board before we get serious. Whoever will be running this inn needs to be here from the beginning."

Jake nodded, his eyes straying to Mimi again. Could he leave Tuscany—as his father had—for a woman?

Chapter 33

Mimi

Paloma announced, "I'm going back in the water. Come on, Mim, join me."

"I'll sit by the pool, okay?"

"Are you afraid to get your bikini wet?" Paloma called over her shoulder as she walked to the poolside outdoor shower, then dove into the deep end and emerged seconds later at the shallow end.

Mimi sat down on the edge of the pool and dangled her legs in the water. It was comfortably warm, and she was thinking about swimming a few laps when she saw Carla coming toward her.

"Hey, how's it going?" Carla asked.

"Great. How did the meeting go?"

"Oh, the usual. Dad held his monologue and we listened. Until he and Jake got into an argument, and Matt and I made ourselves scarce."

"Oh no! What was it about?"

"Dad presented us with some new ideas, and he must've hit a nerve with Jake."

"Is it bad?"

"Don't worry," Carla patted Mimi's arm and laughed, "it's not their first rodeo."

Paloma emerged from doing a few underwater laps and Mimi said, "Carla, you told me you already met Paloma, right?"

"Yes, I was at your café last year and we chatted for a bit." She leaned forward and held out a hand to Paloma, "Hi, you probably don't remember me. I'm Carla."

Paloma shook the offered hand and said, "I remember you. How could I not? We talked about one of my favorite things—fried pickles. Nice to see you again. Are you working here or are you vacationing?"

"Good memory, yes, your fantastic fried pickles! Did you happen to bring any?" Carla laughed. "And I actually slave away my days here. This is my parents' hotel."

"Nice place you've got," said Paloma and lifted herself out of the water. She jogged the short distance to her lounge, grabbed the towel and returned to sit down next to Carla. "I'm kind of bummed that I won't have a chance to stay for dinner, since I've heard such great things about the food. But I've got to catch the last ferry at five or I'll be stranded like this one," Paloma pointed her thumb at Mimi.

"Why don't you come back another time?" Carla asked. She looked to Mimi, "Yeah, that's it. You suggested a few days ago we should have a girls' weekend in Providence so I could meet Paloma. Well, now we've met again, we'll just have it here instead."

Mimi looked at Paloma. "Works for me."

Paloma nodded. "I'll make it work."

"It's a deal, then," said Carla. "Let me know when, and I'll reserve a room for you."

Paloma grinned. "Hey, Mim, I take back what I said earlier about this being a one-time thing. I see myself turning into a regular guest at Bellini's."

Mimi laughed while Carla and Paloma sealed it with a hand-shake. "Deal!"

"What's a deal?" Jake approached them. "I missed you, *bella*." He kissed her soundly.

"Ooh, kiss-kiss-kiss," sang Carla.

"Get a room, kids," Paloma fanned herself, then high-fived Carla.

Their instant camaraderie didn't surprise Mimi; Paloma and Carla had similar personalities. Both were hardworking, but also not afraid to let loose and have fun.

"Why didn't I get the memo about another family meeting?" Matt asked from behind them.

"This isn't a family meeting," Jake held out a hand to Mimi and she stood, only to find herself wrapped in his arms. "I really, really missed you," he whispered.

"I missed you too," she whispered back.

"Ahem, how about introductions?" Matt demanded, but kept his voice down while he elbowed Jake.

Carla bit back a smirk. She turned to Paloma and said, "Paloma, this is my other brother, Matt." She looked at Matt, "Matteo, we live in the twenty-first century, so you could've introduced yourself, no need for a middleman, umm...middle woman, but whatever... Matt, this is Paloma."

Matt held out his hand. "Pleasure to meet you, Paloma."

Mimi chewed on the inside of her cheek when she saw Paloma wipe her hand on her towel before clasping Matt's hand and gushing, "The pleasure's mine."

"Now formalities are taken care of, I need to excuse myself. Duty's calling," Carla said. "Paloma, I hope we'll get a chance to chat soon."

"I'd really like that," said Paloma. "I can't take much time off in the next few weeks, but let me know if you happen to be in Providence. And maybe we can have the get-together you suggested sometime in the fall."

"Absolutely!" Carla said. "I'll get your contact info from Mimi and we'll pick a weekend."

"Sounds good. I'll make it work," Paloma promised, her eyes straying to Matt.

"What are we planning?" Matt asked, while Mimi noticed how he couldn't seem to tear his eyes away from Paloma either.

"*We're* not planning anything. Paloma, Mimi and I are talking about a girls' weekend, no boys allowed," said Carla and slapped her hand on Matt's chest. "Now I really have to go. Bye, Paloma."

"Uh, okay." Matt scratched his head and said, "I also have to run, unfortunately. It was nice meeting you, Paloma."

He waved to no one in particular and strode away, but paused and looked back once before he entered the main building.

Mimi had watched the exchange with interest since she'd never seen her BFF so flustered.

Without letting go of Mimi, Jake said, "How about lunch in an hour or so?"

Mimi nodded.

"Sure," Paloma said, her eyes ping-ponging to the door where Matt disappeared.

"Okay, then," Jake said as he let go of Mimi, but not without kissing her again. "I'll meet you in the lobby."

Mimi and Paloma returned to their lounges, but Mimi's butt hadn't touched down yet when Paloma pulled her own chaise close to Mimi's and said, "Tell me a little bit about Matt."

"I don't know much, other than that he's a year younger than Jake. Usually I only see him in passing. Why?"

"Why? Are you blind? That man is H-O-T," she blew on her fingertips.

"I thought you said Jake is hot?" Mimi grinned.

"Yeah," Paloma waved it off, "but did you see how Matt fills out his polo shirt? I'm so jealous of the Bellini logo."

"Huh?"

"Emily Albizia—think! If I were that logo, I'd be splayed across his heart with my hands all over his body. I bet you my biggest pickle bucket that he's hiding exquisite washboard abs under his shirt."

Mimi was amazed at how captivated Paloma was. Her friend had been single since she separated from Gregory two years ago, with only an occasional short-lived fling thrown in, and claimed that focusing on work was more satisfying than wasting her time with unreliable men.

"Sorry, but I've never seen Matt without a shirt, so I wouldn't know anything about his abs."

"Ah, yeah. Only eyes for your own man. Good girl," Paloma chuckled and flipped her hair over her shoulders. She sighed, "I wouldn't mind hand feeding him some of my cream puffs, though, and then helping him work off the calories..."

Chapter 34

Mimi

WITH HER HANDS CLUTCHED AROUND HER PARENTS' FRONT porch railing, Mimi watched Jake's rental car round the corner and disappear.

Just like that, he was gone.

A cold, clammy emptiness filled her heart and spread through her chest. She shivered despite the midsummer heat and went back to her room, closed the door, and rolled herself into a tight ball on her bed. She buried her nose in the pillow that smelled faintly of Jake's shampoo and wished it were yesterday, so they could have one more day and one more night together.

But it was today, and they left Oak Bluffs on the ten o'clock ferry, drove to Boston, and had lunch with her parents. Now Jake was rushing to Logan Airport, and in four hours, he'd be looking out a small, smudgy, and scratched triple-layered acrylic window while waiting for his flight's departure.

Would the aircraft circle over Boston one last time, or go directly out over the Atlantic Ocean?

But what would it matter if it took Jake away from her for good?

The past week had been extraordinary, and she had a wonderful time sifting through the memories along with the dozens of photos she took on their daily excursions. In a handful of days she'd begun to admire Martha's Vineyard for its artsy vibe, the laid-back attitude of residents—easy enough if one had the money to afford living there—and the mesmerizing views from the cliffs and beaches.

A soft knock interrupted her musings and Nicki poked her head around the door. "May I come in?"

"Of course." Mimi sat up and pushed her hair out of her face. As she yanked a tissue from the box on her nightstand, she noticed the book about Oak Bluffs that she bought on the first day of the bachelorette weekend.

She couldn't wait to start reading it. Jake told her a little bit about the island's history, from the Methodists who started the Campground in the 1800s to the hippie communes in the 1960s to the rise of tourism in the 70s and 80s—not only for high-profile politicians and artists who sought secluded vacation spots for privacy and inspiration.

"I'm about to head over to the house, but wanted to check in on you first," Nicki said and sat down on the bed next to Mimi. She rubbed Mimi's arm. "Anything I can do?"

Tell me the housewarming party is cancelled.

Mimi shook her head and dabbed her eyes. "How is it possible to feel so strongly attached to someone after one week?"

Nicki pressed her lips together and gave her an understanding smile. "I guess those things just happen. But it's obvious Jake shares your feelings. I've only seen him twice, but the fire in his eyes when he looks at you speaks volumes."

One more reason we shouldn't be apart!

"You're not helping," Mimi cried. "What if he meets someone else? He told me he often goes out with his cousin's friends. There's so much I don't know about his life there."

"Don't allow those thoughts to settle. Shake 'em off." Nicki rubbed her thumbs over Mimi's hands. "What's your plan for staying in touch?"

"We'll FaceTime every day, even if it's only to say good night. But with the time difference of six hours, it won't be easy."

"That's a good start. It'll help if you can see him instead of just texting."

Mimi shrugged. "But so much can happen in four months. He met other women before."

"Did he give you any indication that he's not serious about you?" Nicki's eyes bored into Mimi's.

"No, but... We didn't really talk about how we'll make this work in the long run. I assume we'll figure something out when he's back in the States at the end of the year and we've had a chance to get to know each other better."

"Better than after spending a week glued together like Siamese twins?" Nicki grinned.

"Well, yeah, but this was a vacation for both of us. In December I'll be back at work and have a different routine. I can't just drop everything and be with him the entire time."

"Right," Nicki nodded slowly, "You know what? My advice is to believe in him and you. Do you trust him?"

"Yes, but..." Mimi said again.

Then it dawned on her that this was the perfect lead-in for the chat she planned to have with Nicki. "Nic, since we're talking... there's something else..."

Nicki's phone interrupted them, and she said, "'Scuse me, I better take it. It's Ray." She accepted the call, "Hey, honey, I was about to head over. What? No, I don't expect you to do all the work." Nicki rolled her eyes. "Everything for the barbeque just needs to be pulled out of the fridge later. Huh? Yes. I just *said* I'm on my way. See ya." Ending the call, she muttered, "Sometimes I don't know why I bother..."

"Nic?"

"I gotta run, sorry. I've been summoned," she plastered a smile on her face that was so fake and pathetic, Mimi didn't have the heart to insist on her chat with Nicki right now. But after that last comment, she was more determined than ever to keep her sister from walking into the disaster her marriage promised to be.

———

MIMI PARALLEL-PARKED—WITH MODEST SUCCESS—HER VW Jetta on the curved curb, then turned off the engine.

Nicki and Ray's house was located at the end of a quiet cul-de-sac and, according to Ray, much too close to their new neighbors.

"I don't want to have to smell everything they put on their grill," was one of his gripes. Why he put in an offer if the house offended him before he even moved in still baffled Mimi. Nicki had told her the three-bedroom Colonial had a price tag of almost 1.5 million—and was still a far cry from the museum-like mansion Ray grew up in. Mimi had to bite her tongue to keep from adding that she hoped Ray would adjust quickly to having only two bathrooms at his disposal.

She snickered when she recalled one of Paloma's rants, "Never forget, Mim, he has to drop his pants when he takes a dump, just like everybody else. Doesn't make a difference whether he sits on Italian marble imported from Carrara or Home Depot's store brand."

Still sitting in her car, Mimi shook her head. *What a pompous jerk.*

The house's red front door stood ajar, but through a glass storm door she could look through the front-to-back living room and see King Ray holding court, surrounded by his devoted groomsmen.

She knew that in colonial New England front doors were commonly painted red to protect against evil, and that it had also been a signal identifying a home as a "safe house" for escaped slaves during the Underground Railroad movement.

Sadly, a red door wouldn't be able to protect Nicki from getting hurt when she found out about her fiancé's philandering.

Mimi's eyes fell on the car's digital clock, and she wished Jake had been able to come with her. Without him, she felt as if she was drifting. He'd been able to stabilize her, to ground her, and with him she was once more the carefree person she was before the Derek incident.

She leaned her head back and sighed.

Her sullen attitude was starting to annoy her. She would allow herself one more minute of being miserable, and then she'd better get a grip. Feeling sorry for herself wouldn't change a thing and wouldn't bring Jake back.

Pretend he's on a business trip and you'll see him again in a few days.

Yeah, and King Ray is suddenly Saint Ray...

Mimi rubbed her forehead. She didn't feel like pretending to be merry and having fun. Why did Nicki and Ray need to have a house-warming party? Nicki wouldn't even formally move in until after the wedding because Ray's mother didn't approve of living in sin... If only the woman knew what a rotten apple she'd raised.

The slamming of car doors interrupted her reverie, and in the rearview mirror, she could see the ducklings spill out of a car.

Mimi muttered "showtime" and just grabbed the gift bag with a top-notch bottle of champagne off the passenger seat when her cell phone played the ring tone she'd downloaded for Jake, the last song they danced to.

Her heart hammered when she read, ALL CHECKED IN AND HANGING OUT AT THE LOUNGE. WISH YOU WERE HERE. HAVE FUN AT NICKI'S PARTY.

Mimi smiled and imagined him sitting in the business class lounge, sipping a glass of wine maybe, and snacking on hors d'oeuvres. Her fingers flew over the keys, GOING IN NOW. HAVE A SAFE FLIGHT. XO

Signing off with "hugs and kisses" was safe—but what she really wanted was to tell him "I love you" when they met again.

Chapter 35

Jake

"Boarding completed."

The copilot's voice crackled through the cabin before Jake watched the flight attendant close and secure the heavy plug door and then give the ground personnel a thumbs-up through the tiny window.

What would happen if a passenger decided to get off the plane right this minute?

He imagined that very unlikely scenario would probably cause quite a ruckus, and was tempted to find out, but instead drained the last of his mediocre "welcome" champagne and looked out the window. All those airport employees out there, from the signaler to the luggage lugger—*what are those guys even called?*—went home at the end of their shift. While he was heading...where? Home? Away?

How ironic that two weeks ago he was dragging his feet and didn't want to leave Italy. Now he had the nagging feeling that he made a huge mistake by turning his back on America. He just found Mimi—what possessed him to leave her again?

Well, responsibility and family obligations.

Jake pulled his cell phone out of his laptop bag and typed a short message to Mimi. He wasn't sure she'd read it right away. It was only nine o'clock and she was hopefully still enjoying Nicki's party, but he didn't want to depart without sending another note.

IN MY SEAT, WE'RE BEING PUSHED AWAY FROM THE GATE AND I HAVE TO TURN OFF MY PHONE FOR TAKEOFF. I'LL CALL YOU TOMORROW. ARRIVEDERCI, BELLA.

His finger hovered over the Send key. Why didn't he type, "I love you," as he wanted to do? And why hadn't he said those three words to her last night, when they lost track of time in each other's arms?

He raked his fingers through his hair and sucked in a deep breath. Was he about to screw up the best thing that happened to him in a long time? Again, he inhaled and exhaled, then was getting ready to shut off his phone, when her reply popped up.

STILL AT THE PARTY, BUT SITTING ON THE PORCH, TRACKING YOUR FLIGHT. WISH I WAS WITH YOU. XO.

He'd miss her hugs and kisses, but he'd miss her laughter, the sparkle in her eyes, her expressions when she listened to him, and her comforting presence even more.

He'd miss feeling her hands on his skin, her hair tickling his face when she was on top of him, and the way she responded to his touches.

He already missed Mimi. There was no way he'd content himself with FaceTime for the next four months.

Oh, bella, I should've bought a ticket for you and convinced you to come with me.

"Cabin crew, please take your seats for takeoff." The copilot's voice sliced right through Jake's thoughts. Once they were in the air, there was nothing he could do to stop the plane from leaving.

Hell, there wasn't anything he could do at this point, period. Unless he wanted to create an enormous uproar.

Jake watched the flight attendants obey the order while chatting about how they spent their layover in Boston. He looked out the scratched window again to watch twilight give way to night.

"Folks, we have two more planes in front of us, then it's our turn.

There aren't any storms predicted, and the flight should be calm. Our route tonight takes us over Nova Scotia and Newfoundland, then we coast out over the Atlantic Ocean and reach Europe south of England, and from there we'll fly over France. Our estimated flight time to Zurich is seven hours and forty-five minutes."

Jake didn't give a damn about the route. He sat in the dim cabin, and when Chatty Cathy from the flight deck brought their plane to pole position and announced, "flight crew, cleared for takeoff," Jake listened to the engines being fired up, then to the wheels bumping as they sped over the runway. He didn't worry about the rattling and shaking of the overhead bins, the pitiful cries of small children in the coach section behind him, or the rumble of the landing gear being retracted immediately after takeoff.

Instead, he clutched his turned-off phone in his hand and worried about leaving a good thing behind as they climbed higher and higher.

"Scared of flying?" a female voice breathed at his shoulder, the faint smell of cucumber, lemon and juniper telling Jake's sensitive nose that she'd already had more than one gin and tonic.

His head jerked to the side. A woman around his mom's age leaned close—much too close for his comfort—and reached over.

"What? No. I'm..." He pulled his arm out from under her manicured, bejeweled fingers, and, using his elbow, pushed her hand back to her side of the double-wide armrest between their seats.

"If you need some distraction..." her hand returned, her fingers tapping the inside of the console, dangerously close to his leg.

"Let's get one thing clear," he said through his teeth. "I'm not afraid of flying, and I don't need a distraction, and I'd like you to keep your hands to yourself."

"Oh?" she breathed—and winked.

What the... This plane had approximately twenty business class seats, of which—Jake craned his neck—about two-thirds were occupied, and he ended up with this hussy? He shoved his cell phone into his laptop bag and pushed the call button for the flight attendant. He wasn't going to waste any energy fighting off his action-offering Mile-High-Club seat neighbor.

Luckily the flight attendants were already folding up their seats and Joaquin, the Purser, materialized promptly. "What can I help you with, Mr. Bellini?"

"I'd like to switch seats," Jake said.

"Is something wrong with yours?" Joaquin asked with concern.

"Yes, there's an unpleasant draft," Jake said and rolled his shoulders.

"I apologize, sir. 12A is available, which is a single window seat, as you usually prefer."

It had slipped Jake's mind that business- and first-class staff were acquainted with a traveler's seat preferences, and, on eastbound flights he enjoyed watching the sunrise as they approached Europe. "Perfect, I'll go to 12A, thank you."

"Absolutely, sir. If you don't mind waiting until the captain turned off the seatbelt sign, it's no problem at all. Can I bring you something to drink in the meantime?"

"Yes, a seltzer with a slice of lemon, please."

Joaquin nodded, then asked quietly, "Mrs. Robinson, anything for you?"

With her right hand, which was no longer anywhere near Jake's leg, she shooed Joaquin off and pulled her sleep mask over her eyes before raising her leg rest. Great, now he had to climb over her.

Wait until I tell Mimi that Mrs. Robinson hit on me. She'll get a chuckle out of that. Or maybe she wouldn't laugh it off. After her experience with Derek, she was rightfully hyperaware and sensitive about those things. Unwanted advances weren't funny for the person on the receiving end.

Heat built up deep in his belly and his blood boiled, only to freeze instantly when an unpleasant thought crossed his mind. Derek was going to be at Nicki and Ray's party too. What if the guy made another move on Mimi?

Jake could've kicked himself. He should've changed his ticket to depart a day or two later, so he could've been with Mimi at the party. Uncle Fausto would've understood. Between Derek and Ray, there was no way of knowing what might happen at that house tonight.

He trusted Mimi completely, but he didn't trust those two fellas, not after what she told him. And that knowledge would torment him for the next eight hours, because he was trapped in this airplane, unable to protect Mimi.

He'd text her as soon as the inflight Wi-Fi allowed, and suggest she leave the party.

But who was he to tell her what to do?

An image of Mimi in Venice flashed across his mind, how she sat on her stool with that oh-so-cool Casanova in front of her.

There he'd acted on impulse and stepped in without being asked. Now he knew Mimi, and he realized that she wouldn't have needed his help—and that she was very capable of looking after herself. She'd have sent the kid packing without Jake's interference, and he knew she was determined not to let Derek near her again.

Her vulnerable appearance was deceiving and easily misunderstood.

Mimi was like a grapevine. A series of strong storms might give her a rough time, and she might bend under them, but she'd come back stronger and healthier after taking a few dormant months to regain her strength.

And *that* was what made her so irresistible to him.

Chapter 36

Mimi

MIMI ROCKED SLOWLY IN ONE OF THE TWO CHAIRS ON NICKI and Ray's front porch. Loud voices and louder music shattered the otherwise peaceful neighborhood. It was amazing how much noise ten or twelve people could make, especially when booze was involved.

She peeked through one of the two windows, noticing the stacked-up boxes, all still giftwrapped and adorned with elaborate bows. Nicki had told her she didn't plan to open them until after the wedding.

Hard to believe it's only a week away.

"A little birdie told me you got yourself a boyfriend," a voice slurred, and Derek fell into the other rocking chair, shaking off his flip-flops. Mimi looked around, hoping Tanya was with him, but she had the questionable pleasure of his company all to herself. "I also heard he left today."

"None of your business," Mimi said, hoping he'd notice the acid in her voice.

He stretched his leg until his foot touched her bare calf. "If you've changed your mind about having some fun... Nobody needs to know."

"Are you flippin' kidding me?" Mimi jerked her leg away and jumped up.

Derek let out an ugly, creepy snigger. "Shit, seriously?"—it came out as *sheerishly*—"You're so uptight, you can't even say *fucking*."

With unexpected speed, he moved to stand so close to Mimi that his sour breath made her gag. Then, before she could react, he grabbed her butt and breast and squeezed hard.

"Leave me alone," she hissed, trying to swat away his hand while searching for a way out, but he had trapped her in the corner of the porch and gyrated against her. "Feel this? Wanna touch him?"

He towered over her, and she knew she was physically no match for his athletic strength and skills. Being drunk—or high on something else—made him dangerous and unpredictable, but hopefully also slowed down his reaction time.

Disgust fueled her fury, and Mimi brought her knee up as fast, hard, and as high as she could. Derek howled and bent forward, clutching his family jewels, when a flash went off.

Mimi ducked around him and saw Sally, her cell phone pointed at Derek. "Thank you, that was close," Mimi said, and began to rub her arms.

"Dicky, where are you? I got you another drink," Tanya stepped out onto the porch. "Oh, no, what happened, honeybun?" She rushed to Derek, who was crouched and whimpering in the corner where Mimi stood moments ago.

"I'll forward you the photo right away," Sally said. "If you go to the police, I'll be happy to tell them what I saw."

"What did you see?" barked Tanya while she wrapped her arms around Derek.

"How he tried to force himself on Mimi," said Sally.

"Why would he do that?" Tanya asked.

"Hey guys, did you move the party outside?" Nicki stepped out of the house and scanned the scene. "Oh, no. What happened here?"

Mimi took Nicki's arm and led her back inside the living room. They sat down on the side of the room and Mimi said, "Derek groped me and…"

"What? Are you okay?" Nicki paled and ran her eyes over Mimi.

"I'm fine, just a little shaken. My self-defense class came in handy." She gave Nicki a short summary and ended with, "Nicki, I'm going to press charges against Derek this time. Sally took a photo. And I'm sorry, but if Ray allows Derek to be in the wedding, I'll drop out."

"Mim, no! There's no way Ray condones Derek's behavior." Nicki looked frantically around, then called, "Ray, babe, can you come over here, please?"

"What's up, sugar?" Ray sauntered over, a glass of whiskey on the rocks in his hand.

Nicki didn't bother with long-winded explanations, "Derek tried to force himself on Mimi. You have to exclude him from our wedding."

"Maybe he misread something Mimi said or did and took it as an invitation," Ray shrugged and slugged back more whiskey, obviously not noticing that he just implied that it was okay if Derek cheated on Tanya.

"What kind of bullshit answer is that? You don't even know the full story and are already finding an excuse for him?" Nicki stood and slammed her fists on her hips. "Thank goodness Sally interrupted him."

The other two ducklings and Ray's groomsmen gathered around them and followed the exchange. Someone lowered the volume of the music, the house becoming suddenly eerily quiet, except for the blood rushing in Mimi's ears.

Ray squinted first at Nicki, then at Mimi, until his unsteady gaze landed on Sally. "Is that payback for the Vineyard?"

Sally flipped Ray off, then pushed two buttons on her phone and put it on the table behind her. "No, but now that you remind me…"

"Shut up, you teasing bitch," he snarled.

Nicki sucked in a breath and froze. Then she asked softly, "What's this about the Vineyard?"

"Nothing, a misunderstanding," Ray tried.

Sally huffed, "Liar. You knew exactly what you were doing when you followed me to the cottage, put your grubby hands on me, and told me how hot you were for me, you slimeball."

"Ray?" Nicki's brittle voice made Mimi ache for her.

"Sugar, don't believe any of it. Yeah, of course I was hot that afternoon, but only for you. Remember the outdoor shower?" Mimi gasped when he winked at Nicki. "I don't think you can complain. And, by the way, it's your duty to believe me, your future husband, especially when it's her word against mine."

Duty? What era did Ray think he lived in?

"It's not, actually. I was there," Mimi said, quiet but firm. "And based on what I overheard, it wasn't the first time you hit on her."

"You're just frustrated because...uh, it doesn't matter," Ray mumbled.

"It matters to me," Nicki said, and swallowed hard.

Christopher, Ray's best man, who had missed the Vineyard trip, cleared his throat and pulled him aside, "Buddy, I strongly advise you to not say another word." Mimi remembered that he was a defense attorney. "This isn't the time or place, and you better tread carefully. Assault is a Class A1 misdemeanor and can land you in jail for up to 150 days."

"I didn't assault anybody," Ray's temper flared up like a torch.

"Let's not discuss this right now." Christopher eyed Sally's cell phone on the table.

"Now listen, if a man can't show a woman his appreciation..." Ray puffed out his chest, but Nicki stepped up close to him and slapped his face hard.

"What was that for?" Ray shouted and touched his tumbler to his reddening cheek.

Nicki calmly slid her engagement ring off her finger and dropped it in his whiskey, where it clanked against the ice cubes. "Raymond, the wedding is off. I'm sure your mother will be happy to notify your side of the guest list. Tell her not to worry about my side."

"Sugar, don't be foolish." He plucked the ring out of his glass and licked it off. "Here, be a good girl and put that back on." Mimi cringed. "If you're getting cold feet, we can postpone the wedding and go on a nice trip to work out your, umm, issues?"

Your issues? The only ones with issues are you and Derek, you jerk. Mimi couldn't believe Ray's nerve when he tried to blame his behavior on Nicki.

To Mimi's relief, Nicki stepped away and shook her head. "I'm not getting cold feet, and I'm not stupid, either. All this time, I didn't want to believe the rumors about your affairs but didn't want to snoop. I trusted you, Ray! But tonight finally opened my eyes. Your behavior is appalling."

She snagged her purse, walked to the front door, and called over her shoulder, "I'll be in touch about returning the wedding gifts."

"Well done, Emily," Ray spit out. "You can't get your own pathetic life sorted out, so you have to ruin your sister's life too, huh?"

"Shut up, Ray." Mimi picked up her own purse. She nodded at the ducklings and said to Sally, "We'll be in touch. Don't forget to send me the photo."

"Just did."

"Thanks."

On the porch, Mimi saw Derek and Tanya huddled together in the two rocking chairs but didn't acknowledge them. She wasn't going to let him get away as easily as last year, because this time she had a photo and a witness, and she was going to the police tomorrow.

For a moment she was glad that Jake was thousands of miles away.

But had he been here, Derek wouldn't have had a chance to catch her alone.

Maybe Jake being away was a blessing in disguise...

Chapter 37

Jake

"Damn it," Jake cursed in Italian and tossed the innocent canes he accidentally cut off on the ground. He was tempted to stomp on them like a furious child.

Green pruning and cluster thinning, which he'd been doing for three days, was a delicate task which involved clipping off healthy clusters of grapes to balance fruit production so they could achieve a high-quality yield at harvest. But he butchered several plants today, and even though he knew they'd survive and wouldn't threaten the crop, it hurt as much as if slicing off his finger.

The problem was that it was a task done by experienced workers —and he prided himself of being one—but it also left him with plenty of time to let his mind wander. And his latest wanderings took him to Mimi—or more accurately to Derek, and what he wanted to do to the creep. What she told him over the phone could turn the most peaceful man into a revenge-seeking monster.

Jake secured and pushed the pruning shears in their holster, then took a few long swigs from his water bottle. In the distance, someone was singing loud and proud and very off-key, while from a few rows over, Mia's lively banter with Dante drifted through the air.

Dante was Uncle Fausto's age and one of the winery's six full-time employees who helped manage the vineyard, the wine cellars, and do a multitude of other tasks. Because Mia had always been in the fields and worked next to them, even when she was still in school, they respected her, and Jake knew they'd accept her as their boss when Uncle Fausto handed her the reins.

It would be the same for Carla and Matt once their parents stepped down from the helm of Bellini's Cliff House. Their permanent staff regarded his siblings with respect, knowing they pulled their full weight instead of pulling rank.

When Jake was there, he got along well with the staff, and they listened to him, but he wasn't *one of them*. If he added up the time he spent every year on Martha's Vineyard, it'd be difficult to reach a total of ten weeks.

Jake tilted his head back and gazed at the azure sky. The clouds drifted along soundlessly, pushed by the mild breeze. They were headed west, and he wondered if they'd ever reach the East Coast of America or if they'd be pulled apart or diverted on their way there.

His mind had been on the East Coast since he returned to Italy. His heart was there—in a suburb of Boston, to be exact—where Mimi was safely ensconced in her family's arms and home.

How would he be received if he decided to return home—to his family, to his old life, to Martha's Vineyard?

The question had played in an endless loop in his mind since he called Mimi as soon as he made it back to San Gimignano.

Jake recalled her sleep-tousled bed hair when he woke her up at six thirty on Sunday morning. He'd even buried his nose in the shirt he wore on his long travel day, hoping to detect a trace of her, but all he got was a noseful of the ripe stink of clothes worn too long and infused with distinctive airplane stench.

As soon as she filled him in on the events from the party, he wanted to jump on the next flight back.

Now, daydreaming in the middle of the vineyard, his eyes fell on the grapes he just cut off prematurely. He set his water bottle down, picked up a cluster, and squished a grape between his fingers. All while visualizing the grape as Derek's balls. Not that he wanted to touch the douchebag's privates, but it was the first thing that came to mind. How dare that asshole put his hands on Mimi?

He hadn't known about the self-defense class she took last year, and was so proud of her for kneeing Derek. Jake exhaled loudly. It didn't surprise him that she'd been able to protect herself, but it galled him that she—or any woman for that matter—had to endure such treatment. The situation wouldn't have arisen if he'd been there.

Today was Thursday, and he knew she'd already gone to the police and reported Derek for sexual assault. On his advice, she also notified her employer about the incident and her subsequent actions. He suggested she also hand in her resignation, but she countered that she needed more time to think about that part, because she had no other job lined up.

For the first time in years he wished he was still practicing law and in a position to slap Derek with a fat lawsuit. Jerks like him didn't get it until they'd been through an investigation, a trial, a hefty fee, and the prospect of a few months on a state-paid vacation with other scum.

Jake squeezed another grape and grimaced when the mouth-puckering sour juice hit his lips.

"What did those poor grapes ever do to you?"

Jake looked over his shoulder and saw Mia leaning against a thick, round post, taking in the cluster of grapes on the ground and the ones in Jake's juice-stained hand.

"Nothing. They're a stand-in. A placeholder." He dropped the ones he was holding.

"Wanna talk about it?"

"No." He grabbed his bottle and drained the rest of the water. Should he go back to the farmhouse and grab a refill or finish the workday without anything to drink? He easily had another three hours ahead.

"Is it because of the woman you met?"

His head jerked around. "Who told you?"

Mia shrugged. "No one. But you've been so distracted since you came back, it was a fair guess."

"Yeah, well, I met someone. The end." He wasn't going to lay his heart open to his cousin, who was as nosy as Carla.

"Who is she?"

Of course Mia didn't give up.

"Someone I met a few months ago, and we crossed paths again."

Mia ducked and climbed through the trellises. "There's more." She grabbed Jake's arm and dragged him uphill. He knew where she was going—to the ancient, broad-branched chestnut tree.

And he let her drag him there. When he and his siblings visited as children, they spent hours in the tree house perched on one of the lower branches, a relic from his dad's and Uncle Fausto's childhood. The tree house was long gone, but the tree was still there, and the memory lingered.

As soon as they arrived at the old tree, Mia plopped on the ground and rested her back against its enormous trunk. She pulled the tie out of her hair and finger-combed it. "Ready when you are. Spill it."

Jake closed his eyes and counted silently to ten. Then to twenty. Mimi's face appeared in front of him, smirking.

He felt the corners of his lips curl up and he chuckled. Mia won.

"Her name's Mimi. And I think she's The One."

Mia showered him in a slew of exclamations, all in rapid Italian and involving many "*Mamma Mia's*" and "*Maria's*," which could mean anything from "finally" to "oh my goodness" to "are you kidding me" to...well, anything.

After she ran out of steam, Mia put a finger to her cheek and pierced him with the same soul-searching glare as Aunt Francesca when she was onto something. "Then what are you doing here? Where is she?"

Jake looked directly into Mia's eyes and hunted for the right words. He came up empty and said lamely, "I'm here because it's where I live and work. And Mimi lives and works in Boston."

Another avalanche of spicier outcries later about love being more important and Jake being stupid—he began to regret not going to the house for a water refill, because this could go on awhile—she said, "Invite her to visit us. I want to meet her."

Jake chortled. "What if she doesn't want to meet you?"

But the wheels in his mind started turning, and pretty fast. It was only July, and Mimi didn't go back to work until the beginning of September. The *vendemmia*, the Tuscan grape harvest, was anywhere from mid-September to late October.

Mia was right. He was an idiot, and why hadn't he thought of it himself?

He jumped up and hugged Mia. "Thank you." He kissed her cheeks, then jogged down the hill, ignoring the curious looks from Uncle Fausto and the other workers. His cell phone was in his jeans pocket, but he wanted to run to the house, refill his water, and text Mimi without Mia peering over his shoulder.

Chapter 38

Mimi

MIMI SAT AT A WROUGHT IRON BISTRO TABLE AT THE PICKLE, Paloma's artisan bakery and café in the heart of Providence, and sipped iced tea in the shelter of a large red umbrella.

She didn't waste more than a glance at the greenish-brackish Providence River, and instead listened to the lively chatter at a nearby table, where several Brown University students debated the pros and cons of spending a semester in Bologna, Italy. Mimi wanted to lean over and urge them to do it. What she'd have given for a chance to study at the oldest university in Europe, whose famous alumni included Copernicus, Dante, and Erasmus.

And which happens to be not too far from Tuscany.

"Don't let Paloma see that you haven't touched your sandwich yet," Gregory passed her table with a tray laden with more yummy-looking sandwiches and salads.

Mimi chuckled and bit into her chicken and avocado panini. It was delicious as everything from Paloma's kitchen, and Mimi wasn't surprised that the café was brimming with activity. The menu consisted of simple comfort food and a few eclectic choices, and everything was freshly made with seasonal produce.

She remembered how Paloma and Gregory started dating in culinary school and opened the café after graduation. Luckily, they managed to continue a harmonious business relationship, even after they broke up as a couple. It helped that Paloma considered Gregory a better business partner than boyfriend—at least most of the time. His laissez-faire attitude didn't always work in his favor.

Mimi picked up the pickle on the side of her plate and savored the garlicky dill flavor. She never asked Paloma for her recipe—knowing it was very bad taste to ask a chef to share their secrets—and she wasn't the only one who loved them, because people bought the pickles by the jar.

Her mouth was watering from the perfect balance of sweet and tangy and the crunchy, firm texture of the pickle, when her phone announced an incoming message.

Her heart did its typical jig. But this was an unusual time for Jake to text her, since they always FaceTimed after he showered and had dinner. She hoped everything was okay, and opened the app with somewhat shaky fingers.

BELLA, I HAD A FABULOUS IDEA TODAY (WELL, MIA HAD IT, BUT I WON'T ADMIT ITS SPLENDIDNESS TO HER). I MISS YOU SO MUCH THAT I'M CONSTANTLY MESSING UP MY WORK. I'M AFRAID UNCLE FAUSTO WILL PULL ME OFF PRUNING AND MAKE ME SCRUB MOLDY OAK BARRELS WITH A TOOTHBRUSH AND ACIDIC WASH.

Mimi snickered as an image of Jake crawling into a dark wooden barrel with his sweaty T-shirt clinging to his torso popped up in her mind's eye—and sent heat waves through her belly.

She continued reading, SO I THOUGHT, WHY DON'T YOU COME JOIN ME FOR A FEW WEEKS? YOU CAN STAY WITH ME—he inserted winking emojis—AND I'LL SHOW YOU AROUND FLORENCE AND TUSCANY. THE VINEYARD IS BUSY, BUT I'LL MAKE TIME. PLEASE SAY YES, I'LL BE HAPPY TO COVER THE COST FOR YOUR PLANE TICKET.

He attached a selfie that showed him with steepled hands, as if praying—making her chuckle again, because he'd mentioned once that he wasn't overly religious, and neither was she. But the raw pleading in his eyes was what made her bite her lower lip while she longed to kiss away his agony.

His idea was tempting, but she couldn't commit on the spot. This needed some thinking and planning, and luckily Paloma was the perfect person to brainstorm with.

She quickly replied, *I LIKE YOUR IDEA A LOT, BUT LET ME GET BACK TO YOU. WE'LL TALK TONIGHT, OKAY? I MISS YOU.*

Mimi closed the app after he sent three red hearts, and slid her cell phone back into her purse just as Paloma approached her table. She frowned at the almost-untouched panini, snagged one of Mimi's fries, dipped it in buttermilk dressing, and popped it in her mouth. "Hmm, someone around here makes delicious zucchini fries."

"They are really yummy," Mimi agreed and ate one too. Paloma used the perfect amount of Italian seasoning.

"So, what's new with you?" Paloma asked before taking a sip of her iced tea. "And how's Nicki holding up?"

"Nicki's mood depends on whether she's had to deal with Ray or not. She's gone to the house twice and sorted through the gifts, took those that came from friends on our side, and is about to return them."

"Is she going to the house by herself?"

"No, Mom had already taken this week off from the office because of the wedding, and she's going with her. She's much better at dealing with Ray's mom—who actually showed up once—than I could be." Mimi ate some of her sandwich before it got soggy. "It's not easy for Nicki to deal with this shit, but she's standing by her decision to give Ray the boot..."

"He's such an...ugh, you know my opinion of him," said Paloma and rolled her eyes.

"Yes, and I've always shared it. But outside of this mess, Nicki seems to be her usual self. I know she's also hanging out with Sally, who I'm beginning to see in a different light. She's not as superficial as I thought she was."

Paloma snagged another fry and pointed it at Mimi. "And you? How are you doing after your newest run-in with The Louse?"

"Who?"

"The Louse. The Parasite. Derek."

"Ah!" Mimi nodded. "I'm glad I went to the police this time, and now it's out of my hands. My school's headmaster called me and made a few rather curt remarks. The administration's implying—again—that I encouraged him by going to a party where he was."

"What kind of lukewarm piss comment is that? It was your sister's housewarming party, for Pete's sake, why wouldn't you go?" Paloma hissed.

"You know it, and I know it, but they just don't want to slap their golden boy's wrist." Mimi finished her sandwich and snatched a napkin off her tray.

Paloma dipped another zucchini fry in the dressing and ate it. "I can't believe you're still planning to return to work in September."

Mimi shrugged. "Not you, too. Jake says I should resign."

"Smart man. I knew there was a reason I liked him."

"But it's not practical. What am I going to do if I quit my job?" Mimi swirled her iced tea and watched the ice cubes spin in circles.

"You'll find another one. Schools are hiring like crazy." Paloma leaned back and stretched her long legs under the table. "And you don't have to stay in Boston."

"What do you mean?"

"Mim, do I need to point out to you that your teaching license is valid in the entire Commonwealth of Massachusetts? You can work anywhere from Pittsfield to Provincetown."

Mimi's gaze drifted away, and she imagined the state line of Massachusetts, ending in Provincetown on Cape Cod—and from there her mental cursor jumped to Martha's Vineyard...

"Yeah, maybe I'll look into that option." The idea was tempting... But why would she want to work there if Jake wasn't with her?

Paloma's deep sigh made Mimi focus again on the now.

"Jake texted me just a few minutes ago and asked if I'd like to visit him in Tuscany." She scrunched up her face with an and-I-really-want-to-do-it expression.

"You should do it!" Paloma clapped her hands, making several guests look over.

"Pickle, I can't just up and leave."

"Why not?"

"Because of the wedding..." Mimi started to say.

"Which has been cancelled."

"Exactly, and it would be shitty to leave Nicki alone right now."

"You said she's hanging out a lot with Sally."

"Still..."

Gregory called from the open café door, "Paloma, I could use an extra set of hands in here..."

Paloma, sitting with her back to him, rolled her eyes. "I bet he can't find the mustard," she said. "Coming," she called over her shoulder, and squeezed Mimi's hand. "Thanks for swinging by. Keep me posted about Italy."

Mimi got up and hugged Paloma. "I'll call you."

During the forty-five-minute drive back to Boston, she ran the possibility of an impromptu trip through her head. The next four or five weeks were wide open on her calendar, and going back to Italy—and to Jake—would be a dream come true.

At home, Mimi got comfortable on the couch in the family room and laid out her planner and laptop on the coffee table.

———

AN HOUR LATER SHE LEANED BACK AND FOLDED HER HANDS behind her head, staring out into the lush green backyard. Considering the short notice, the tickets weren't exactly cheap, but it was doable.

She startled when the front door opened and shut with a *bam*, then Nicki breezed into the room. "Hey, what are you doing?" She plopped down next to Mimi and craned her neck to peek at the laptop. "You're going to Italy?"

"Jake asked me to come visit him at his uncle's winery." She couldn't hold back her huge grin.

"And are you?"

"It's tempting, but I don't see how," Mimi said truthfully.

"Why not? What's stopping you?"

"I can't just drop everything and fly halfway around the world."

"Why not?"

Mimi shrugged. "It feels wrong with everything you're going through."

"Psh..." Nicki waved if off. "I mean, yeah, it hurts, and I'm nowhere near forgiving Ray, but..."

The corners of Nicki's mouth curved as high as possible while she reached into her purse and pulled out a rectangular envelope. "Know what this is?"

"No."

Nicki tapped the enveloped against her palm. "Our tickets to Europe."

"*Our* tickets to Europe?"

"I'm coming with you!" Nicki smirked.

Mimi drew a blank, and her face must've shown it.

"Remember my honeymoon? Five days in Paris and five days in Rome?" Nicki asked.

"Yeah, you've been so excited about that trip," Mimi said, wanting to smack Ray all over again for ruining more than one of Nicki's dreams.

"Indeed! And since...umm..." Nicki scratched her head, "unforeseen circumstances prevent Ray from going on the trip, I'll call the airline and return his ticket. Then we'll buy your ticket using his credit card."

"Whoa, is that even legal?" Mimi asked.

Nicki made deer-in-the-headlight eyes, "Of course, most business-class tickets are returnable for a refund until the day before departure."

"You know what I mean."

A wicked look spread over Nicki's face, "You heard him when he suggested going on a trip to work through my issues…" She air-quoted the last two words. "Too bad he won't be part of my entourage."

Mimi couldn't help but laugh out loud, then sobered and said, "He'll never agree to it."

"He doesn't have to, because he won't know until after I've done it, and I dare him to make even one peep." Nicki held up her index finger and narrowed her eyes. "I just came back from meeting him. He said he can't trust me not to take out things that don't belong to me and demanded my house keys."

"No, he did not!?"

"Yup, he did. And I told him there's nothing in the house that I want, including him."

Nicki reached over and gave Mimi's hand a squeeze. "So I say let's fly to Paris together and I stay there—because the hotel also happens to be paid for—and you get yourself a one-way ticket to Florence. After Paris, I'll fly to Rome as planned, and enjoy time in another already-paid-for hotel, all courtesy of Ray's parents."

"He'll be so mad, Nic, you really shouldn't do that," Mimi cautioned. She didn't want to add to Nicki's troubles.

"Just watch me… And don't feel bad for him—"

"I don't, it's you I worry about."

"No need. By the way, I told him to keep the engagement ring, which is worth more than the two tickets and hotels combined, so he better be very quiet," Nicki said. "And I don't think his mom wants dirty details about the breakup to start circulating, so I've got them by their slimy balls." She pinched her fingertips together and twisted her wrist.

"I never knew you had such a wonderfully mean streak in you," Mimi grinned.

"You never two-timed me, so I had no reason to show it to you."

Mimi cast another glance at Nicki's face, "You sure you don't mind being in Paris and Rome by yourself?"

"Mim, I've been looking forward to this trip for so long, and you'd be proud of me to see how I have it planned out meticulously, including group tours." She chuckled, "I might cancel the romantic dinner reservations we have, though...or maybe not."

Mimi saw excitement in Nicki's eyes—and a lot of mischief. For someone who was just dealt such a huge blow, she was admirably composed.

"Okay then, I think we've got a plan. I can't wait to tell Jake."

Nicki reached for her cell phone. "Let me call the airline right away."

"Wait until I double-check with Jake that it's okay if I show up as early as this Monday or Tuesday."

"Do you expect him to say no, silly?" Nicki asked. "How long do you want to stay there?"

"Well, for the duration of the time you're in Paris and Rome."

"Wanna add another week? That gives you almost three weeks with Jake, and I don't mind touring Tuscany after I'm done in Rome."

"Are you serious?"

Nicki nodded and pointed to her face. "Does this face look as if I'm kidding?"

Mimi chuckled. "No."

"Okay, I'm going to my room. Let me know after you two have talked."

Nicki strolled out of the room, singing, "Here comes the mad bride," and Mimi pinched herself hard enough to yelp, "Ouch."

This wasn't a dream. It was really happening.

In five more days, she'd be in Jake's arms again—if all went well.

Chapter 39

Jake

Jake paced back and forth in the arrivals area of the Florence Peretola Airport, craning his neck in the direction of arriving passengers every four to five paces.

Mimi landed in Paris yesterday and stayed there with Nicki for one day. No matter how much he wished she'd taken the next available connecting flight, he had to agree when she told him, "I've never been to Paris, and this is a perfect chance to see some sights. Plus it'll ease my mind to know Nicki's fine by herself."

And when he saw the smiling selfies she forwarded from atop the Eiffel Tower and from beneath the glass pyramid at the Louvre, he was double glad she stuck with her plan. It also proved that she had a healthy backbone and didn't let anyone run her over—a character trait he regarded highly.

He glanced at his watch. *Where is she?* According to the arrivals board, her flight landed ten minutes ago.

Dude, give the plane time to taxi to the gate.

Had it been up to him, she'd have been on the first flight out of Paris this morning, but again she explained—rightly so—that she wanted to have a leisurely breakfast with Nicki before heading to the airport, and also wanted to give him time to put in half a workday.

Did she have any idea how much he longed to hold her in his arms?

He'd wolfed down a quick lunch—providing Mia with the golden opportunity to tease him about his impatience—and left the winery as giddy as a child on Christmas Eve.

Wrong! As giddy as a man in love.

He wiped his sweaty hands on his khaki shorts when he finally spotted her—looking fresh and rested and smiling broadly—and he crossed the distance in a few strides.

His heart clenched and his belly tightened when she flew into his arms and their lips touched. He inhaled her scent—citrusy from her shampoo, with a hint of almond from her hand lotion—tasted her sweet lips—stale airplane coffee and something chocolaty—and felt lightheaded when his blood rushed—very inappropriately—to his groin area. "I missed you so much, *bella*."

"I can't believe I'm really here." She touched his face, and he leaned into the palm of her hand. Instead of words, he took her mouth again, gentle and slow, as if it was fragile. When he broke off, he whispered, "Do you believe it now?"

She nodded. "Yes, but I might need a reminder or two later."

"I'll be happy to refresh your memory."

HOURS LATER, MIMI WIGGLED AS CLOSE INTO HIS ARMS AS THE uneven rock wall they perched on allowed—after years of sitting here in the evenings, he'd learned which hollowed-out spots were more comfortable than others—and sighed.

"I love everything here...the view, the vineyard, the sunset. It's as spectacular as you described it," she said.

"I love *you*."

207

The words slipped out quiet and light but carried the full weight of a heartfelt confession.

She stiffened almost imperceptibly, then turned her head and gazed at him. In the receding light, he saw a watery veil glinting in her eyes, and he rubbed the pad of his thumb under them.

"I love you too," she whispered.

It was the first time he said those three words to a woman, and he knew in his heart that he'd never say them to any woman but Mimi. To hear them from her was sweeter than the sweetest grape he'd ever tasted, and a tsunami of emotions raged through him.

"*Ti amo più di quanto le parole possano dire*," he said, naturally slipping into the language of love.

"If you don't have words for how much you love me," she translated with a smile and twisted in his arms until she settled in his lap, "why don't you show me?"

Jake shot glances in all directions. In all his years of watching the sunset from here, almost no one had interrupted his solitude. But...

"Here?" he pushed her hair back and nuzzled her neck. "I have a very comfy bed and a cold bottle of prosecco waiting for us in my room."

She shook her head. "It has to be here. Then it'll always be our special place."

Through the thickening fog of horniness, it didn't escape his attention how she said *always*, implying they'd still be together when they looked back to this moment many years from now. And just the thought made him harder than the ancient rock wall under his butt. If he didn't want to risk walking into the farmhouse using his best John Wayne stride—and he could imagine Mia's snide commentary, should she happen to witness it—he needed to pull the emergency brake now and get Mimi off his lap.

He inhaled the sickly-sweet scent of the rotting grapes on the ground, heard far-away church bells tolling, got lost in Mimi's beautiful eyes—and decided to surrender control and let her be in charge.

A jolt zipped through him when she slid a hand under his T-shirt to touch his abs. How did his entire body turn into one single erogenous zone when she was near?

Jake's hand copied hers and snaked under her tank top, her sharp intake of breath tightening his balls so dangerously, he worried they might already be turning blue.

With Mimi sitting firmly in his lap, all he could do was run his hands over her back and butt and stroke her hair while his shaft burned a hole through his khakis.

Mimi kissed him and raked her wicked fingernails through his chest hair. Her kiss escalated from nipping to hungrily devouring him, and his tongue tangled with hers and did what his erection wanted to do: explore and dig deep.

He wanted her naked, needed to see her while the last rays of fading sunlight kissed her soft skin—and was perilously close to tears because it wasn't possible.

Without breaking their kiss, Mimi raised up on her knees, somehow wiggled out of her underwear and tossed them aside. Lightning fast she unzipped his pants and reached inside his boxer briefs. His throbbing shaft jumped free like a Jack-in-the-box, and before he could react, she lowered herself onto him until he was buried to the hilt under the cover of her flowing skirt.

Jake closed his eyes and swallowed the stinging tears behind his lids. Even if he'd been able to move with her straddling him, he didn't dare. Just like at their first time, feeling her adjust to him brought him dangerously close to climaxing, so he distracted himself by imagining the mouth-puckering taste of immature grapes on his tongue.

When she finally began to rock against him and begged, "Make me come now, don't wait," he sent a thousand praises to the gods of love.

Pushing up her tank top, he freed one of her breasts, drew it deep into his mouth and suckled until she tensed around his shaft. Her hiccupping gasps were music to his ears, and the powerful contractions of her innermost walls set off his own potent orgasm just as the sun dipped below the horizon.

Once both of them were spent and trying to catch their breaths, she slid off his lap, slipped back into her panties, and snuggled back under his arm. "This is the most memorable sunset I ever experienced."

"You had your back to it."

"I watched it in your eyes," she smiled lazily. "Can we come back tomorrow?"

"It's a possibility," he croaked, and pulled Mimi closer.

Chapter 40

Mimi

Mimi scrubbed her hands in the deep kitchen sink, taking her time to lather on the olive-scented hand soap and let her eyes glide over the feast on the counter.

"Francesca, if this is how you always feed your staff on Friday evenings, I might be tempted to apply for a job with you. I've become a proficient vegetable peeler in the past three days, don't you think?"

"*Va bene*, you are hired, Emilia." Francesca's eyes sparkled when she looked up from mixing homemade pesto into penne.

When she arrived on Tuesday, it had startled Mimi when Jake's aunt used the Italian version of her name, but now, Mimi found it rather endearing and took it as a stamp of approval, an initiation into the family. After she mentioned it to Jake, he laughed and said, "*Bella*, it's just the way things are around here."

"Ah, so you're saying it's the Italian way?" Mimi had teased.

"No," Jake kissed the tip of her nose, "it's Francesca's way."

And Mimi had no problem with it. It wasn't much different from how Jake always called her *bella*, almost as if it was her first name. She loved that he had his own name for her, and she liked it much

211

better than pet names like honey, sugar, or babe. Many of them sounded derogatory and were lacking imagination.

"When are you and Jacopo leaving for Florence?" Francesca interrupted Mimi's straying thoughts and set a hand-painted glass bottle filled with golden-yellow olive oil on the table—*mental note: buy two of those for Mom and Paloma, together with some of Francesca's olive-scented soap!*

"After breakfast tomorrow. I'm really looking forward to our weekend away," Mimi said. Then she slapped a hand over her mouth and added quickly, "Oh no, that came out wrong... I love being here and everything is wonderful, but it will also be exciting to explore Florence. Jake put an itinerary together."

Francesca patted Mimi's forearm, "I understand, and you should have time for yourselves. And he always enjoys going to Florence with friends." Mimi soaked up the tidbit and couldn't help thinking about how little she knew of his daily life.

Fausto and Jake, conversing in rapid Italian and raising their voices to interrupt each other, appeared at the back door, and Mimi grinned when both men, perfectly in sync, toed off their muddy boots before stepping onto the kitchen's cool terracotta floor.

From the corner of her eye, she watched Fausto hug Francesca while Jake enveloped and kissed her soundly. Mimi savored the earthy, outdoor smells in his hair and felt the warmth of his sun-kissed skin seep through her shirt.

"Are you guys done?" she asked, wrapping her arms around his waist.

"We're done in the fields, but I'm not done with you," he said with a suggestive eyebrow raise while he snatched a cube of cheese off a nearby platter. "And I'm starving."

Holding the cheese between his teeth, he lowered his mouth to hers, feeding her like a baby bird while kissing her at the same time. The gesture was so intimate it made Mimi's girl parts tingle, and she fervently hoped they'd be able to continue that level of closeness until they were old.

"Where are your thoughts, *bella?*" Jake asked close to her ear.

"Oh, here and there." She didn't want to shock him by blurting out stuff about spending her life with him. "Maybe I'll tell you later."

He winked at her, "Ahhhh, need some more incentive again to talk? I'll remind you later, but now I'll go freshen up or Aunt Francesca will forbid me to sit at the table." He pecked her lips and jogged off, playfully buffeting Fausto's shoulder on his way by.

A smile plastered itself on Mimi's face as she watched him disappear, and she didn't care that it spread from ear to ear. Why should she hide her feelings in front of Jake's family? They had welcomed her with open arms, and what she said to Francesca earlier was the truth. She loved being here.

"Ooh, what did he do now?" Mia asked from behind Mimi. "You have that, what do you call it? The google look," she said in English while she crossed her eyes.

Mimi paused, then smiled, "Oh, you mean googly-eyed," and copied Mia's silly face.

"Yes, like my friend Gianna."

A searing pain pierced Mimi at the same time as Mia winced.

"What do you mean?" To distract herself, Mimi reached for the oven-fresh bread and began to slice it with shaking hands.

"It was stupid and meant nothing," Mia said, and then threw up her hands and sighed. "Gianna is sweet on Jake. When I saw you following him with your eyes, it just slipped out."

"Okay." Mimi arranged the thick, still-warm slices in a large wooden bowl. She shouldn't care if other women crushed on Jake, and had no reason to distrust him, but she did panic for a second. It was another reminder that there was so much they didn't know about each other, and it made her worry about what would happen after she flew back to Boston.

Mia peeled the knife out of Mimi's hand and put it on the cutting board. "I'm very sorry. Sometimes I just say things that come out the wrong way."

"Which is why I keep telling you to watch your tongue."

Francesca joined them and took Mimi's hands in hers, "Emilia, don't listen to this silly girl. Jacopo loves you. I can see it, and nothing else matters." She glared over her shoulder at her daughter, told her in rapid Italian to make herself scarce and to take the food outside.

Blinking away tears, Mimi let Francesca pull her into a bear hug, then she straightened and said, "Thank you. I'm okay, really. I don't know what came over me."

"You're in love, Emilia. Sometimes love is sweet, and sometimes it is painful. But always listen to your heart and trust yourself." Then she pulled Mimi into another crushing hug and mumbled, "*L'amore non è bello, se non è litigarello.*"

The course of true love never did run smooth.

Mimi chuckled at the quote from *A Midsummer Night's Dream.* Given her and Jake's short relationship, it was too early to speak of a course or dating history. But she wholeheartedly agreed with Francesca—she was in love like never before, and shouldn't let Mia's guileless remark upset her.

"Our love runs very smoothly where I'm concerned, *bella.* I'm not asking why you lovely ladies are quoting Shakespeare, but I want to know why you're crying. You were smiling when I left to shower," Jake said from the doorway and crossed the distance to Mimi in a few long strides.

Mimi wiped a finger under her eyes and shrugged. "It's nothing. Really."

"*Nothing* doesn't make you cry, and that's two things now I want answers for." He guided her hand around his waist and held her close. "How about a stroll under the full moon later?" His lips touched her earlobe, "Maybe we'll go to our special place..."

She nodded and grinned, aware that he'd coax everything he wanted to know—and more—out of her as soon as they were alone, and she didn't mind telling him about her silly insecurity—or her secret longing for a future with him.

"*Ti amo,*" he said, low and sincere.

"I love you too."

214

Raucous laughter and the sound of happy chatter ended their quiet conversation, so they grabbed the remaining platters and joined the family and rest of the team under a vine-covered pergola.

Long, sturdy wooden tables already held numerous colorful ceramic bowls and platters laden with grilled vegetables, cheese, salads, pasta blended in fresh pesto, bread, marinated olives, creamy butter, and sliced salami and prosciutto. Bottles of tap water and glass carafes with red and white wine were interspersed with the feast.

In awe, Mimi realized that almost everything on the table had been produced by this vineyard except for the meat, which came from a nearby farm.

She pulled out her phone and took several photos, and couldn't wait to send them to Paloma, who would love this scene. For years she'd been a passionate supporter for alfresco dining versus over-priced "nibbling at a star-rated restaurant that serves nothing but fancily arranged ikebana on a plate"—as she liked to call it.

Mia materialized at Mimi's side and hugged her. "Will you forgive me?"

"There's nothing to forgive," Mimi smiled and squeezed Mia's hand as they sat down next to each other. "My reaction was childish. It's been a few crazy weeks, and my mind's messing with me." She caught Jake's eye as he sat down on her other side, their thighs touching. He poured red wine from an unlabeled bottle, first for her, then for himself, and they joined the rest of the family and friends in passing the delicious-smelling food around until Fausto called out, "*Buon appetito!*"

Hours later Mimi listened to the rustling of leaves and under-growth caused by foraging nocturnal critters—she wasn't too keen to encounter porcupines or wild boars—and was very comfortable sitting with Jake, Tonio, and Mia around the glowing coals remaining in the firepit. Gazing at the star-sprinkled sky, she sipped her wine, the flavors of cherries, herbs, and oak lingering on her tongue, and her thoughts circled back to her earlier conversation with Mia.

Too bad she couldn't bottle her current contentment and take a sip of it every time her childish wariness reared its head in the months ahead.

Chapter 41

Jake

THE SMELL OF FRESHLY BREWED COFFEE PULLED JAKE TO THE kitchen after yet another short night. By the time he and Mimi retreated to his room last night, they weren't too tired to... He smirked at the memory. Every second spent with Mimi was well worth a little bit of fatigue.

Humming "*Senza una Donna,*" he pulled two oversized mugs out of the cabinet. The 1980s earworm was playing on the radio when he and Mimi indulged in a few more minutes of cuddle time before he got up to shower.

Without a Woman. The song's lyrics didn't match their situation, but he knew he didn't want to be without Mimi ever again, and hoped to make their weekend in Florence unforgettable.

"Ooh, someone's in a good mood," Mia's singsong voice interrupted his thoughts.

Jake spotted her leaning against the counter sipping a latte. "Ah, Miss Chatty, I'm glad to catch you alone." He decided to get straight to the point before she could bail on him. "What possessed you to suggest to Mimi that Gianna and I had something going?" He'd been livid when Mimi finally told him about Mia's comment, and hoped he'd been able to rob her of the notion that there was even a trace of truth in Mia's stupid remark.

"I didn't mean to imply anything, and I apologized to Mimi. We're good."

"But you and I aren't. What did you think you'd achieve by mentioning it?" He began to froth milk for Mimi's cappuccino, knowing she'd be downstairs any minute.

"I said I apologized. No need for you to puff out your chest like a rooster." Mia pushed away from the counter and put her cup in the dishwasher.

"How would you like it if I gabbed to Tonio about how Cesare constantly sniffs around you?" Jake knew it wasn't the same. Cesare, a seasonal worker from a nearby town, was aware that Mia was dating Antonio, which didn't prevent him from flirting with her endlessly. It was mostly innocent, but with an occasional spritz of sexual innuendo. From what Jake heard, Cesare enjoyed tasting the fruits offered to him—something Jake could relate to, since he hadn't been much different until he met Mimi.

"Tonio knows Cesare, and that he's just teasing me. It doesn't worry him." Jake knew it was true. And Mia had no trouble handling Cesare's flirting.

"And why? Because he's been with you for years and is aware of it. But Mimi doesn't know anyone here and could easily misinterpret what you're saying."

"So why don't you invite a few people so she can meet them and know who you're hanging out with?"

An invisible hand smacked Jake's forehead. Why hadn't *he* thought of it? "Perfect idea! We'll throw a small party next weekend, when Nicki's also here."

"Yes, I like it," Mia clapped her hands. "Can I organize it? We could go to Montisi as a group for the festival, then end up here and..."

"No!" He had something casual in mind, and the *Giostra di Simone*, a medieval festival with jousting tournaments and parades, was a fun tourist magnet but didn't give Mimi a chance to connect with his friends.

"Suit yourself," Mia shrugged and walked to the back door.

"I heard you mention Nicki, what about her?" Mimi strolled into the kitchen, taking Jake's breath away in her yellow sundress and white leather flip-flops.

"Miss Chatty gave me an idea. I'll fill you in when we're in the car." Jake kissed Mimi briefly and handed her the mug of steaming coffee, topped off with a thick layer of milk foam. "Everything okay with Nicki? I expected you to be on the phone with her longer."

"She was in a hurry. Apparently she met some women from Boston on one of her pre-booked tours and is hanging out with them. They're visiting Versailles today."

"Is she still flying to Rome tomorrow?" he fixed his own coffee and brought a plate of breakfast pastries to the kitchen table.

"Yes." Mimi eyed Francesca's assorted *sfogliatelle,* picked one, and bit into the flaky puff pastry. She licked a dab of custard off the corner of her mouth and grinned, "I have to get this recipe for Paloma. Knowing her, she'll tweak it and play with seasonings and herbs so she can sell it all day." Mimi chewed so reverently, Jake half expected her to close her eyes to savor the taste.

Choosing a Nutella-filled pastry, he said, "I'm not sure the powdered sugar will go too well with anything savory."

"Don't underestimate Paloma, she'll find a way. But I wouldn't know, I'm only a veggie scrubber and peeler," Mimi laughed and sipped her cappuccino.

Jake wanted to devour her, she looked so adorable with a smudge of powdered sugar and a dash of milk foam on her lips. He cleared his throat and tried to redirect his thoughts.

"They make *sfogliatelle* with meat and vegetables in Sicily," Francesca said as she entered the kitchen. "But I want to hear about what your friend invents."

"I'll let you know." Mimi snagged another pastry and gobbled it, then she wiped her mouth and said to Jake, "That should hold me over until lunch."

IT WAS TOO EARLY TO CHECK IN AT THE SMALL BOUTIQUE HOTEL on the banks of the Arno River, so they changed into comfortable walking shoes and stowed their bags in the hotel luggage room.

After a couple of hours of exploring the exhilarating maze of streets, Mimi said, "I've lost all sense of direction and I'm starving."

She looked around and started to cross the square in front of them. "Come on, I've also got to pee."

"Then where are you going?"

"To find a restaurant."

"Good thing you're with me, *bella*," he smirked and took her hand. "But let's go that way." He pointed to an alley opposite of where Mimi had gone.

"Oops..."

Within a few minutes Jake led them back to *Piazza del Duomo*, the busy tourist square dominated by *Santa Maria del Fiore*. No matter how often he was in Florence, he never tired of seeing the magnificent thirteenth-century cathedral with its red-tiled Brunelleschi dome and three-colored marble facade, the adjacent Baptistery—itself considered a minor basilica, and two centuries older than the *duomo*—and Giotto's bell tower. These marvels of architecture, the timeless grandeur of those monuments, simply humbled him.

He steered them toward one of several restaurants—all lined up neatly like pearls on a string—and after a short conversation with the maître d', including a discreet tip—they were seated at a front-row table, sheltered from the bright but relentless midday sun by an eggshell-colored awning.

Jake leaned back in his chair, ran a thumb over his lower lip and couldn't tear his eyes away from Mimi. The way she watched tourists, gazed at the cathedral, took photos, and oohed and aahed when she discovered something she liked, would be forever branded in his mind.

"*Bella*, if you have a moment, let's toast to us being here," Jake smiled.

Her head snapped around. "Oh, of course, I'm so sorry. I can't believe we're actually sitting here." She said it almost reverently. "This restaurant has a fantastic reputation, and it's packed."

She glanced back at the *duomo*. "I could look at the pink, green, and white marble panels all day long. It's so busy, yet it...works. Just look at the detail in all the sculptures and ornamentations. We'll have to walk around it one more time after lunch so I can take more pictures, especially of some of the molding around the portals and windows." She reached for her prosecco flute and clinked it to his *Apérol Spritz*. "I guess I'm babbling. *Cin-cin!*"

He knew he was grinning like a fool. "Cheers, my love."

Her glass hovered briefly midway to her lips, and he could've sworn he saw her eyes welling up before she said, "To us and to Florence."

She'd taken the words right out of his mouth.

———

AFTER A TO-DIE-FOR PASTA LUNCH AND A FEW MORE HOURS OF sightseeing, Jake gave the door to their hotel room a push with his hip and dropped their two bags on the floor.

Mimi went immediately to the floor-to-ceiling glass door and stepped onto a narrow balcony. "Oh, wow, Jake..." She beckoned for him to come. "Look, we're facing the Arno River and *Ponte Vecchio*."

Jake stepped behind her, wrapped his arms around Mimi's waist, and nodded into her hair. "I know."

"Have you been to this hotel before?" She twisted her head enough so his lips touched her forehead.

"Yes. When I have an evening business meeting, I often stay here." Jake turned Mimi in his arms.

"Ah, okay." Her expression conveyed relief, but also a silent question.

"Did you think this is where I take women to impress them?" Jake smirked, hoping she didn't think he was being smug. "My secret love nest?"

Mimi shrugged and looked heart-meltingly sheepish. *Aha, Mia's stupid remark went deeper than she intended. Let's nip that in the bud once and for all.*

"Jake…" she started, but he placed a fingertip on her warm, soft lips.

"Mimi, I told you I haven't been in a serious relationship since law school. Finding out my ex had something going with one of my best buddies cured me of the urge to date." He ran his finger along her lips. "I haven't been celibate in the eight years since then, but I swear I haven't looked at any woman since I met you in May. I couldn't get you out of my mind."

"You told me, and I believe you." She dropped her forehead to his chest and mumbled, "I've never been the jealous or clingy type, and have no clue why I'm reacting the way I do." Mimi raised her head again and he saw so many emotions in her trusting eyes. And hoped he'd never be the reason for her anguish.

"How is it possible that I love you so much after only two weeks? One on Martha's Vineyard, and now at Bellini's vineyard," she grinned.

He tipped her face up with a finger under her chin, and his eyes roamed over her eyes and mouth as he drank her in. As much as he wanted to show her how much he desired and loved her, this moment required talk rather than action.

"And we have another two weeks." Of which he planned to make every second count.

"Mimi, *bella*, love. One hour was all it took to know you're unlike anyone else I've ever been with, and I can't think of anyone I'd rather be with."

She swallowed hard and nodded. "But how are we going to make this work?" A trace of worry traced her quiet voice. "I can't fly back and forth, and school starts in a few weeks."

"We'll find a way. I'm coming to the States as soon as possible after the harvest. In the past I waited until Thanksgiving since there wasn't much to pull me there. But now there is, and it's going to be damn long three months."

Jake lowered his mouth to hers, and just before they touched, he asked, "Will you wait for me?"

"Of course," Mimi's voice was barely a whisper, and Jake wished he could close the distance between the two continents as easily as he closed the distance between their lips.

Chapter 42

Mimi

MIMI STEPPED OUT OF THE BLACK AND WHITE-TILED SHOWER and wrapped the thick, soft terrycloth towel around her. Standing in front of the wide mirror, she slowly combed styling cream into her hair with her fingers, then smelled the complimentary lotions and picked one with a hint of gardenia.

Sitting down on the wooden stool—so out of place in the elegant, marbled bathroom, but strangely complementing the look—she moisturized her legs and arms, finalizing everything with a spritz of the also-complimentary eau de toilette on the inside of her wrist.

The luxury items were a wonderful...well...luxury...and she was tempted to snag the miniature eau de toilette—just like everybody pocketed the guest soaps.

She imagined Jake saying, "*Bella*, it's already paid for, just take it." And he would be right... Of course she knew it was calculated into the room rate, but she was also a little queasy about Jake spending so much money.

Mimi had offered to cover half of the expenses for the weekend, but he wouldn't even let her pay for one meal. Her little victory today was when she paid for their gelato. Her white chocolate ice cream with pistachio sauce had been out of this world, and Jake's tiramisu gelato was a close second—yes, she'd sampled some of his.

She sighed and massaged the remaining lotion into her hands.

"Mimi, did you fall asleep in there?" Jake's silhouette appeared outside the frosted glass door.

"No." She slid the door open. "I need to blow-dry my hair, then I'm good to go."

"Really?" His right eyebrow shot up.

"What?"

"Are you going like this?" He pointed at the towel.

"Oops, no." She skipped out of the bathroom and pulled her dress out of her small carry-on. "Be right back."

"Feel free to dress in front of me." Legs crossed at the ankles, he leaned against the doorjamb, smirked, and folded his muscular arms. Wearing a pair of khakis with a short-sleeved shirt, he looked...drool-worthy. And he was hers!

"Jake?" she flirted. "What time is our dinner reservation?" She reached for the tucked-in corner of her towel.

"In...umm...half an hour." His calm posture changed in front of her eyes, and he uncrossed his legs, then cleared his throat. "Why?"

"How long does it take us to get there?" She opened the towel enough to give him a peek.

"Ahh...I'd say fifteen minutes." He grabbed her towel with one hand and pulled her to him.

"I better hurry and dry my hair, then." She stood on tiptoes and kissed him. "Sorry."

"We'll finish this later, *bella*," he chuckled.

"I was hoping you'd say that." Mimi wiggled her eyebrows and slipped out of his embrace, then closed the bathroom door to muffle the sound of Jake's laughter.

THE RESTAURANT HE CHOSE WAS PERFECT—LIKE EVERYTHING else so far. To get there, they crossed *Ponte Vecchio* and entered a small front yard, separated from the Riverwalk by a tall black wrought-iron gate.

Small tables were set up with white tablecloths, votive candles, and the usual array of glasses. But best of all was the view. From the terrace on the second floor, they overlooked the Arno River and saw the majestic dome of the *duomo* in the background.

After a leisurely dinner—Mimi was grateful for the European habit of allowing guests to sit for hours and enjoy meals unrushed— they strolled back to their hotel. The jewelry stores on *Ponte Vecchio* were closed this late in the evening, but Mimi couldn't help glancing at the displays. She'd never be able to afford any of the diamond- and pearl-studded pieces, but admiring them didn't cost a cent.

With Jake's arm around her shoulder, and her nose almost touching the glass pane, he asked close to her ear, "See anything you like?"

"No...well, yes." A Florentine-style ring—two-tone gold with a delicate cross-patched pattern, dotted with about six or eight small, bezel-set diamonds—was stunning. Maybe she'd check online once she was at home if this style was available in more wallet-friendly silver.

"Which piece?" His stubble rubbed temptingly against her cheek.

Mimi straightened and stepped away from the window. She didn't want to give him the impression that she was fishing for a gift, especially not jewelry, and most definitely not a ring.

"*Bella?* Just tell me." He pulled her against him, and she melted into his embrace.

Her eyes went back to the ring. "The Florentine ring. It's looks so fine and subtle, but is sturdy because the strands are interwoven."

He checked out the display, then nodded and took her hand. "I agree. It's beautiful." He kissed the back of her hand. "Like you."

Butterfly wings fluttered in her belly. It didn't seem to matter what he said or what he did—she was a goner.

Back at their hotel, Mimi dropped into a chair, kicked off her kitty-heel sandals, and flexed her feet. She mumbled, "We walked so much today, I'd marry you in exchange for a foot massage."

Geez Louise! She slapped both hands over her mouth and tucked her feet under her hip.

"Good to know your priorities," Jake laughed as he sat down in the other chair. He patted his lap and beckoned for her to put her feet there.

"I'm sorry, I didn't mean..." she stuttered.

"Stop apologizing, *bella*. Now give me those feet, and we'll see what happens."

MIMI WOKE UP TO LOUD VOICES FROM THE STREET BELOW THE hotel. Still half asleep, she stretched her arms above her head, only to be grabbed and tumbled on top of Jake.

"Good morning, my love." He nibbled on the side of her neck, his voice husky.

"Hmm? Oh, good morning. What was the screaming about?" She wiggled around, her body on autopilot.

"No idea. I only have eyes and ears for you." His hands roamed over her, leaving a trail of fire.

"Smooth answer, Mr. Bellini." She wanted to touch him everywhere at once, but had to settle for running her fingers through his hair, then working her way down...

He tugged on her tank top. "Can we get rid of this?"

"M-hmm..." She let him pull it up and over her shoulders and head and then stretched out, relishing the skin-on-skin sensation, grateful that he only wore boxer shorts to bed but no T-shirt, because she'd never tire of seeing and feeling him half-naked.

People flocked the *Accademia* Gallery to see the statue of David

—or contented themselves with the naked butt of his replica on *Piazza della Signoria*, the L-shaped plaza outside of *Palazzo Vecchio* —but all she wanted was Jake.

"Can we also take this off?" He hooked his finger into her panties.

She twisted to help shed them, then squealed when he flipped her on her back and positioned himself between her legs.

When did he take off his boxers?

"I need to be inside you. Now," he almost pleaded.

She nodded. They often took their time at night, but were impatient in the mornings, and she didn't mind. Last night, after a truly heavenly foot massage, he made love to her so sensually she wanted to weep when she came. Both times.

Now Jake held himself up on his forearms and entered her at an agonizingly slow pace, his eyes never leaving hers. When he was deeply buried, he muttered, "You're everything to me, *bella*."

Later, trying to catch her breath while their legs were still tangled, Mimi vaguely heard church bells ringing, as if in blessing.

In that moment, she silently promised her heart and soul to Jake. She couldn't imagine ever loving anyone more than she loved him.

———

"WHAT'S ON TODAY'S AGENDA?" MIMI ASKED AND NODDED A thank-you to the waitress who served her another cappuccino. Having breakfast at a small café on a quiet side street, and surrounded by locals, Mimi felt like a Florentine rather than a visitor.

"I thought we'd walk to *Borgo degli Albizi*, the street named after your ancestors. They were wealthy merchants between the fourteenth to nineteenth centuries, and even though their palazzo, family residence and the tower aren't open to visit, we can at least get a look at them. Then we'll spend the afternoon on the other side of the river."

"They had a palazzo *and* a family residence?" she laughed.

"Then they're definitely not my ancestors. I have a more modest background."

"Your last name derives from their name, which is good enough for me."

"That's so far-fetched, there are probably hundreds of other possibilities."

"The mimosa tree, *Albizi julibrissin*, was named after an eighteenth-century naturalist, Filippo degli Albizzi, who was a member of the Albizi family from Florence. Although nobody seems to be able to make up their mind whether to spell the name with one or two z's."

"Are you making that up? If you are, I must say you sound rather convincing," Mimi said. As much as she enjoyed history, he constantly surprised her with his nuggets.

"I read. Especially when I want to impress lovely ladies."

"Ah, I see, so that's your secret," she smirked and let her eyes glide over him. "But you have so many amazing qualities, you can't impress me any more than you already do."

Jake clutched a hand to his chest. "Are you saying you want only my body, not my brain? Mimi, you...you... I'm shocked."

"You'll get over it, you're a big boy," she patted his cheek and laughed, realizing her double entendre.

His bark of laughter made several people turn to look at them. "What do you want me to say now? If I agree with your comment, you'll accuse me of being cocky." He wiggled an eyebrow. "If I say you're wrong, I'd be lying. I guess I'll let you be the judge, *bella*."

Mimi felt her cheeks warm up and hoped she didn't look like a ripe tomato. "I guess I asked for that one." She tried to steer the conversation back to less provocative topics, "Have you ever researched the origin of your name?"

"No. I mean, everyone has heard of Giovanni Bellini, the fifteenth-century painter who revolutionized Venetian painting. Others may know Vincenzo Bellini, the nineteenth-century composer, who was supposedly some wunderkind who composed his first five pieces by the time he was six years old."

"Huh? What? Get out... But why am I surprised? Mozart started composing when he was five."

Jake shrugged. "So, in other words, I have no idea if our family goes back to anyone famous. Ancestry isn't high on my list of interests. I'm more fascinated by the now—and in the future." His eyes bored into hers—and jumbled her insides like the scrambled eggs on her plate.

———

AFTER DRIVING UP A WINDING ROAD—THROUGH A neighborhood of grand houses hidden behind tall hedges and walls that only allowed occasional glimpses of the mansions' grandeur—Jake parked the car on a large terrace, led her past a bronze sculpture of *David* and came to stand at a stone balustrade.

All Mimi could do was gasp.

And look.

And take slow breaths.

Florence was sprawled out below them, basking under a bright blue sky in the midday sunshine, showing off her timeless beauty, with the glimmering Arno River meandering through her.

Behind the City of Lilies, the Tuscan capital's nickname, the green hills of Fiesole and Settignano provided a picture-perfect backdrop.

Mimi took numerous photos with her cell phone, including selfies of her and Jake, but no matter where she turned, her focus was always pulled back to the looming *duomo* surrounded by a sea of red rooftops.

"I take it you like the view from *Piazzale Michelangelo*?" Jake stood behind her, with his hands loosely folded around her.

She nodded and, without looking at him, asked, "Why didn't we come here yesterday? This is absolutely stunning."

"I wanted to save the best for last."

She turned in his arms. "*You're* the best." If she wasn't already so in love with him, the mischievous sparkle that lit up his eyes would've sealed it. "I'll never forget seeing this with you."

"Me neither. I hope it's the first of many memorable moments. Even though I'd say we've had a few already," he kissed her softly.

Mimi wanted to beg him to assure her they'd always be as happy as they were right here and now. But a promise like that was impossible to make, because no one could know what the future held, so she kept quiet—and poured all her love into the kiss.

"Mimi," he held her tightly, "there's something I want you to know."

Chills seized Mimi's heart and stalled her breath.

"I love you so much, and I'll do anything to make this work. Make *us* work," he said.

Warmth replaced the cold, and her heart jumped with joy.

She must've let out an audible sigh, because Jake held her even tighter and asked, "What did you think I was going to say?"

"I…" she sighed again. "I don't know. But I also promise to do my best to make us work." She said cautiously, "So I guess you're stuck with me."

"Which is exactly where I want to be, *cara mia.*" Jake's use of Italian terms of endearment was so special, and Mimi instinctively knew they were sincere.

He reached for her hand and they strolled across the square, passing several artists capturing the view with pencil, crayon, chalk, or paint, then crossed the street and walked toward a neoclassical-style building with three tall windows and a rooftop terrace.

"This is the *loggia*," Jake said. "When *Piazzale Michelangelo* was created, this building was intended to house a museum of Michelangelo's work, but it was never realized. Nowadays it's a restaurant."

Mimi turned around—ignoring the busloads of tourists flocking to the piazza like pigeons to breadcrumbs—and admired the sweeping views of Florence anew.

Jake said, "I thought we could have a late lunch here, and then I have two suggestions for this afternoon."

"Yes to lunch! And what are the options for the rest of the day?"

"We could visit Boboli Gardens, an outdoor museum-slash-park that was created in the 1760s for the Medici and inspired many European courts. It's filled with statues and grottos and isn't far from here."

That sounded interesting. "And the other option?"

"By the time we finish lunch, it'll be midafternoon. We could drive home, and I'll take you out to dinner in San Gimignano. We haven't spent nearly enough time in my favorite town."

"I chose number two," Mimi said without hesitation. They'd gone to San Gimignano once, but not in the evening. The town was spectacular during the day, the views from *Torre Grossa,* one of Tuscany's best-known medieval towers built in 1310, were awe-inspiring, and she was bursting to see it all illuminated at night, needing to collect more memories she could revisit during the months when they'd be apart.

During lunch, Jake continued to feed her more history, like when Florence was Italy's capital from 1865 to 1870, and underwent massive expansions, including the removal of fourteenth-century city walls to make room for six-lane, tree-lined streets plus the installation of river walks on both sides of the Arno River.

Mimi soaked it all up, and her thoughts strayed back to when she took Anna to the historic locations around Verona.

"Am I boring you?" Jake asked, sounding amused. "You're getting your faraway look."

"Oh, gosh, no, I'm sorry."

"Don't apologize, *bella.* Just tell me what's going on in that pretty head of yours."

"I was thinking about how much more fun it is to learn about history by visiting places and creating a personal connection with them. It's what I did with Anna, the girl I was tutoring in Verona. But the spoiled brats I'm teaching at home would never appreciate it because they take jet-setting around the world for granted. Yet all their parents do is deliver another stamp in their passports, almost like the pins kids collect at amusement parks."

"What would you do? How would you teach the kids?" Jake leaned back and scratched his chin—one of his habits—and Mimi's heart overflowed with affection.

"Are you referring to the kids in my classes, or if I had kids of my own?"

"I meant the kids in your school, but what are your thoughts about both?" Did she imagine that his gaze became more intense?

The butterflies in her belly fluttered like crazy. Of course she hoped to have kids one day, but she never talked about it, and hearing Jake ask about children—even though it was only a hypothetical question—made her feel light as a helium balloon.

She focused on the cathedral in the distance, as if the golden copper ball and cross that topped the oculus held the questions to all answers.

"I'm afraid there's not much I can do for the kids in my school, since I have to follow a pretty strict curriculum. If a trip to Plymouth is on the syllabus, that's where we go. For my own kids, I'd expose them to as much traveling as possible. Because even if they don't appreciate hiking up that hill or climbing the ancient castle wall at that moment, the memory will always stay with them."

Mimi sipped from her sparkling water. "But what I'd really like to do is give children who aren't privileged enough to travel a chance to get out and explore. Like summer camps that provide more than mornings spent in a musty gym and afternoons at a bacteria-infected town pool."

"That's a very laudable wish."

"I know. I can't even explain where those thoughts are coming from. Maybe I'm a social worker in disguise."

"*Bella*, I'm sure you'll figure out a way to do it."

Chapter 43

Jake

JAKE WIPED THE SWEAT OFF HIS FOREHEAD WITH ONE OF THE hand towels he carried as consistently as his water bottle. Chugging some water, he eyed the cerulean sky, today unmarred by clouds. The abundant sunshine and temperatures in the eighties were helping the *veraison*—the onset of grape ripening and subsequent change of color —and he was grateful for the perfect conditions. Already, many berries had turned from green to purplish or yellow, depending on their variety, a process he never tired of observing.

For the next two to three months, all eyes and hands would be on the grapes, and there was no counting how many times he, Fausto, and the other vignerons would walk up and down the endless rows of vines, meticulously checking the crop while staying abreast of the weather forecast.

He picked up his pruning shears again and continued cutting away excess leaves and occasional clusters of grapes—to give the other fruit more sun exposure—when a commotion drifted up the hill.

Jake smiled and lowered his tools—he could recognize that voice anywhere and often found himself listening for it everywhere. Just like kissing its owner first thing in the morning and last thing at night had become rituals he depended on like breathing.

He was tempted to go and check out what was happening—no excuse was too feeble to justify sneaking a quick kiss—but Francesca's exuberant and repeated exclamation of *"Maledetto,"* accompanied by Mimi's clear-as-glass laughter, made him guess that some of the chickens had escaped the coop and hid eggs in his aunt's sacred vegetable garden.

Jake chuckled. He didn't see it as a big issue, but knew his aunt's opinion. *If you want frittata for breakfast on Sunday, Jacopo, you better pray we have enough eggs.* He imagined Francesca chasing the stray chickens with a worn, scrubby broom, and Mimi crouching down to coax them to come to her.

If I was the chicken, I'd jump right into her waiting arms.

Listening to Mimi and Aunt Francesca was priceless, even if he couldn't make out words besides the cursing of the chickens. The two women were almost inseparable—except for when Mimi was with him.

Sharp pain gripped his chest, and he sat down on the low stone wall, rested his elbows on his knees, and inspected the weeds between his shoes. This was how he imagined family life. Not necessarily including the chickens—all those feathered little devils did was attack his fingers whenever he was sent to collect eggs—but a life of genuine happiness and love. With Mimi at the center and a bunch of kids surrounding her.

Mimi...his *bella.*

Their time together was soon coming to an end. In another week his arms would be as empty as Mimi's side of his bed.

The past two weeks had been an unexpected gift, but she couldn't stay forever. Of course he knew it was inevitable. She needed to return to her life stateside, but he didn't know how he'd be able to let her go.

I'd marry you in exchange for a foot massage. Mimi's sweet, innocent remark in Florence came back to him. Could he...? No, that was insane...

Jake took off his baseball cap and rubbed his towel over his hair. More unrestrained laughter from downhill made his insides knot up.

Mimi fit in so...flawlessly. Into the winery just as much as into his life and his heart. And at night they were also a perfect fit...

He scooted around on the merciless stone wall.

"Jacob, what's the matter?" Fausto's voice startled him, and he looked up into his uncle's dark eyes, so warm and caring.

"I can't let her go," Jake said. No reason to beat around the bush. His uncle knew who he was talking about.

Fausto sat down next to him, took off his hat and fanned himself. "Do you want to go back with her?"

Jake flinched, opened his mouth, and closed it again. "No... Yes... I'm torn."

He breathed in, blew the air out slowly, and said, "I won't leave before the harvest, you know that. This vineyard is as important to me as—"

"Don't say as important as Emilia is," Fausto said sternly. "Nothing...there is nothing more important than the person you love. Nothing. When you find her, you don't let go of her. Ever."

Fausto's vehement advice didn't surprise Jake. Mimi won Francesca and Fausto's hearts on the first day, when she greeted them in fluent Italian and pitched in right away, assisting Francesca in the kitchen and at the B&B.

"Uncle Fausto..."

Fausto shook his head. "Jacob. Listen to me. I love you like a son, and I'm forever grateful for what you have done for us and the winery. You uprooted your life and risked your father's anger, but you can't let the woman you love slip away because of us. If you want to have a future with Emilia, you must be with her, and it doesn't matter where."

Jake let his uncle's words settle in.

Until now, Jake hadn't given too much consideration to where he'd spend his life, or what he'd do for work. But he always knew—in the deepest part of his heart and soul—that, as much as he loved it, it wouldn't be at this vineyard.

"Dad and I had a long conversation a few weeks ago. I think we cleared the air, and now I understand better where his opinion about my leaving law is coming from," Jake said. "He wants me to come back—"

"As he has wanted for years," nodded Fausto.

"Yes, but this time he pulled out the big guns." Jake pressed his lips together. "He wants me to manage a new business he's about to open in Uncle Charles's memory, and he needs my answer by Thanksgiving."

"Is it something you want to do?"

Jake shrugged. He wasn't sure what he wanted—besides Mimi, of course.

"Have you discussed it with Emilia?"

"I told her a little bit about Dad's plans, but we haven't brought it up since then."

"Talk to her. She might have ideas that you haven't considered yet. Be open, be flexible, but above all, include her. Do it *with* her."

Fausto put his arm around Jake's shoulders. "And learn from your father."

"What do you mean?"

Fausto's eyes strayed from Jake's face to the farmhouse. "I was lucky to have found Francesca, and that she wanted to make our home on this land. But Roberto wasn't happy here. When he met your mother, he was in the same situation as you are now. And he didn't hesitate. He listened to his heart and pursued his dream. And you need to do the same."

"I don't think opening a hotel on Martha's Vineyard was his dream."

"No, I don't think so either," Fausto smiled. "I doubt he had any idea what he wanted to do—he was drifting, like you."

I'm drifting?

Jake paused.

Yes, I am. I have a home and work, friends and family, but I'm still drifting!

"Roberto realized that he didn't want to be without your mother, and the hotel was her family's business. It was important to her, so it became important to him too. Then and now, he wants to make your mother happy, and they set the course of their lives together," Fausto continued.

"But didn't he end up just like *nonna* and *nonno*, something he wanted to avoid and ran away from? He's working 24/7 and worries constantly about the business."

Fausto shrugged, "Jacob, he didn't run away from work or responsibility. He searched for his purpose and his fulfillment. And he found it. When I FaceTime with him, he looks happy and content. He stands completely behind what he's doing, and it shows."

Jake recalled his father's explanation. *I promised your mother we'd travel more once she turns sixty.*

His parents deserved it—they should be able to step back and take time off for themselves. Which meant he needed to step up and do some serious soul-searching about where he saw himself a couple of years from now.

Fausto was correct, he was a lot like his father—he might not know yet what he wanted, but he knew who he wanted to have with him while he searched, and when they put down roots in the right place.

"I think I want to marry Mimi," Jake uttered, then suppressed a chuckle when Fausto threw his hands in the air and praised several saints Jake had never heard of. For all he knew, his aunt and uncle made them up as they needed them.

"Do you think, or do you know?" Fausto asked heatedly.

"I know."

"Then do it."

"I can't. We only started dating."

Another slew of saints' names left Fausto's mouth, but in a

harsher tone than before, underscoring Jake's belief about their real existence. "Have you not listened, Jacob?"

Fausto asked very slowly, "Do...you...love...her?" as if he didn't trust Jake's mental capacity to process more than one word at a time.

"Yes."

"Then time doesn't matter. I asked Francesca after a few months of dating. Your father proposed to your mother after only two weeks."

"Because she was leaving," said Jake—and ducked his head when Fausto jumped up and threw his arms in the air again. "Bellini men do or don't do something, but we don't waste time trying. Make up your mind what you want, Jacob!"

Jake grinned, and not just because his sixty-three-year-old uncle just quasi-quoted Yoda.

And it was true, what Fausto said about his parents' fast engagement. His dad proposed to his mom at the end of her vacation, then followed her to the States, where they tied the knot within six months, and Jake arrived within a year of their wedding.

If his uncle and aunt's, as well as his parents', marriages were any indication, Jake had no reason to wait. Besides, nobody could guarantee a happily-ever-after, but there was one surefire way to not have one: being indecisive and not going after what he wanted.

"Do you mind if I take off for a couple of hours?"

Fausto reached into a bucket at their feet. He eyed the cut-off clusters of grapes and said, "I think you're actually doing me a favor by taking the afternoon off. What was wrong with this fruit?"

"Nothing..." Jake got up and kissed his uncle's weathered cheeks. "Thank you."

"Go," Fausto pushed him away with a huge smile and muttered something about "being useless" while Jake collected his tools and jogged toward the farmhouse. He agreed with his uncle. He was useless if he continued to butcher the plants, and he wouldn't be able to concentrate again until he mapped out the path for his future.

Chapter 44

Mimi

THAT SOB! HOW DARE HE?

Mimi stomped over the gravel driveway muttering every exple-
tive she could think of—which weren't very many, because she
couldn't stand cursing.

She glanced at the guesthouse, hoping none of the boarders were
there, or at least didn't understand the finest of English swearing,
although everyone knew the f-word. Not even calling and bitching to
Paloma—who had introduced her to a plethora of new swearwords—
had calmed her down sufficiently.

"Mimi, what are you doing? Even Jake didn't leave such tracks in
the gravel when he took off like he's being chased by the devil," Mia
came out of the farmhouse. "Speaking of, where did he go to in the
middle of the day? He and *babbo* are supposed to be working in the
Sangiovese section."

Mimi stopped pacing and wrinkled her forehead. "What do you
mean?"

"Half an hour ago I saw him run into the house and leave shortly
after."

Ah, that must've been when I was on the phone with Nicki and then Paloma.

"But you still didn't tell me what's going on," Mia said.

Mimi held up her phone. "My sister's been in Rome for two days and I hadn't heard from her, which worried me, so I started filling her inbox with messages. She finally called and said her ex-fiancé showed up."

"Oh, did they make up?" Mia's hands went to her heart.

"I doubt it. Nicki said he texted her constantly when she was in Paris, telling her he wants to talk to her, but she told him to leave her alone. Now he's showed up in person."

"How did he know where she is?" Mia asked.

"This was supposed to be their honeymoon, and of course he has an itinerary and list of the hotels." Mimi shook her head.

"I can't believe he has the nerve to follow her," Mia's eyes widened.

"He's unbelievable—and not in a good way. Nicki said he booked a room in the same hotel and surprised her this morning at breakfast."

"What's she doing now?"

"Right now she's sitting in her room looking out the window, spitting mad."

"She needs to leave immediately," Mia said without hesitation. "Tell her to come now instead of in a few days."

Would Ray try to follow Nicki to Tuscany? Mimi wouldn't put it past him. But then she shook the thought off. Ray didn't know anything about Jake or where his family lived. Unless he called Mimi's parents and boohooed to them. Which, of course, wouldn't get him anywhere.

"Call Nicki. Now," Mia said. "Tell her not to worry about getting a train ticket online, she can buy one at the station."

"Maybe she can exchange the one she already had for the end of the week to today."

"Maybe. Maybe not," Mia shrugged. "We need to know when

she arrives in Florence so we can send someone to pick her up. And since we don't know where Jake is, I'll send Tonio."

Mimi laughed. "You can't expect Tonio to drop everything and leave work just like that. I can drive if someone lends me a car."

Mia tut-tutted, "Of course I can expect it." She smirked at Mimi and snapped her fingers. "If you call Nicki now, she'll be here in time for dinner!"

"You're amazing!" Mimi hugged Mia and laughed. "But perhaps I should check with your mom first."

"Nonsense, she loves to have guests. Now let me call Tonio."

A few minutes and a torrent of words later, accompanied by frantic hand gestures, Mia said, "He doesn't mind driving if we need his help."

Mimi was speechless. She hit gold when she found Jake—and his entire family—and wished with her whole heart that Nicki would find the same.

She speed-dialed Nicki and gave her the short-and-sweet of Mia's suggestion while Mia tapped rapidly on her own phone before waving it in Mimi's face.

"Nic, Mia's showing me the train schedule. There's an *italotreno* leaving Rome at two forty, one at two fifty-five, and another one at three forty. Let us know which one you're on. I'll pick you up."

"It's only 1 p.m., so I should be able to make the two fifty-five train," Nicki said. "That gives me enough time to get to the train station and figure out how to exchange or buy a new ticket. On second thought, I'm sure the hotel can arrange that for me."

"I wouldn't involve the hotel, Nic. Someone might let it slip to Ray when he asks for you. The less he knows about where you are the better."

"Good point. You're right. Text me a screenshot of the timetable, and I have all the info I need to look it up. Now I'm packing my stuff."

"Okay, text me when you're on the train."

"Will do. And... Thank you, Mim."

"Love you. Take care."

Mia reached into one of her cargo shorts pockets and gave Mimi a set of keys. "Here are my car keys. It's relatively clean inside and I just filled the tank." She smirked, "Now I've got to go back to work, since we can't all play hooky."

Accepting the keys, Mimi hugged Mia again, "Thank you so much!" Which Mia only waved off.

Speed walking toward the house, Mimi started a mental to-do list: 1) Get the guest room ready to make sure Nicki's early arrival didn't dump more work on Francesca's shoulders, 2) Let Jake know why she was driving to Florence, 3) Text her parents to tell them about Nicki's change of plans, although Nicki might also let them know.

About an hour later, she was unlocking Mia's VW T-Cross when Jake's car came to a stop next to her and he jumped out. "Where are you going?"

"Didn't you get my message? I'm driving to Florence to pick up Nicki." She tossed her purse and water bottle on the passenger seat.

"No, I didn't." He pulled out his phone. "Shit, my battery died. But what's going on?"

As much as she wanted to know where he'd been, she also itched to get on the road. "Ray showed up in Rome and is being a pest. Mia said Nicki should come here earlier than planned."

"Of course!"

"Her train comes in around four thirty, but I thought I'd leave early to allow for traffic or construction."

"Do you want me to drive you?"

"No, thanks, I'm fine. And maybe she needs some girl time to talk. Apparently he's been harassing her since she arrived in Paris."

"That has to stop!" He narrowed his eyes and displayed the same don't-mess-with-me expression she'd seen on Martha's Vineyard when he was being protective.

Jake grabbed her around her waist, and she snuggled closer to him. "Where did you go?" she asked. "Mia said she saw you leave in a hurry. Everything okay?"

"Yes, everything's fine. I had an unexpected errand to run. Did you miss me?" He nuzzled her neck.

"I did. It's unusual for you to take off like that." Then she snickered, "Actually, Mia wondered first where you went and asked me. That's how I found out you had left."

"Mia needs to mind her own business."

"She helped me a lot with Nicki an hour ago. But maybe it happens all the time that you have to run somewhere, and I just didn't realize it."

"Nah, it was an unusual circumstance." He kissed her. "I'll fill you in another time."

Mimi laughed. "Great, now I'll be playing guessing games while I'm driving."

"Then I should probably come with you. I don't want you to be distracted while driving."

"And you think I'd be less distracted with you in the car?" Her arms went around his neck. He felt so good, so solid, so safe. *They* felt wonderful together, the way their bodies met and molded.

"It wouldn't matter if you were distracted, because I'd be driving."

Mimi laughed again, "Mia would say you're being all macho if you automatically assume you'd be driving."

"Don't listen to her. She doesn't know how a man in love feels." Did she imagine it, or did his eyes get bigger, as if they wanted to swallow her? They definitely left no doubt about the truth behind his statement.

"I've got to go," she whispered.

"Then you're going in the wrong direction, *bella*," he muttered while he cupped her butt with both hands.

"What is it about you that I love you so much?" she asked against his mouth while she pressed herself closer, loving the solid proof of his response.

"I'd like to think it's everything, but we can discuss it in more," he cleared his throat, "depth later. When I have you all to myself."

"Another macho line," Mimi whispered. "But I'll remind you."

It took a lot of willpower to break away from him. "I'll text you when I'm in Florence. And you'd better charge your phone, babe."

As soon as Mimi spotted Nicki, she met her halfway and pulled her into a bear hug, then held her sister at arm's length—immediately alarmed by the dark rings under her sister's eyes.

Nicki nipped any questions in the bud when she said, "Let's not discuss Ray right now, okay? I had lots of fun in Paris and wish I could say the same for Rome. Too bad I couldn't do everything I planned, but it's also cool that I get to spend a few extra days in Tuscany."

There'd be plenty of time to talk, and Ray's bruised ego—what other reason could there be for why he trailed after Nicki like a dog in heat?—shouldn't be allowed to overshadow this trip.

After an easy drive back, Mimi turned off the main road and wound her way through the vineyard to the farmhouse, noticing that everything was as familiar to her now as their neighborhood at home. And it tickled her when she heard Nicki's sharp inhale when she brought Mia's car to a stop.

"Welcome to Bellini's Winery," Mimi said as they climbed out of the car. "Isn't it gorgeous?"

"Yes, it is. I mean, you already heard me gushing at every turn of the road once we left the *autostrada*, but this is just...wow."

Nicki spun in a circle, covered her heart with her hand and asked, "And who is that cutie?"

Mimi spotted a few men sitting under a pergola, enjoying a beer as they always did at the end of the workday. On her first day she asked Jake why they didn't drink some of the table wine they produced, and he explained that it was common to drink beer, because it was both cold and refreshing.

"Those are Emilio, Dante, and Cesare. I'll introduce you to

everyone—if not today, then tomorrow."

"No, I didn't mean the guys," Nicki did a double turn, "even though the younger one is kind of cute. I wouldn't close my bedroom door in his face."

"I'm afraid Cesare is used to that reaction from women," Mimi said easily, recognizing that he would be Nicki's type. But his reputation preceded him, no matter how nice he was, and she'd better give Nicki a heads-up.

Mimi called a greeting to the men, not missing that only Emilio and Dante replied, while Cesare sat up straighter, his eyes following Nicki.

"I was talking about the dog," Nicki twisted her hair in a messy top bun and walked toward the fawn Boxer snoozing near the farmhouse's entrance.

"That's Geppetto," Mimi crouched down and scratched behind his ears. "He's the winery dog and a big lovebug. Huh, Geppetto? That's what you are, right?"

"What's a winery dog?" Nicki held out the back of her hand to Geppetto, who graciously lifted his head, sampled a noseful, and approved Nicki's scent.

"Winery dogs are used to keep critters and deer away from the grapes, and some can also sniff out pests. But you can see how well this one's doing his job. You can mostly find him out here waiting for his daily ration of attention from B&B guests and winery visitors."

"I'll pat you every day," Nicki promised, and got a big yawn in response, as if there was no other conceivable response.

"And you're already his new best friend," Jake strolled out of the house. He greeted Nicki with a peck on each cheek, then pulled Mimi into his embrace. "I missed you, *bella*."

"I was only gone four hours." She melted against him, having missed him equally.

"Four too-long hours," he muttered before he kissed her soundly.

Niki rolled her eyes. "Sheesh, how are you two going to make it through the next three months?"

Chapter 45

Mimi

Mimi turned off Mia's car in front of the farmhouse but didn't get out. She dangled the key fob on one finger and said, "I can't decide whether I liked Volterra or Pisa better."

"Hands-down Volterra for me. Just imagine... The town goes back to the Etruscans, and here we are, thousands of years later, strolling through the ancient streets and eating ice cream," Nicki said. "Which was to die for. The ice cream, that is."

"It was," Mimi said. "By the way, help me think of a thank-you for Mia for letting us use her car."

"Wouldn't it be fun if she and Tonio would visit us in Boston, and we could show them around?"

"Yes, it would, but I still want to give her something. Any suggestions are highly appreciated." Mimi collected her water bottle and purse from behind the driver's seat when she glimpsed Cesare lingering between a cluster of the tall cypresses—so characteristic of the Tuscan landscape—at the end of the driveway.

"Your fan club's waiting," she chuckled. "He better not let Francesca catch him smoking near the guest house."

Nicki turned her head and waved through the open window

before she looked at Mimi again. "He asked me to go to a party in town with him after supper tonight. Do you mind?"

"You're twenty-seven, newly single, and on vacation. Three good reasons to do whatever you want." She didn't need to remind Nicki of Cesare's playboy reputation, they had that chat already, but added, "Just be careful."

"I am," Nicki said. "And it's not as if we're having a wild affair. But he's nice, and if I'm not around, you and Jake can enjoy an evening alone. You don't have many more before we leave."

"Wait a minute!" Mimi dropped everything in her lap. "Are you saying you're going out with Cesare because you think you're in our way?"

"No, of course not. He told me about a festival in town tonight, where people walk through the streets wearing medieval clothes, play drums, and present their neighborhood flags, and it sounds fun. He said we're meeting a group of his friends there and hanging out at a bar afterward."

Mimi picked up her bottle, purse, and sneakers again. Maybe she and Jake could also go to the festival, but she didn't mention it now, lest Nicki would think she planned to spy on her.

"Okeydokey, then," she chirped. "Time to go in and help Francesca with dinner."

Nicki also collected her things and said, while she climbed out of the car, "I've never seen you spend as much time in a kitchen as you do here. Wait till Mom hears and puts you on kitchen duty."

Mimi laughed out loud. "She won't hear about it unless you tattle. And you're right, I never had much interest in cooking. But it just happened. I love all the fresh produce." She didn't bother locking the car...nobody did on the farm during the day.

"I wish I could come back in the spring, when Francesca plants the seedlings and everything starts growing," she mused.

Nicki stopped walking. "Nobody's holding you back, Mimi. A blind man can see how much you love being here. And I know you didn't want to return home last May. You could move to Italy, be with Jake, and do what you did in Verona."

"What I did in Verona?" Mimi asked slowly, as if the late afternoon sun didn't only warm her face but shrank her ability to comprehend simple English words.

"You can tutor again, maybe in Siena or Florence, and you'd be much closer to Jake."

When Cesare strolled over, Mimi was tempted to hug him. Because she didn't have a reply for Nicki.

AN UNEXPECTEDLY COOL BREEZE MADE MIMI SHIVER AS SHE leaned her head on Jake's shoulder and looked around, creating a series of mental photos to provide her with strength and comfort during the upcoming weeks.

Through the kitchen window, she could see Mia and Francesca putting away leftover food. Next to Mimi, Tonio chatted amicably with Dante and Fausto around the firepit, and Cesare and Nicki had taken off in his Fiat Panda not long ago.

"Want to go check out the grapes, *bella*? I think the sunset will be spectacular tonight." Jake's whispered words brushed her skin and triggered a flood of goose bumps.

If they ever needed a code for sex or just alone time, "check out the grapes" would be it. Even though she'd been effectively cured of outdoor sex after Jake mentioned the scorpions and snakes—and no matter how often he assured her they weren't poisonous and stayed away from people—the allure of rolling around on a blanket among the vines had dulled dramatically.

Mimi smiled, the cool breeze forgotten and replaced by the warmth spreading through her. "I was just gonna ask if we should also watch the festival in town. What Nicki told me sounded fascinating."

"The festival isn't only today," he kissed her forehead. "Tomorrow's the cookout with my friends, but we can go on Sunday."

"Oh. Nicki made it sound like it's only today."

"No, it's going on all the summer, mostly for the benefit of tourists."

"I see. Well, I hope Cesare doesn't think she's easy to trick. I'd be pissed if he played Nicki." And she would let him know it, too. The last thing they needed was another guy who thought Nicki was gullible.

Luckily they hadn't heard a peep out of Ray since Nicki fled Rome—except for one text message asking where she was, and to which Nicki replied that it was none of his business, but using more colorful language.

"He probably skipped that detail, but it's still something worth seeing. I should've thought of it earlier. And don't worry about Nicki being with him. He might enjoy the company of many women, but he would never force himself on anyone." He cleared his throat. "He reminds me of myself, before I met you. Of course, I'm a changed man now."

"I'm so glad to hear that," Mimi grinned, "And of the two of you, I must say you're the better-looking one."

"Phew," he laughed and took her hand. "On that note, let's go for a walk so you can have my good looks all to yourself."

"Ooh, what am I going to do with so much gorgeousness?" she snickered and let him pull her to her feet.

"Surprise me!"

And, *darn*, those two words sent another wave of warmth through her, this time pooling between her legs.

She tossed her light scarf over one shoulder, slid her phone in her skirt pocket, and they took off for their habitual evening walk. But when they reached their usual spot, Jake kept walking instead of sitting down on the stone wall.

"Where are we going?"

"You'll see." Jake breathed a kiss on Mimi's lips and marched on, his thumb rubbing the back of her hand.

"I guess I will," she murmured, startled by his non-answer.

He led her down a utility road—more a wide path, really—through the vines, up the hill, past an old storage shack that looked as if the next strong storm could blow it over, and toward a solid line of tall chestnut trees, when Mimi spotted a wrought iron table and two matching chairs.

"How come I haven't seen this before?" she asked while Jake steered straight to the setup, glancing over his shoulder several times.

"Are you expecting someone?" she laughed, "or is something chasing you?"

"Just checking the time," he said.

"Isn't that what your watch is for?" she asked—but didn't get an answer.

Reaching the table, Jake pulled out a chair and gestured for her to sit. "Please excuse me for a moment, and don't go anywhere."

"Where would I go?" she asked as he disappeared behind the massive trunk of the ancient chestnut tree. Leaves rustled nearby, making her wonder which creatures were already out for their nightly hunt.

She twisted in her seat to see what Jake was doing, but only heard more rustling and clinking of what sounded like—ice cubes? Before she could ask, he emerged with a bottle of prosecco and two glasses.

"We've got to hurry," he nodded to the fiery sphere that almost touched the hills in the distance, bathing the landscape in surreal light.

The splendor in front of her—combined with Jake's nervous energy—baffled her, so she simply folded her hands in her lap and watched while he quickly opened the bottle and filled both flutes. Still standing, he handed her one and penetrated her with his eyes, making her knees quiver.

"To sunsets and sunrises, and to us." He clinked his glass to hers, creating a lovely, angelic chime, then raised his glass to his lips.

Before Mimi could take a sip, the last rays of sunlight—blood-orange red and beyond beautiful—hit her glass, sending sparkles everywhere.

She gasped and got up.

These are the colors from my vision in Venice.

Colors that would forever symbolize her happiness.

She turned to Jake, who watched her intently, then gulped down his prosecco and set the empty glass on the table. He abruptly wrapped an arm around her waist and pulled her to him, the glass in her hand tipping over and sloshing the prosecco on the ground that had produced it. "Mimi..."

"What are you doing?" His behavior confused her, and this had to be the weirdest sunset they ever watched together.

"I want to ask you to stay with me, but I know you can't," Jake said solemnly.

She opened her mouth, but he put a finger over her lips.

"I want to give you the sun and moon and the stars, but I guess sunsets are the best I can do." He looked at her with such tenderness, she was afraid her heart would burst with love.

He shifted, glanced away, and then looked back at her. "I want to ask you to marry me, but I can't."

She couldn't stifle a gasp, and her glass shattered on the ground.

Chapter 46

Jake

WHEN HE SAW HER EYES ALMOST JUMP OUT OF THEIR SOCKETS and felt her stiffen in his arms, he knew he'd messed up. He had envisioned this evening as being very different and wanted to push the rewind button.

Instead, his mind replayed his last words, *I want to ask you to marry me, but I can't.*

What an idiot he was! He deserved a slap on his face, but sweet Mimi was still here. Frozen, and with glass shards at her feet, but here.

"I'm sorry, *bella*. That came out wrong." He hugged her closer, realizing too late that she probably didn't need to feel his ill-timed hard-on right now, when what she really needed was clarification.

He couldn't believe that he had butchered one of the most important moments in their lives. Guiding her onto a chair, Jake grabbed the other one and positioned it to face her. Their knees touched, and he felt the warmth radiating off her.

He said, "I want you in my life. Now and forever. In good times and in bad times. But when I said I can't marry you, I meant not right this moment."

Jake gripped her hand with his clammy one.

"Under Italian law, foreigners can marry in a civil ceremony within two or three days, but I assume you don't travel with your birth certificate, which we'd need for the marriage to be legal."

He raised one hopeful eyebrow in question—people traveled with the strangest things—but her regretful head shake bummed him out, nonetheless.

Still, the smirk she—unsuccessfully—tried to hide gave him hope that he hadn't completely screwed up. "Your knowledge of Italian law is astounding, but sadly I had no way to know I'd need it."

The smirk turned into a smile so sweet it was like honey sliding down his throat, and encouraged him. "Maybe I should've started with this." He pulled a ring out of his pocket and presented it to her.

"This is a promise ring. The promise of us. To pledge our commitment to each other." His heart pounded in his throat. He couldn't breathe and itched to loosen the invisible, nonexistent necktie that slowly choked him.

"Mimi?" he whispered. "What do you say?"

When she remained silent, he wanted to bang his head against the fat tree trunk behind her. The chestnut had sheltered his tree-house and so many other childhood memories, and he'd hoped it would be a pillar of his future when he pledged his love to Mimi beneath its canopy of thick branches and broad leaves.

"Say what? You didn't ask me anything," Mimi fake-whispered back with a fire in her eyes that matched the heat in his chest. "You only told me several things you can't do."

Man, he was so out of his league!

College and law school had taught him how to work out elaborate business contracts, set up sometimes despicable prenuptial agreements, and other, often pitiful, documents of life and death.

But they hadn't taught him how to ask the most important question of his life! Good thing this was the only marriage pledge... because it wasn't a proposal yet...he'd ever make.

Consider this the dress rehearsal for when you propose for real, and make sure to nail it then.

In the distance, church bells tolled when she wiggled her fingers and asked, "Can I try it on?"

"Does that mean you'll say yes?" Finally able to breathe, he slid the ring on her finger with shaky hands.

"Of course I'll say yes," she beamed at him. "If you ask me, whenever the right moment comes," she sassed his earlier words back to him and twisted the ring around, running a finger over the delicate swirls. "Is this the ring...how...where did you find it?"

"The other day, when I took off for a couple of hours, I went to a local jeweler and asked him to contact the store in Florence, and they overnighted it to them. We'll go shopping for a proper engagement ring once I'm home for good."

"Home for good?"

"Fausto and I had a long conversation the other day. I'm leaving Italy after the harvest. There are so many things you and I need to discuss, like where we'll live or what I'll do for work, but my place is with you. Everything else is up for grabs."

He cradled her face in his hands. "I love you more than words can say."

"No more than I love you."

He pulled her out of her chair and into his lap. "I can't wait to make you mine," he said and nibbled on her earlobe.

"I *am* yours," Mimi said, wrapping her arms around his neck.

But Jake knew he wouldn't rest until they'd both signed on the dotted line.

Chapter 47

Jake

Two days before Mimi's inevitable departure, Jake woke hours after they fell asleep to find the moon casting his room in a cold, eerie light. Automatically, he reached for Mimi, but his hand hit the empty mattress just when a breeze rustled the curtains, giving away the partially open door to his balcony.

He slipped out of bed and found Mimi on the balcony, bundled up in a cotton throw blanket, sitting in one of his two canvas folding chairs.

"What are you doing out here, *bella*?"

"I couldn't sleep, my mind's going a thousand miles a minute," she looked up at him and attempted a smile.

"The idiom's a hundred miles an hour," he grinned, knowing she'd get his humor.

"I know, but mine goes faster."

"Anything I can help you with?" He leaned his shoulder against the wall. She looked so vulnerable in the pale, blueish light, but looks could be deceiving, as he'd learned before.

"Maybe," she got up and walked past him into his room. Instead of going back to bed, she sat down on his love seat.

"Have you ever seen tumbleweeds race across the plains?" she asked, but didn't wait for a reply. "Nobody knows where they're coming from or where they're going, and they move at the mercy of the wind."

When he opened his mouth, she chuckled, "Don't worry, I'm not losing my marbles and comparing myself with a noxious, invasive plant. My mind's just like a million threads of thoughts tangled up like a huge ball of...tumbleweeds. But unlike a tumbleweed, I don't want to be at the mercy of something—or someone—else. I want to be in control of my own life."

He wasn't quite sure about where this was going but his intuition told him to let her continue following the threads of her thoughts.

"When I was lying awake tonight, I remembered what you said after you gave me the promise ring, something about making me yours.'"

"Do you feel you have to give up a part of yourself if you're with me?" he could hear his voice shake.

"No, the opposite!" She shook her head vehemently. "A healthy relationship isn't about imposing one's will or opinions on the partner, but complementing each other. You're completing my life without making me feel caged in or manipulated.

"And as one thought led to another in my tangled mind," she whirled a finger on the side of her head, making his heart clench with love, "I played around with our names and eventually I thought, 'If I belong with Jake, then I'm Bellini's Mimosa. And I love it, and I love you."

He couldn't stop himself from taking her sweet face in his hands and kissing her. *Bellini's Mimosa.* Damn right she was!

After their kiss, she said, "Another thing you said was that you want me to stay with you. Now. Here. And there's nothing I'd like better than to do it. But I need to bring closure to old business, which includes facing Derek."

Yup, the conversation went exactly where he'd suspected. The bastard's name brought Jake's blood to a different kind of boil than when he kissed Mimi only moments ago.

"And that's where you're going to come in handy." Her smirk left no doubt in his mind that she'd chosen her words intentionally.

"Glad to hear you need my hands," he tried to joke with her.

"Now I've reported Derek to the police and started an investigation, I expect the school board will make my life living hell when we go back in August. I'm not scared of them, but I need to be prepared and need to know my rights. And since you happen to be a lawyer..."

"I'm doing everything I can to help you. As I told you before." *Though I'd still prefer you tell them where to shove their arrogant, unacceptable behavior.*

"Thank you."

Sensing she had laid the topic to rest, for tonight at least, he took a deep breath and glanced at the neon green digital numbers on his alarm clock, torn between his need for a couple of hours more sleep or continuing their talk. Because he also had things on his mind, things about their future.

But—in good attorney fashion—he decided to compromise and settle. Start with a short rundown tonight and wrap it up in more detail another time.

"Seems like you're not the only one who's been doing a lot of pondering," he said.

"Let's hear it."

"It's about when I come back to the States." He looked at her, and when she nodded, continued, "To keep it short... I've been thinking about my uncle Charles's property—"

"Where your dad wants to build an inn and have you manage it."

"Yup. I still don't see myself as an innkeeper, but I have some ideas I want to toss around with Carla and Matt. You and I will discuss the details another time, not tonight, because there's too much at stake and it can't be rushed, but I promise to fill you in on everything before I talk to them."

She only nodded.

"Aaannnddd..." he reached for her left hand and played with her new ring. "I've also toyed with the possibility of going back to practicing law. Which I can do anywhere in Massachusetts."

"Jake?" Mimi said quietly, "can I say something?"

"Of course, silly."

"All of what you said sounds good, and you're right, none of this should be rushed, but can we live on Martha's Vineyard?"

"And your job?"

"I don't want to back out of a commitment, so I'd like to wait and see how things are going at the school in the fall. But come spring, I'll start looking for teaching positions on Martha's Vineyard for the following year."

He swallowed hard, trying to get rid of the lump in his throat. She just paved the path to their future, and he couldn't wait to set the other wheels in motion.

Chapter 48

Mimi

FOUR WEEKS LATER, MIMI LISTENED TO THE DOOR CLOSE behind her for the last time ever. She stopped in the middle of the wide walkway at the sight of the first red maple leaves on the trees and opened her arms wide.

She did it! And it felt *amazing*!

As much as she had wanted to make it work, but being called into the Headmasters's office like a naughty child and having to listen to their sermon about "try and get along with Derek" were the proverbial last straw. Of course, the cowards waited until the end of teacher training and professional development to have the chat with her, just before the scions of Boston's elite filled the hallways again starting next week.

The look on her supervisors' faces when she calmly got up after their rant, reached into her purse, withdrew the prepared letter —*thank you, Jake, for your foresight*—and said goodbye was priceless.

Mimi had to suppress a chuckle at the memory of them sitting neatly lined up behind the enormous walnut conference table, only missing puffy Shakespearean collars.

"Mimi?"

She turned around and saw one of her co-workers coming up behind her. "Hey, Sarah, what's up?" They weren't close friends, but friendly with each other.

"You quit?" Sarah asked.

"Wow, that didn't take long to start making the rounds," Mimi said. "Yes, I handed in my resignation. Effective immediately. I told them I'll collect my accumulated sick days. How did you hear?"

"Erin was in the office when Bill the Almighty hurled your letter on the secretary's desk and said to make sure to have a substitute lined up for you."

Mimi smirked at Sarah's use of the unofficial nickname for their boss. And Erin, another English teacher, was known to have her ear to the ground. It didn't bother Mimi anymore. News and gossip always spread like wildfire, and now everyone would know before the end of the day.

"I want to congratulate you for having the balls to do what you did. Go after Derek, I mean. I wish," she looked over her shoulder, then back at Mimi, "I'd had the same courage."

"What do you mean?" asked Mimi, goose bumps erupting on her arms.

"He tried something similar with me a few months ago," Sarah blushed.

"Oh, no. I wish I'd known!"

"It happened while you were away, and wasn't something I wanted to broadcast, especially not after the way the administration treated you last year. I kept quiet because I need this job, but I'm beginning to second-guess my decision."

Mimi shook her head, "I'm so sorry, Sarah. Listen, you shouldn't have to put up with any of that crap. It's not too late to report it. If there's anything I can do to help, let me know."

"If your case goes to court, I'm willing to testify. Even though I wasn't there when he manhandled you, I can speak up in your favor and share my experience. And," she looked over her shoulder again,

"I heard rumors about him also doing it to a substitute teacher, but it will be harder to find her."

"We should stay in touch," Mimi said.

She hadn't intended to start an avalanche when she reported Derek, but if what Sarah said was true, they needed to team up, because there was power in numbers. Jake would advise her on the best strategy when she called him later.

"Absolutely," Sarah nodded. "What are you doing now?"

"Looking for another job, I guess." She'd brought along the resignation letter as a safety net, so she was fully prepared for a showdown. But it ended up being only the first step, and she didn't have any second or third steps figured out.

"Are you going back to Italy to your boyfriend?"

The thought of surprising Jake tickled her, but she didn't want to get in the way of the harvest. Even though she could entertain herself very well while Jake and the others brought in the grapes... And maybe Francesca would be grateful for an extra set of hands to help feed the team of year-round and seasonal staff...

"No. As much as I want to, but I can't jet back and forth all the time. And he's coming home next month."

In six long weeks, a little voice whispered in her ear.

Would you go if Jake asked you to come? the voice didn't give up.

Let's discuss it later, she replied to the little voice.

Mimi hugged Sarah, "If I go, I'll send you a postcard."

———

Two weeks later Mimi was browsing job openings on her phone and sipping an iced latte while sitting at one of Paloma's outdoor tables. With schools and colleges in session again, the café was busy, and she scarcely had a chance to say hi to her friend when she ordered her meal.

So far, the job search had been unsuccessful, but Mimi was in no rush. She could always sign up as a substitute teacher until she found another permanent position.

"I'm surprised to see you here," Paloma said as she pulled out a chair.

"Where did you expect me to be?" Mimi put her phone away.

"In Tuscany, sipping *vino*, watching your bare-chested boyfriend sweating and laboring, filling bucket after bucket with lush, juicy grapes."

"I don't know what movie you watched, but when I was there, nobody worked shirtless. And I'm impressed with your graphic descriptions, even though you didn't give my boyfriend," she made air quotes, "any attributes."

"Don't tell me you don't picture Jake wearing only a pair of low-cut jeans, flexing his biceps. You can fill in those attributes better than I can."

Mimi chuckled. She might have had a fantasy or two along that line.

"Ha! I knew it!" Paloma clapped her hands. "You're blushing, Mim."

"Okay, you win, now let's talk about something else." Mimi hid behind her beverage and sipped slowly, glancing at Paloma over the rim of her extra-large to-go cup. "Carla reminded me the other day about the girls' weekend we talked about in July."

"I have next week off and zero plans."

Mimi nodded. "Works for me too. Want me to text her and ask?"

"Sure. We're staying overnight, right?"

"Yes, absolutely." She typed a short message to Carla and received a prompt reply.

"She says she's not working Thursday and Friday," Mimi said.

"I'm in. Where are we staying there?"

"Umm...good point." Mimi tapped her finger to her chin. "I don't think we can rent a cottage for a night or two on such short notice, but we can try. Should I ask Carla if they have vacancies at the hotel? We only need one room."

"That's iffy. I don't want her to feel obliged to let us stay at a special rate or even free," Paloma said and took her own cell phone from her pocket. "Let's check other hotel options."

"That's just as weird, since they run a hotel." Mimi's phone vibrated in her hand. "It's Carla again. Ha! Problem solved! She writes we're welcome to stay in the guest room at the house." She looked questioningly at Paloma, who nodded. "It's a nice room, I've seen it."

Yeah, and that's all you did since you slept in Jake's room across the hall...

Thankfully Paloma didn't comment on the blush that most likely covered Mimi's face because of the memories and only said, "Sure, if you think it's okay with the family. I mean, you're kind of family since you're sort of engaged to Jake. But they don't know me."

"That's a lot of kind-ofs and sort-ofs..." Mimi laughed. "But Carla wouldn't have offered if she thought her parents would mind."

She typed back that they appreciated and accepted the invite. Then she looked straight at Paloma, "And you know Jake and I aren't officially engaged."

"What do you call it when a man asks a woman to marry him? You told me those were his words. And you said yes."

"Yes, but he also said he'll propose properly when he's here."

"Does it make a difference to you? He asked. You answered in the affirmative. You're wearing his ring." Paloma pointed to Mimi's left hand, as if she needed a reminder of where the ring was. "Voilà! Engaged. Have you decided on a date for the wedding?"

"Whoa, hold your horses."

"Mim, I've known you for how long?" She held up a hand, "Don't answer. Long enough to know you've given it plenty of thought. So?"

"Ugh, okay." Mimi looked down at the tiny diamonds sprinkling the sunlight. "Maybe in May on the anniversary of the day we first met in Venice."

"There! Was that hard to admit? And why do I have to pull it out of you bit by bit? You know you can tell me anything," Paloma leaned back in her chair. "Where would you like to get married?"

Since she'd started babbling, there was no need to hold back with the rest. Yes, she had already given the subject quite a lot of thought.

"Just Jake and I in Italy, and then have a huge party on Martha's Vineyard with family and friends." She narrowed her eyes at Paloma. "But we haven't talked about any of it yet, so don't you dare say anything to anyone."

"Who would I tell?"

"Who knows? You can be a bit chatty at times," Mimi swirled the drink in her cup and listened to the ice cubes rattling. "I'd like you to be my maid of honor, Pickle. Or wedding witness, in our case, because we'll need two witnesses for a civil ceremony, and, under Italian law, they can't be family members."

"How do you know the technicalities? I thought you hadn't discussed it with Jake yet."

Mimi shrugged one shoulder and gave Paloma her best *seriously?* look. "Google, of course. So, what do you think?"

"It will be a privilege to be your maid of honor, my friend. I'll even brush up on my Italian for the occasion."

"You don't speak Italian," Mimi laughed.

"Eh, but some Spanish, so I'll just tweak it a little. And if there's a problem, I'll flash my goodies at the court official to distract him," Paloma laughed with her. Then she asked, "Who is Jake's best man?"

"I don't know, I told you we haven't had this conversation yet. You and I are a step or two ahead. And let's hope we're not jinxing it."

"Oh, stop it. You've got that man wrapped around your pinkie."

"Pickle, please!" Mimi regretted telling Paloma anything.

Chapter 49

Mimi

MIMI AND PALOMA STEPPED OFF THE RHODE ISLAND FAST Ferry, took synchronized, deep breaths of the briny air, and reached for their wind-tousled hair.

"I should cut my hair super short," Paloma muttered. "This mane is becoming a nuisance."

"Do you have any idea how many women envy you those curls?"

"I don't care. They don't have to deal with them daily. And most of the time I have to tie my hair back anyway because of work." Paloma wrapped a bright green headband around her hair, holding her black curls at bay. "Ah, better. Which way?" She stuck a pair of massive sunglasses on her nose.

Mimi looked around and shrugged. "I don't know."

"Huh? Are you kidding me?"

"Well, I sort of assumed we'd arrive at the Steamship ferry dock." Noticing a street sign declaring them to be on Circuit Avenue, she said, "Okay, I remember this is one of the main drags. Let's follow the street."

"How far is it to the Bellinis'?" Paloma swung her duffel bag over her shoulder and peeked over the rim of her sunglasses at Mimi.

Mimi tapped on her phone, then said, "From here, about fifteen to twenty minutes."

"Maybe we shouldn't have declined Nicki's gracious offer to pick us up," muttered Paloma.

"Oh, come on, it's September, not July and blistering hot." Mimi hoisted the handles of her own bag over her shoulder and started walking toward the gray-shingled houses to her right.

Ten minutes later a wave of nostalgia washed over her when they passed the street leading to Bellini's Cliff House Hotel—and the flower-named cottages. How could it be only a little over two months since she visited this town and her life was entirely overturned?

"Remind me to buy a gift certificate at the hotel while we're here. Nicki and I want to surprise Mom and Dad with a relaxing weekend. I should've gotten it in July, but I forgot."

"Ha! No, Mim, you didn't forget! You were distracted," Paloma grinned. "But now they have one more reason to come."

"Why?"

Paloma peeked over the top of her sunglasses. "A meet-and-greet to scope out the other in-laws?!"

"Where do you get those ideas?"

"I have lots of people coming and going at the café. And they looove to talk. And I looove to listen."

Before they could ring the bell at the Bellini home, Carla threw the door open and beckoned them in. "Come in, come in. I've got to hurry back to the kitchen."

Paloma dropped her bag in the foyer and raced after Carla. "What is this heavenly smell?" She sniffed more, reminding Mimi of a search dog who'd picked up a lead.

"I'm playing around with old recipes from my grandmother and great-grandmother. This one's a quiche with a twist," Carla said and pushed a fork into Paloma's hand. "Try it."

Mimi plopped down at the kitchen table, took a photo of the two women, and sent it to Jake.

FIVE MINUTES INTO GIRLS' WEEKEND AND THEY'RE ALREADY COOKING TOGETHER. GO FIGURE.

Her heart jumped when he replied instantly.

THAT GIVES YOU PLENTY OF TIME TO THINK OF ME AND MISS ME. AS I MISS YOU. ARE YOU SLEEPING IN MY ROOM? CAN I IMAGINE YOU UNDER MY DUVET, NAKED?

NO, SORRY. NOTHING TO SEE OR IMAGINE. CARLA ASSIGNED US THE GUEST ROOM.

TELL HER YOU WANT MY ROOM.

YEAH, RIGHT.

"What are you doing, Mim?" Paloma waved the fork in Mimi's face.

"Take that rake out of my face. And I'm texting Jake."

"Ask him about his best man." Paloma turned her attention back to the quiche, clearly not bothered by her lapse.

Mimi's jaw dropped. "Pickle, really?" She mimicked zipped lips.

"Oops," Paloma shrugged—and didn't look the least bit apologetic.

Carla licked her own fork and nodded to Mimi, "Which reminds me, can I see the non-engagement ring?"

Mimi held out her left hand and Carla nodded approvingly, "Very nice. As to Paloma's question, I bet my secret spice jar that he'll ask Damian to be his best man."

"Damian?" asked Mimi, momentarily drawing a blank.

"They've been friends since school, but with Jake in Italy and Damian living in California, they haven't seen each other as often as they used to. But Damian moved back recently."

"Oh, wait, is he the architect friend?" Mimi asked, glad to connect the dots. Now she remembered when Jake mentioned him regarding the inn.

"That's him." Carla elbowed Paloma, "He's cute. I crushed on him as a teenager, but he told me he wasn't into dating baby sisters."

"Does he know you're not a baby anymore?" Paloma said and

sampled more of the quiche. "Sage...there's definitely sage in here and...nutmeg. But there's an underlying hidden spice...hmm..."

"Yes! And, yes," Carla said. "I'm not telling the third one. You have to figure it out yourself."

"So, this sister-snob guy," Paloma said, and licked her lips. "What does he look like?"

"Think Hemsworth brothers."

"No thanks, not my type." Paloma's pinched face made Mimi chuckle. "He's all yours, sister."

"Great. Now I only need someone to tell him I've grown up," Carla said.

"You still want him after he snubbed you?" Paloma's eyes widened.

"I wouldn't say no to him..."

"Okay then. Should he and I ever cross paths, I'll tell him you wear lacy 36 B/C bras. Let's see if that wakes him up."

"Helllooo?" Mimi had followed the banter with amusement, but once Paloma started this kind of meddling, there was no stopping her. "When you're done with the horse show, what's our plan for the day?"

"You'll start with meeting Grandma. She wants to see you ladies after breakfast, or brunch, or whatever you're having," a deep voice said from the doorway.

Mimi whipped around, expecting to see Jake, only for her heart to plummet to the bottom of her belly.

Matt grinned. "Grandma heard there's another chef in the house and wants to meet you." He pointed a finger at Paloma.

"Me? Why?" Paloma asked.

Matt shrugged.

"You'll like her. Cora started the B&B that turned into Bellini's hotel," Mimi said. "She's told me many fascinating stories of the early years."

"Girls, let's eat," called Carla and put the baking dish on the kitchen table that was set for three. "Matt, you're not invited. This is a girls' weekend. Goodbye."

Matt ignored his sister's jab and said, "Ladies, I'll catch up with you later."

Mimi noticed his gaze lingering on Paloma, just as it had at the pool a few weeks ago. And Paloma's fork hovered in front of her open mouth while she stared at Matt.

Grilling her BFF later would be. So. Much. Fun!

AFTER BRUNCH MIMI, PALOMA, AND CARLA STROLLED together to the Daisy cottage.

"I didn't realize your grandparents were also here this week," said Mimi. "It'll be nice to see them again."

Carla said, "Grandma and Grandpa are usually here around the anniversary of Uncle Charles's death, which is coming up."

"Oh," was Mimi's not-very-intelligent reply. But sometimes it was impossible to find the right words on the spot.

"Are you sure she wants to meet with us?" asked Paloma.

"You heard Matt. He said she insists," said Carla as she stepped up onto the yellow cottage's porch, to be greeted by Jake's grandmother, who was sitting in a recliner with her purse next to her on the table, as if ready to go out. "Carlotta, did you bring a car? I want to show you something."

"Matt didn't mention a field trip," said Carla, "But I can run to the hotel and borrow Matt or Mom's car."

"Please do," said the old lady. "Bring your mother's, I don't want to twist my hips getting in and out."

Carla winked at Mimi and Paloma and said, "I'll be back in a jiffy."

"Emily, please come and sit. And this must be your friend?" asked Cora.

"Yes, ma'am, this is Paloma."

"It's a pleasure to meet you," said Paloma and held out her hand to Cora. "We just ate the most delicious quiche, and Carla told us it's a family recipe. She also mentioned you have a box full of handed-down recipes. I'd love to have a look at them if you don't mind."

"I don't mind at all. That's why I wanted to see you girls." Cora smiled like a cat watching a bird, tail twitching.

WHERE ARE WE? MIMI CLIMBED OUT OF THE SECOND-ROW SEAT. From her copilot's seat in the SUV, Cora had directed Carla to a huge clearing in the middle of nowhere.

In July, when Jake showed Mimi around Martha's Vineyard, she'd been amazed by how much of the island was still undeveloped —and appreciated the efforts to preserve the island's habitat.

But nothing she'd seen equaled the size of this spread of over-grown meadows, neglected vegetable patches, barns in different stages of shabbiness, all surrounded by tall oak, hickory, beech, and pine trees.

Images of Bellini's Winery popped up in her mind—the gentle slopes of cultivated vines, Francesca's lovingly tended garden, and the ancient chestnut trees standing sentinel over it all.

The similarities between the two properties were almost eerie—if one bothered to look past the first impression of the property in front of her.

"This land belonged to my son Charles," Cora's voice pulled Mimi out of her musings, and she followed the old woman as she walked slowly toward a Victorian-style home, which Mimi assumed must've once been the farmhouse. "It was his dream to make this into a comfortable inn and to build family-friendly cabins farther down near the pond."

Mimi fell in love as soon as she saw the brick-colored roof over the extra-wide front porch, and the gray cedar shingles. She was in awe of the house's simplicity, and grateful for the lack of fairytale ornamental woodwork that made some of the gingerbread cottages somewhat kitschy.

More unbidden comparisons to Tuscany popped up, this time to the farmhouse, all clean and well maintained.

Yet even after years of sitting empty, this weathered structure appeared solid, and had most likely withstood more than one stiff Nor'easter.

"Girls, come on inside, but watch out for loose floorboards and nails sticking out," Cora said, and tsk-tsked. "I should send James in here with a hammer to take care of them." She stepped over said traps with the agility of a woman half her age, as if being here rejuvenated her.

Mimi, Carla, and Paloma followed her, but before Mimi stepped onto the porch, her eyes were drawn to a raised area at the far end of the lot, and she walked toward the spot until she found herself in a thickening of knee-high weeds—and overgrown vines carrying thick, dark purple fruit.

She picked a grape and held it to her nose, then squeezed it and let the juice dribble on her tongue—while missing Jake so much it hurt.

On impulse, she took a selfie with the vine and the farmhouse as a backdrop and sent it to Jake—glad to have cell service in this rabbit hole.

"Mimi, what are you doing there? Come here," Paloma's voice drifted across the quiet land.

"Coming," Mimi called back and set off to join the others, then stopped halfway and did a slow three-sixty.

She wished she could see all this through Jake's eyes, to know what went through his mind when he stumbled upon this during the summer.

Did he notice the same beauty, potential, and promise as she did?

Or did he see it as nothing but a burden, a shackle, a way for his father to force him into taking charge by overseeing the manifestation of Charles's vision?

She knew Jake still struggled with what awaited him after he left Italy and that he had decided to table decisions about his professional future until he came home in a few weeks. He'd told her he refused to commit to his father unless he could stand one hundred percent behind it.

As if summoned, a text message from Jake arrived. *WHAT THE HECK ARE YOU DOING ON CHARLES'S LAND?*

Chapter 50

Jake

JAKE STEERED HIS RENTAL CAR DOWN THE SAME STREET HE SO reluctantly drove away from in July. This time he watched Mimi waving in her parents' driveway, getting bigger by the second, instead of getting smaller in the rearview mirror as she did then.

He didn't see the golden locusts and blood-red maple trees lining the street, and only paid minimal attention to the little princesses and ghosts who stretched Halloween by still wearing their costumes.

Jake only had eyes for the woman who welcomed him home.

As soon as he brought the SUV to a full stop and turned off the engine, he bolted out of the car and finally embraced Mimi again. Their bodies molded together just as he remembered, their lips locked, and it wasn't only her tears that dampened their faces.

"I missed you so much, *bella*," he said against her mouth. Having to extend his stay in Italy by ten days had stretched his nerves thinner than the silkiest fiber, to the point where even Mia stopped teasing him and let him brood in solitude.

"No more than I missed you."

Without letting go of her hand, he got his overnight and laptop bags out of the passenger seat.

"Where is everyone?" he asked when they entered the quiet house.

"Mom and Dad are still in Oak Bluffs. Instead of two days, they decided to stay the entire week," Mimi said. "And Nicki is spending the weekend with the ducklings." She leaned closer and said, with what she hoped was her most seductive voice, "So we have the house to ourselves."

His eyes roved over her face, down to her creamy chest, and he was bursting with the mad urge to undress her.

"I wasn't sure how hungry you'd be after the flight, so I made something to eat, but it's mostly finger food." Her fingertips caressed the back of his neck, driving him crazy.

"I'm ravenous for two things," he put his hands on her hips and let her feel one of the two. "A quick shower, and you. And satisfying my hunger for you may take a while." He watched her pupils dilate.

"Ooh, straightforward, Mr. Bellini, I like it. Why don't you go take your shower while I put a tray together?"

He breathed another kiss on her lips, then picked up his duffel and said, "Give me ten minutes, *bella*."

Standing under the jets of hot water, he forced away fantasies of Mimi's hands doing the lathering. Pent-up longing made it hard to think straight, and even though he hadn't intended to jump her within a half hour of arriving, he was helpless in the face of his desires. Finally he shut off the water, dried off, and wrapped a dry towel around his waist.

Stepping through the bathroom door, he found Mimi sitting on the edge of her bed, struggling with the cork of a prosecco bottle.

"*Bella*, don't hurt yourself," he stepped closer and, with a twist of his wrist, released the stubborn cork.

Mimi laughed. "I usually wrap a kitchen towel around the cork to pull it out but forgot to bring one." She tugged lightly on his towel, "Maybe I should've waited and used yours."

Jake sat next to her, poured the bubbly liquid into the flutes on the folding table she'd set next to the bed and handed one to her. She accepted it with her left hand, the Florentine ring sparkling in the dimmed, recessed light.

"To us, *cara mia*," he said as he kissed her, then sipped and set his glass down before leaning down to pull a square box out of his duffel bag.

Mimi covered her mouth to—unsuccessfully—stifle a giggle. "We haven't used condoms in the past. Why did you bring a box now?"

He retrieved a foil package and said, "I wanted to get through customs as fast as possible and didn't want to waste time declaring goods."

"I don't think Uncle Sam has an issue with travelers bringing condoms into the country," she said in a hushed voice.

"No, but maybe with this," he peeled the foil open and pulled out a ring.

She gasped and stared at the ring. "You, Mr. Attorney-at-Law, committed a crime? What if the airport scanners would've detected it?"

"I prefer to call it a minor...umm, gentlemen's...offense and hoped they're not in the habit of digging through protectives. Had they caught me, I'd have blamed lovesickness. Now, may I continue, please?"

Mimi nodded and glanced at the ring, then back at him.

He reached for her hand, "Emily Albizia, will you do me the honor of becoming my wife? To let me love you and spoil you and watch sunsets with you until we're old and doddering?"

She nodded.

"You have to say it," he said and raised his eyebrows.

"I gave you my answer in Italy, but I'm happy to say it again. Yes, I will marry you."

He slid the solitaire on her finger to join the Florentine ring and tilted her face up so their eyes met. "I know I said we'd go shopping for a ring together, but then I saw this one, and wanted to surprise you, and—"

"It's perfect."

Very slowly, he kissed her eyes and tasted the salty tears. His lips found hers, and when she returned his kiss, he gently pushed her down on the bed, draped an arm around her waist and lifted her up until her head rested on a pillow.

He took his time undressing her, his mouth touching where his fingers touched. Her gasps when she shuddered under his tongue spurred him on, but only when he was dangerously close to bursting from love and need did he slide into her.

Her tightness forced him to close his eyes and hold his breath, but waiting was impossible and, after a few deep thrusts, he released deep inside her, taking her again over the edge with him. They continued to move through the waves and prolonged the skyrocketing sensations before collapsing in each other's arms.

When he trusted himself to speak again, he asked, "Do you think we can eat some of the snacks you prepared?"

Mimi nodded and crawled over the bed, rewarding him with the loveliest view of her backside, and set the tray between them. They snacked, they drank prosecco, they talked and kissed, and when she yawned and nestled into his arms, he drifted off, knowing he was home for good.

"Jake?" her voice seeped through the veil between wakefulness and sleep.

"M-hm?"

"Remember the selfie I sent you from Charles's land?"

"M-hm."

"Can we go there this weekend?"

"We can do anything you want, *cara*."

"Why do you call me *cara* now instead of *bella*?"

He kissed the top of her head and shrugged, "Not every question has an answer."

Chapter 51

Mimi

MIMI WOKE UP TO THE SOUND OF RAIN. SHE COULD SEE DARK, menacing clouds through the partially open curtains but the window was dry. Something heavy hit the bathroom floor and was followed by a muffled Italian curse word, making her smile. *Jake!*

She sat up and stretched her arms in front of her. The round, bezel-set diamond dazzled, and she snapped a photo and sent it to Paloma, along with *I SAID YES.*

Paloma's reply came promptly. *I THOUGHT YOU ALREADY DID. BUT WOW. YOU'LL NEED A BODYGUARD FOR THAT BLING. CONGRATS.*

WHAT ARE YOUR PLANS FOR THE WEEKEND? WANNA JOIN US ON MV TO CELEBRATE?

MY PLAN IS TO STAY AS FAR AWAY FROM GREGORY AS POSSIBLE. FOR HIS OWN SAFETY.

Confused, Mimi hit the "call" button.

Instead of a greeting, Paloma started talking as soon as she picked up the phone. "The short version is that Gregory forgot to pay the rent for the café. And our slimebag of landlord was just waiting for that to happen. He wants to sell the building, but our contract wasn't up for renewal for another two years. Now Greg has played nicely into his hands, and we have to close the café. And it's only because Dickory can't keep his hands off his newest bimbo long enough to pay attention to our business."

"Whoa, take a breath, Pickle," Mimi put the phone on speaker, slipped on her yoga pants and sweater, then grabbed the phone and went to the kitchen. "There has to be a way to fix it. Can your land-lord evict you after a one-time occurrence?"

"That's the problem. It wasn't the first time, and idiot-me should've known better than to trust Greg. He had one—ONE—responsibility, and still managed to screw it up!" Mimi heard Paloma rummage around her kitchen. "I'm so tired of this shit and have been up all night tossing around ideas."

Paloma's sharp, "Ha, I got it!" made Mimi flinch, but before she could ask what her friend got, Paloma slammed a drawer shut—Mimi heard the silverware rattle and hoped it wasn't the professional chef knives—and said, "I'll buy a Wienermobile, paint it green, and drive around selling sandwiches."

Then she sang, "Pickle, pickle, little cuke, can you please make Gregory puke?"

Mimi cringed, then snickered, despite the situation being anything but funny. Jake's arms came around her from behind and she leaned against him and blew him an air kiss. "Seriously, Paloma, why don't you come to Oak Bluffs for a day or so? We'll be there all week."

"I might do that. Now I've got to run. Someone has to open the café—while we still have it."

"Okay, but call me."

"I will."

"Pickle swear?" Mimi asked, using one of Paloma's favorite pledges.

"Pickle swear!"

Mimi turned in Jake's arm and filled him in on the part of the conversation he hadn't overheard. "Can you help her?"

"I'll be happy to advise her, but I can't represent her if she decides to take this to court. I haven't been admitted to the bar in Rhode Island."

Mimi was so furious at Gregory, and so sad for Paloma, that she needed something to do with her hands, so she stepped out of Jake's embrace and started measuring coffee.

When she spilled the second measuring cup of coffee grounds on the counter instead of into the filter paper, Jake stilled her hands and asked, "Why don't you go take your shower while I start breakfast? We have plenty of time to discuss this later. I have friends who practice in Rhode Island, and we won't let Paloma deal with this alone."

———

LATE SUNDAY MORNING JAKE AND MIMI RUMBLED DOWN THE road to Charles's property.

"Remind me again why we're here?" he asked as he dodged hazardous tree branches scattered everywhere like Mikado sticks.

"No special reason, I only wanted to see it again," she said, suddenly reluctant to admit it was because she had dreamed—and not just once—of building a house on one side of the lot. "When I came here with Carla and Paloma, I wished you were with me."

"So did I, *bella*."

Jake parked next to the old house—Mimi's eyes immediately drawn to the yellow and golden leaves sprinkled over the brick-red roof—and jogged around the SUV to meet her. A mad wind whipped above their heads, trying to shake the last leaves off trees which now resembled raised fists, but through a few openings in the dark clouds, Mimi spotted promising patches of the special kind of blue sky that could only be found in the winter.

A good omen?

Mimi zipped up her fleece jacket, tightened the woolen scarf around her neck, and called, "Hello? We're baa-aack."

Jake draped an arm around her shoulders and laughed. "Who are you talking to?"

"No one, but I imagine Charles is watching us, wondering what's going to happen here."

"That makes two of us," Jake mumbled.

"Have you, Matt, and Carla decided how you want to respond to your dad's proposition?" Mimi asked. If Jake said no, she wouldn't tell him about her dreams.

"Sort of."

Well...that didn't help her much.

She knew Jake and his siblings had held many FaceTime sessions in recent weeks to discuss their father's idea for an inn. They had invited her to join the group chats, but until Jake was certain what his role might be, she stayed out the discussions, only acting as his sounding board when he was frustrated after hitting another wall.

Jake was the one who would have to undergo the biggest change by literally overturning his entire life. Again. She could work anywhere, as her new job as substitute teacher for Waltham Public Schools proved, and which also allowed her the luxury of choosing her own work hours and even taking the occasional week off, like this one.

"Come on, let's walk around. It's too cold to just stand here," he tugged on her hand, and they walked down a dirt and gravel path, past the dying vegetable patch, away from the spot where she hoped her dream house would stand someday.

Jake stooped to pick up a red-cheeked apple, small but firm, and turned it in his hand, then tossed it into the woods with a fluid over-hand pitch.

"Quite a few things are uncertain right now, but the only thing I know for sure is that I don't see myself as an innkeeper," he said.

"They're not called innkeepers anymore," she winked at him, shaking off lingering daydreams.

"Doesn't matter, *bella*. I'm not gonna do it."

"So you're turning down your dad's offer?" A pebble of regret sat heavy in the pit of her stomach.

"Let's just say that until Matt, Carla, and I talk to Dad this afternoon, all bets are off."

Chapter 52

Jake

"Come in." As usual, Bob Bellini stood behind his massive desk and beckoned Jake, Matt, and Carla into his home office, a replica of the one at the hotel except for more family portraits on his desk.

Jake watched his father kiss Carla's cheeks and exchange a man-hug with Matt before it was his own turn to be enveloped in the same strong arms that held and comforted him so many times when he was a little boy. "Your engagement to Emily makes your mom and me very happy, Jacob."

"Thank you, Dad," he smiled. "Me too."

"Where is she?"

"In the living room with Mom, discussing the pros and cons of taking our last name versus hyphenating it with hers."

"Albizia-Bellini sounds terrible," Jake's dad said, his shock visible.

Jake agreed one hundred percent and laughed, "It wasn't Mimi's idea, Mom brought it up. Together with a photo album of your wedding."

"Oh, then they'll be busy for a while."

"Excuse me, but could we get to business? Or do you need more time to also discuss children's names? In that case, I'll go grab a round of coffee," Carla said, but plopped down on one of the several high-back upholstered chairs in front of their father's desk.

"Mimi is pregnant?" Matt sat down in the chair next to Carla, stretched out his legs, and crossed them at the ankles.

"Not to my knowledge," Jake glared at his sister. He and Mimi hadn't been together in three months, and if it had happened during her visit to Italy, she surely would've told him by now. But her belly was flat as always, as he'd seen up close last night when he kissed his way down...

He cleared his throat.

"Do you know something I don't?" he asked Carla.

"I don't know a thing, but it sure stopped you in your tracks," she smirked. "You're such a goner."

"Carlotta, stop it." Their dad sat down behind his desk again, leaving Jake to pull up a chair and join Carla and Matt. His dad picked up a pen, put it down on a blank notepad in front of him, then picked it up again. Jake had never seen him so fidgety.

"You said you want to talk to me about something. Am I correct in assuming it's about Charles's inn?"

Jake looked at Matt first, then at Carla. They hadn't appointed roles for who would say what or answer which question. Deciding to take charge—since his participation in the project loomed over them like a sword of Damocles—Jake said, "After you surprised us with your plans, we've been doing some thinking."

His father's face didn't give away a thing, but his pen tapped a fast staccato against the notepad.

"Did you know that Grandma took Carla, Mimi, and Paloma there?" Jake asked.

The pen-tapping paused, the pen frozen in midair. "No. When?"

Carla nodded, "In September, when Mimi and Paloma visited. Grandma asked if we could take her there, and we spent an hour or so poking around. Mimi spent most of the time outside, but Grandma, Paloma, and I explored the house."

Jake sighed. He wasn't interested in a minute-by-minute rehash of that visit. What was important was what happened afterward.

"Carla called me a few days later with a first idea for an inn," he said, in an attempt to move the conversation along.

"Yes!" Pen in hand, their father pumped a fist.

"But not exactly as you envision it, Dad," Carla said. "The location is too secluded, and to draw guests to it, we need to offer more than an average inn and glorified campground with a firepit in the middle. We need to set ourselves apart from those that already exist on the island."

"What do you mean?" their father's focus turned to Carla.

"The house is gorgeous, the first floor is bright and airy, the bedrooms on the second floor have stunning views of the pond and landscape. At least they will, once it's all cleaned up a little—or a lot," she said.

"What's your idea, then?" The annoying pen-tapping resumed when his dad leaned forward in his chair.

Jake wanted to tell him to chill but swallowed the rude remark. He'd save the head-butting for when it was necessary—because it would, as sure as "amen" in church, come eventually. Matt must've thought along the same lines, because he shot him a "hold your horses" look, making Jake wonder when Matt would join the debate. So far he was just sitting there with his chin resting on the back of his hand, taking it all in like a mere bystander.

Carla sat up straighter and said, "I see a high-end inn, maybe eight to ten rooms with all the imaginable amenities. Think luxury packages for honeymooners, etcetera. We'd only offer breakfast for the guests, but we'd have a modern, full-size industrial kitchen so we can host smaller events for up to maybe fifty people. Anniversaries, second weddings, or reunions. Maybe we can add a four-season room, which gives us more possibilities year-round."

"Hmm, so we'd need at least one, if not two, part-time cooks and a catering service on hand." Their dad made a note on his notepad, then scratched his chin. "Matteo, you've been quiet. What are your thoughts?"

"I like Carla's idea, but we'd be stupid if we don't utilize our own catering service," Matt said.

"Carlotta already manages hospitality and event planning. She has her hands full. In peak season, when the hotel is hosting several weddings on weekends, plus catering private parties, it would be too much for her," their dad said.

"I could do it if I leave my job at the hotel and concentrate on the inn," said Carla. "I can coordinate the catering business from here as well as from the inn."

"Are you abandoning me and our hotel?" Their father's face was dangerously pale and a stark contrast to his heated voice.

"You didn't listen, Dad," Carla said. "Yes, I would give up my *administrative* position for hospitality at the hotel, but I'd continue being in charge of catering." As an afterthought she added, "And not only because CB Catering is in my name to begin with."

"Umm..." Matt raised his hand. "Before you get all worked up over nothing..."

"Nothing?" their father barked.

Matt shot him a pointed look. "Please listen! I'm not planning to go anywhere, Dad, and will continue as sales and marketing manager at the hotel. To be quite honest, I have no interest in the new project."

"You can't handle what you're already doing, plus Carlotta's job —plus mine, eventually."

"Ever heard of hiring someone new? You can't expand and expand without adding more staff. We're already stretching ourselves thin. We have over a year until Carla drops out of the hotel position and is busy with the inn. Isn't that enough time to train a new manager?"

"I don't like to bring in outsiders," their dad's voice was flat, almost defeated.

"Times are changing, Dad," Matt said. "And you said yourself in July that we'd hire staff to assist us."

Their father turned his focus on Jake. "Jacob, this was meant to be your job. What the three of you have presented so far tells me that you're not doing it. Are you pushing it at Carlotta so you can wash your hands of our family businesses?"

Jake held his dad's withering stare and mentally counted to five—he'd never make it to ten without blinking.

It was take-it-or-break-it time!

Steeling himself, he rested his forearms on his thighs and said firmly, "Working full-time at the hotel or at the future inn isn't for me. But I offer to manage the business side of Charles's inn, dealing with the town and conservation committees, getting permits, being the liaison for construction companies, everything that's needed during the renovation. You said you already talked to Damian. He and I would work together closely."

Surprised that his dad didn't deliver the anticipated outburst, Jake continued, "After completion of the project, I see myself in a supporting role, but not in a permanent management job, at the inn or at the hotel."

Jake didn't take his eyes off his father when he closed with, "I want to scout out possibilities to join a local law office and practice again. Only a few cases at the beginning to allow me enough time for Serenity LLC."

"What is Serenity LLC?" his father asked.

"The company that Matt, Carla, and I are founding, and which stands behind Charles's inn. We want to separate it from your hotel company. To give us autonomy, but mostly to protect the hotel should anything with the inn go belly-up."

His dad nodded slowly, as if replaying and processing everything he just heard. "I like your idea of going into law again. But it doesn't solve our problems, it makes it worse. We'd be understaffed if Carlotta leaves, especially once your mother and I step back."

Jake glanced at his father. Did he look defeated? There was no reason for it, he just had to take off his "I'm the boss" hat and accept that he had three grown children who thought outside the box.

"Dad, we won't leave you and Mom high and dry. Start bringing Matt into your daily dealings more, let Jake help Matt with marketing and sales—" Carla said.

"Which I did very successfully at Uncle Fausto's winery, if I may add that," Jake said, and earned himself a frosty glance from his dad.

"*Paparino*," Carla said softly, "why don't you think about everything and let's sit down again in a few days to brainstorm ideas for how to shift the responsibilities, hire someone new, and try to make life easier for all of us. I've been longing to get back into the kitchen, and the inn would allow me to cook again."

The pen dropped to the notepad and rolled to the side.

"So let me summarize," their dad said in a choked voice.

"Jacob, you are offering to oversee the construction of the new inn, with everything it includes. And you are also taking on some responsibilities at the hotel. You will be busy, especially because you want to go back into law, but I think you can do it."

Jake nodded. "I never shied away from working hard, and I want to at least try it again. The law, I mean."

"Matteo, you continue as before, with Jacob's support as needed. You will become the new face and force behind Bellini's Cliff House Hotel once your mom and I step down."

Matt nodded. "Yes, sir."

"Carlotta, you'd be responsible for hospitality at the new inn and continue to run your catering business. Once you are full-time at the inn, we hire someone for your management position at the hotel."

Carla nodded. "Yes."

Jake looked from his brother to his sister to their dad. It was crystal clear that none of what his dad heard was exactly what he wanted, but it was what his children offered.

Would he take it?

Chapter 53

Mimi

Mᴍɪ ʙʟɪɴᴋᴇᴅ ᴀᴡᴀʏ ᴀ ʀᴜsʜ ᴏꜰ ᴛᴇᴀʀs ᴡʜɪʟᴇ sʜᴇ ʀᴇᴀᴄʜᴇᴅ over and clasped Jake's mother's hand. Anne squeezed back while the women stood in the doorway to the office and listened to Bob's summary.

With her free hand, Anne knocked softly on the door and pushed it open. "Do you mind if we join you?"

"Not at all," Bob said, and he and Jake jumped up and came toward the women.

"We didn't mean to eavesdrop, but the door was ajar, and we caught the tail end of the conversation," Anne said as she accepted Bob's peck on her cheek.

Jake pulled Mimi to a chair next to him and linked his fingers with hers.

"May I add something to the discussion?" Mimi asked.

"Of course, please do," Bob said.

"From what we heard, you talked about the different responsibilities at the hotel and the inn, but what about the cabins that were also important to Charles?" Five pairs of eyes were on her.

"Let's hear it," Bob said.

"Guests at a luxury inn don't want to have a cluster of cabins interrupting their view. Which doesn't mean they can't be on the property..." she paused to decide how to proceed.

When Jake's mom nodded encouragingly, Mimi said, "This island is not only a favorite vacation spot for well-to-do folks, but has an even longer history as a cultural center. Just think about when Colonel Sprague established the Martha's Vineyard Summer Institute as a summer school for teachers in the late 1870s."

Mimi leaned forward, "He strove to combine scientific and literary studies with rest and relaxation. Sounds lovely, doesn't it? I'd certainly sign up."

Jake gave her hand a gentle squeeze, and she continued, "Musicians, painters, and other artists have also been attending retreats here for decades. But I'm sure you know all that, so I'll stop the introductory part of my sales pitch right here."

"Oh, and Matt is very familiar with the visiting artists," Carla chuckled, earning herself a crude gesture from Matt, pretending to scratch his nose, and a stern look from her father.

"Go on, Mimi," Jake's mom said.

Mimi took a deep breath, "So, back to the cabins... No matter how nice they look, high-paying inn guests would probably consider them an eyesore"—she made air quotes—"and wouldn't want them showing up in their wedding or celebration photos."

"What are you suggesting?" asked Bob.

"Build them off to the side of the property, and offer them to aspiring chefs fresh out of culinary school for a minimal fee. They would be responsible for tending to the vegetable gardens and orchards, and in return get to take cooking classes with Carla."

Carla sat up straighter.

"Instead of only breakfast, the inn could offer a three-course fixed menu exclusively for inn guests on five days a week. Everything would be prepared by the young chefs under Carla's supervision, using only produce grown here, fish fresh off the boat, and so on. Like farm-to-table, but a cut or two above the average."

"I love it, why didn't I think of it?" Carla gushed. "Hmm, it makes me wonder if we could use your farm-to-table idea for the hotel, too. Gosh, I wish I had someone to toss those ideas around with."

"I know someone," Mimi said and looked at everyone in the room. "Paloma is losing her café, so she might be able to help out until she decides what to do next."

"Oh, wow! I'll call her right away," Carla said.

"Fantastic idea, *bella*," Jake said and kissed Mimi.

Anne covered her mouth while tears rolled down her cheeks. "Everything you suggested, Mimi, is exactly what my brother would've wanted. Mom and Dad will be so happy to hear it."

"Then it's decided," said Bob. "Let's do it."

"You saved the day today. My father wasn't happy that we didn't go along with his plans," Jake said when he and Mimi strolled through Charles's property an hour later.

"It's a culmination of ideas that had crossed my mind in the past weeks, but I wasn't sure they'd be doable."

"It's always worth it to speak up, especially in this family."

"It sounded as if you and Matt and Carla are pretty certain about your respective responsibilities."

"I think it was more that we know what we *don't* want to do. And Dad needs to accept that we're too old to be told what to do. It's no longer his way or the highway."

"I'm proud of you for lawyering again." Mimi snuggled closer and wrapped her hands around his arm. It made walking on the uneven ground more difficult, but she didn't care.

"Lawyering?" he smiled.

"You know what I mean. I'm only worried that you're adding too much to your plate between that and the new inn."

"I can do it. But I rely on you to tell me when you think it's too much," Jake said and kissed Mimi's forehead.

"I will, I promise!"

"When I was here in July, I was at first shocked how run-down everything is. Then I stumbled across the vines, though," he pointed to the little hill with his chin, "and an idea began to take shape. You cemented it when you sent me the selfie."

The wind—milder than yesterday, but no less blustery—blew leaves around, making Mimi shiver. A vision of them in front of a blazing fire in a wide fireplace popped up in her mind's eye, warming her from the inside out.

"I want to run another idea by you," Jake said. "What do you think about building a house for us here? I imagine something with a wall of floor-to-ceiling windows so we have a lake view from the living room and our upstairs master bedroom, a jacuzzi with view of the woods and the lake, a huge fireplace and a comfy sofa..."

Mimi's heart stopped beating for a second or two. He just sketched her dream.

"Where exactly would you want to build our house?" she asked.

"Over there," he pointed to the slope that ended at the small hill, on the far side of the property.

She followed the direction of his finger with her eyes. "Yes, absolutely yes, to building our house there." She said in a hushed voice, "Exactly where I dreamed it would be."

"Perfect, then you can start making notes about everything you want it to look like."

Mimi looked back to the old farmhouse. "I'd like something like that. A Victorian without the frills, and of course walls of windows."

"You got it, *bella.*" He leaned closer and asked, "Can I share another secret with you?"

She nodded.

"I want to resurrect those old vines and grow grapes. It'll take years, and they won't produce more than a few bottles of wine, but I need to try. If the results are promising, I'll look into expanding it, either by buying a larger parcel for more vines or by combining crops with another winery."

"Go for it. I would've been surprised if you didn't at least try. You turning your back on winemaking seems impossible." Mimi thought for a moment. "You know, if we live here, with the inn close by, we can take advantage of the fresh produce. We could even raise chickens, like Francesca does."

"You can have as many chickens as you like, *bella*, as long as you don't make me collect eggs. I'll do anything else for you, but chickens are beasts with mean beaks and don't like me."

"Duly noted." She giggled—the man who told her not to worry about scorpions and snakes in Tuscany was afraid of chickens.

Mimi scanned the expanse surrounding them and tried to picture how it would look in a year or two from now—and had a good feeling about it.

"This will be so beautiful," she said. Then a sobering thought struck her. "If only happiness was contagious."

"What do you mean?" Jake asked while he pulled her closer and wrapped his arms around her.

"Everything's coming together for us. But Nicki and Paloma aren't in such great places right now. I want them to be happy too."

"Give it time. They'll find it when they least expect it. And who knows? Maybe your idea of bringing Paloma into the hotel is the first step."

"We still need to ask her, and it would only be temporary, but I'd love to have her around. I can see Paloma, Carla, and me spending a lot of time together."

When Jake didn't reply, she looked over her shoulder and found him gazing at her. Then he turned her slightly, cupped her chin and kissed her so gently, Mimi's knees turned to pudding.

"This is the perfect place to raise our kids, don't you think?" he asked softly. "Can you see them tumbling over the lawn, chasing a dog, doing all the stuff kids do?"

"Yes, I can," she nodded. Children had been part of her dreams. "When do we start?"

"I'll talk to Damian next week."

"Why do we need him for making babies? Last night you certainly knew how to do your part. Exceedingly well, by the way."

"The house, *bella*. I want to talk to him about the house." His eyes were the color of a clear winter sky and left no doubt about his sincerity. "I'll take care of the rest all by myself, as soon as you give us the green light."

"Green light," she whispered. She longed to carry his baby. Sure, most couples waited a few years before they started a family, but this was their life and their decision. And it felt right.

"Really?" His arms tightened around her. "Wait, don't you want to get married first?"

"Nah," she shrugged, then laughed at his startled expression. "I mean, yes, I want us to marry. By the way... Remember your suggestion about a civil ceremony in Italy? Just us and two friends? I really like the idea and first thought we could get married at the anniversary of our meeting in Venice—"

The gleam in his eyes almost took her breath away. "I hear a but..."

"I don't want to wait until May," she admitted. "And I want our families to be with us."

"I'm happy with whatever makes you happy, *bella*."

Mimi smiled, "Then let's marry here with a Justice of the Peace and honeymoon in Tuscany!"

"Perfect! And we'll be able to spend four or six weeks there. I have to go back to the winery in January anyway to discuss the transfer of my obligations with Fausto and Mia," Jake hugged her closer. "Pick a date, and the sooner the better."

"Are you in a hurry?"

"Yes, I want you to be mine."

"I *am* yours. Did I never tell you?"

"Tell me what?"

She thought she'd drown in the depths of his eyes. "You had me at '*Ciao, cara.*'"

THE END

Thank you

FOR READING THIS BOOK.

Nothing helps an author more than a review.
A sentence or two at Amazon, Goodreads, and/or BookBub is much
appreciated.

If you're interested in more bookish news, please sign up for my
newsletter at www.AnnetteGAnders.com

Author Notes

In the 1990s, while my husband and I lived in Zurich, Switzerland, we spent several weekends at Lake Maggiore in Ticino, the Italian-speaking region in Switzerland. The combination of centuries-old towns on the shores of palm-lined lakes, the snow-capped Swiss and Italian Alps, and medieval castles is simply awe-inspiring—and unforgettable.

In 2011, long after we moved to the United States, we vacationed with our son in Italy and spent time in the Veneto region (Verona, Vicenza, Venice) and Tuscany, and I fell in love with it all. A second trip in 2016 to the ancient hilltop towns of Tuscany and the spectacular cities of Florence and Rome—both bursting with history, architecture, and art—cemented my passion for the country.

My 2020 debut novel, TURN BACK TIME, takes readers to France, and I knew while still working on it that I also wanted to write a book with a setting in Italy to relive my fond memories of the country that is so much more than pizza, vino, and gelato. But a writer depends on a little thing called muse—and mine stoically refused to whisper an Italy story idea in my ear.

Until 2021, when I saw a photo of someone drinking a Bellini. I knew of two Bellinis (the nineteenth-century opera composer and the Renaissance painter), but I'm not very cocktail-savvy and, after looking up the recipe, learned that it's like a mimosa. Then I started to play with the words: bellini...mimosa... Next, the cocktail's colors conjured images of sunsets, and sunsets made me think of vineyards.

And from there, the plot for BELLINI'S MIMOSA quickly took shape in my mind.

It was in Venice in 2011 when my son and I overheard an exchange that is now the opening scene of BELLINI'S MIMOSA. Somewhere near the Bridge of Sighs, a young German tourist bragged to a few young women about his fluency in "Dumb, Moron, and Stupid" and even though I didn't know then that his remark would one day become the opening line of my novel, it clearly snoozed somewhere in the back of my mind—waiting to be brought to life a decade later. Even funnier is that we ran into the kid again a day later in Vicenza, a city about ninety minutes away from Venice— it really *is* a small world sometimes.

Mimi's experience in the cockpit of an airplane is also based loosely on personal experience. I visited Egypt in 1988 and had the opportunity to spend the entire flight from Cairo to Sharm el-Sheikh on the Sinai Peninsula in the cockpit of a—thankfully—much larger plane than the one described in this story. It was an amazing experience, including a glass of champagne.

Like with my other books, I am beyond grateful for my husband's and son's support. Axel and Mika, thank you for being you, for encouraging me to follow my dreams, and for being such awesome travel buddies! I can't wait to go back to Italy with you!

And, of course, thank you to you, my readers! Please email me and let me know if you liked Mimi and Jake's story. To stay in touch, sign up for my newsletter and join my book group, MORE THAN ONE STORY, on Facebook.

Annette G. Anders
May 2022

References and Acknowledgments

In BELLINI'S MIMOSA, I respectfully quote from William Shakespeare's *Romeo and Juliet* and Tom Coryat's 1608 *"Coryat's Crudities: Hastily Gobled Up in Five Moneths Travells in France, Savoy, Italy, Rhetia Commonly Called the Grisons Country, Helvetia Alias Switzerland, Some Parts of High Germany and the Netherlands: Newly Digested in the Hungry Aire of Odcombe in the County of Somerset, and Now Dispersed to the Nourishment of the Travelling Members of this Kingdome."* Both works are in the public domain, as is George Sand's quote at the beginning of the book.

Bellini's Cliff House Hotel is a product of my imagination, but I sure wish it was real and I could spend a few days there. The Ginger-bread cottages in Oak Bluffs are real and worth a visit if you're on Martha's Vineyard. When I saw them for the first time many years ago, I felt like being in a different world with all the whimsical décor and candy-colored paint.

Menemsha is a small, breathtakingly picturesque fishing village on Martha's Vineyard.

Thank you to:

- Faith Freewoman for always being just an email away.
- Brandi Doane McCann for fiddling with my cover design ideas until I'm content.
- Joyce Greenfield, Nancy Porter, and Kathleen Weekes for providing me with amazing feedback and detailed, constructive critique.

- My A-Team for helping me spread the word.
- The community of authors; we're not competition but friends who share the love of writing.

About the Author

Annette G. Anders always liked the idyllic world created by Astrid Lindgren and the sassiness and independence of Jane Austen's heroines. She is a huge Charles Dickens fan, but also admires many contemporary authors.

In 2018, Annette turned her love for books into a freelance editing career, and in 2019 had the inspiration and found the courage to write her first novel, TURN BACK TIME.

Her first two books have received multiple awards: 2021 National Indie Excellence Awards Winner, 2021 Readers' Favorite Award Silver Medalist, 2021 Pencraft Award 1st Place Winner, 2021 Independent Author Network Award Finalist, and the 2022 Eric Hoffer Award Honorable Mention for Romance.

Annette is the author of *Full Circle* series as well as the *Colors of Happiness* series.

An avid traveler, Annette loves to write about locations she visited and to take the reader there together with her protagonists.

When Annette isn't working on a new novel, she enjoys having lunch chats with friends, photography, and reading—often under the watchful eye of her boxer buddy, Ecco.

Stay in touch with Annette by visiting her website, sign up for her newsletter, follow her on social media, or just send her an email. She loves to hear from readers!

Website: www.AnnetteGAnders.com
Email: author@AnnetteGAnders.com

Also by Annette G. Anders

COLORS OF HAPPINESS SERIES

BELLINI'S MIMOSA

PALOMA IN A PICKLE

NICKI GOT SPUNK

CANDIDLY, CARLA

THE FULL CIRCLE SERIES

TURN BACK TIME

IN DUE TIME

TIME IS ETERNITY

TIME WILL TELL

Available as e-book, paperback, and audiobook.

Made in the USA
Monee, IL
06 April 2024